HOW TO SUCCEED IN

SKELETON BUSINESS

BY STEVE BERNARDI

BOOK ONE IN THE BONESBURY CHRONICLES

HOW TO SUCCEED IN SKELETON BUSINESS

Cover Illustration by Tommy Devoid

Full-Page Interior Illustrations by Jenna Skold

Typesetting and design by Jen Frankel; glyphs by kjpargeter / macrovector / Freepik

1st Xeno edition 2024
ISBN: 978-1-988393-62-9

Published by Jen Frankel & XenoProductions
        71 Mayflower Avenue Hamilton ON L8L 2K5
        info@jenfrankel.com

This book is dedicated to Matthias, Allissa, and Garett... the finest party a Skeleton could ask for.

Table of Contents

CHAPTER 19 – Give Back to the Community
Chadwick basks in his newfound success and establishes
himself as a figurehead in the community.

CHAPTER 20 – The True Meaning of 'Skeleton Business'
Chadwick and the reader learn a terrible truth about his company.

CHAPTER 21 – Never Stop Reaching For New Heights
In an attempt to push past his guilt, Chadwick becomes invested
in a dangerous new endeavor which could spell his doom.

PROLOGUE — So You Want to Succeed in Skeleton Business

It's a fine thing to be a skeleton. Hello, and welcome to the prologue of my novel. I suppose some introductions are warranted before we go any further. My name is Chadwick Bonesbury, the first and only, which I'm sure comes as a relief to many.

In my long existence, I've become a modestly successful businessman, a decently powerful spellcaster, and a well-traveled, only seldom maligned adventurer! And, as suggested by the title of this tome, I am a specialist in the field of Skeleton Business. I also happen to be a Skeleton.

You might be asking at this moment, what exactly is Skeleton Business? If so, then congratulations on being a sapient creature capable of asking complex questions! If your first guess was either 'the business of being a skeleton,' or 'regular business done by skeletons,' then I'm afraid you're not a particularly bright sapient creature. No, Skeleton Business is far more substantial than either of those answers would suggest.

You see, the important part of the title is not 'Skeleton Business' but 'How to Succeed.' My time in this field has brought me astounding triumphs, and a good number of tribulations as well. It is the latter which I hope to shield you from, dear reader. Though we are times and worlds apart, if I can make but one miniscule, positive impact upon your life, I'd like it to be this.

So read on, friend. Or don't; if you've gotten this far, chances are you've already bought the book, and your coinage now fills my already deep pockets! Redistribution of wealth aside, I will say that the novel before you is something I'm quite proud of. It's deeply personal, covering some of my best moments, and many of my worst. Read it for a laugh, if you like; you might learn something, not least of which being Skeleton Business.

I have heard the bards say that "what's past is prologue." With chapter one nearly upon us, they'll soon be right. At the risk of sounding pretentious, I ask you now to read my story; know me as few others do. Do you feel it? The impulse just beneath your skin, urging you towards the next page? Don't worry. There's a skeleton in all of us; yours might just want to see what happens next…

CHAPTER 1 – Take Stock of Your Available Resources and Capital

I want to start this chapter with an important point of clarification. There is a considerable degree of overlap between Skeleton Business and regular old business, or what you plebeians simply call 'business.' Therefore, most of my patented and surefire advice may seem geared towards the latter, but I assure you, there is a method to my material.

Of course, I don't expect you to see the correlation just yet, because that's what this book is for! I assure you, by the penultimate chapter the true meaning of Skeleton Business will become clear. So, in the interest of getting you there, let us begin.

What exactly are 'resources' and 'capital'? It is far too easy to fall into the delusion that you have nothing, and therefore must either start from nothing or never start at all. After all, is it not the purpose of getting into business (or Skeleton Business) to attain and amass such assets? Wealth, success, to have all the things your tiny mind believes you need to be happy!

I say 'no!' This delusion is a cancerous blight! Everyone has something. An able-bodied poor man can still work until he is richer than he was. A broken body can house a beautiful soul, whose songs and poetry touch hearts and minds. If a Dragon has no treasure hoard of its own, it may trade its scales, which shed and regrow in cycles, to mortals for shiny baubles until it has a respectable collection. Even a particularly economical squirrel can make the most of a tree full of acorns.

Whether you attained them through trickery, chance, or hard work, you too are in possession of assets which can be utilized to achieve success. All that's required is ambition, and the will to use your assets to their full potential. And luck. You're going to need a little luck.

Take my start, for example. You've likely heard the expression 'make the most of a bad situation,' but there is such a thing as making the most of a good situation too. I learned this years ago, during my first days as a Skeleton.

My last recollection prior to awakening was that I had been alive. Naturally, the revelation that this was no longer the case left me shaken and befuddled. But I didn't catch on right away, and instead wandered throughout my surroundings, a dingy underground structure with grey stone walls and dirt floors, for what must have been days. My first suspicion was that I had been poisoned, or possibly bewitched, since none of my senses seemed to be working quite right. Sound came to me like my ears were filled with wax, and touching the walls felt as if I was wearing thick leather gloves. My vision was impeccable, with no need of a lantern to see through the layers of shadow around me, but there was no colour to be seen in my new world.

In hindsight, I should have been grateful I could see at all. But when I spotted another resident of this maze-like dungeon, I began to wish I couldn't. The sight of the corpse made me gasp, but the action didn't feel right, like it was simply performative. Whoever this was, they were long dead. There was no moisture left in the partially-mummified body; even through the dim shadows that surrounded the scene I could see bits of skin and hair stretched taut over bones and gristle. It wore a knight's armour that was caked with years of grime and filth. A large sun insignia was still visible on the breastplate, and a shield lay long discarded next to the body.

I picked up the shield, disregarding the fact that there was no chance of me actually being able to identify its origins. Still, seeing a dead body led me to believe that there were dangers within this cave-like realm, and I might need some basic form of protection. Besides, it was shiny, and I found myself drawn to it, so I tried to scrape off the dirt. It made an awful sound when I did, like I was dragging a rock over the metal. When I final-

ly returned some of its reflective sheen, I could see why, although I would not accept the fact for some time.

I saw my reflection, and I let out another one of those performative gasps before dropping the shield. The clatter echoed on and on, suggesting there was a lot more of the dungeon to explore, but I had other things on my mind at that particular moment. I began shaking, and my body rattled as I did. The shield, now face down in the dirt, was an object I grew to fear immensely. Any reflective surface would have revealed the same wretched scene, but that shield was the first, and for that I hated it.

I paced around the room for several minutes, as if that would somehow change the reality of my present situation, or give me inspiration to do anything but the one thing I knew I must. Dreading what my mind might do to me if I evaded it any longer, I grasped the shield and looked into its steely depths.

Staring back at me was the face of a Skeleton.

To say I screamed would be inaccurate. I opened my mouth and attempted to expel the fear out of my body, as is the purpose of a scream, but what came out was an uneven, insidious humming sound. I thought it had been a proper scream for a second or two, but then I questioned how I could scream at all; I could see no throat or lungs anywhere.

"How can I see?" I cried out to no one. "How can I… speak?" I grew dizzy, but was careful not to let the shield fall again. If it did, I feared I would lack the resolve to pick it up a third time. I studied my reflection carefully, analyzing its movements for a trick or wizard's spell. But we moved in perfect synchronicity, and I could see my own hands were indeed nothing more than dull, white bones. There was a chance the shield had been enchanted, somehow, but surely I could trust my own…

"Eyes?" The word hung in the air, and before I knew it I began to laugh hysterically. The sound was broken up with that same humming as before, but otherwise my laugh sounded as it had in life, albeit more manic and stricken with terror. "What eyes?" I questioned madly before continuing my cachinnation.

Surprisingly, the brief loss of my mental capacities (can you still have a mind when you're not even skin and bones, but just bones?) had the unexpected benefit of easing me into the next big surprise. As I grappled with this new sense of existential despair, other figures were moving about in my peripheral vision. It turned out I was not the only undead creature on the premises, and had I been more sane in the moment, that fact might have been greatly upsetting. Instead, I merely took note of it while I exhausted my non-existent lungs.

It took some time but I regained my wits, and I decided to investigate these living-impaired companions fate had saddled me with. Some were much like me, bare bones pacing between rooms. Others were more modest, covered in sections of flesh which were rotting but relatively intact. These Zombies were more difficult for my already fragile mind to accept; their resemblance to once-living people was more realistic, and therefore more terrifying, than seeing a pile of walking bones — or perhaps I was projecting? But who were they? By what means had this tomb been filled?

Any attempts at communicating went largely unreciprocated. A few gave a reflexive groan or wrench of the head when I addressed them, but none could look me in the...eye. Initially I began to suspect my consciousness was merely imagined, that I was a shambling corpse lost in a dream like them. But my voice echoed exactly how I expected it to, and I could move as freely as I ever had. If this was a dream, it would be futile to try and oppose such a powerful dream weaver.

What alarmed me most was how armed my cohorts were. Many wore armour and carried weapons, forlorn from what must have been years of neglect. None of it matched, either, as I could see styles and designs from all manner of eras and dynasties, though none were terribly intricate. Some even carried tools for farming. This suggested my present location was not where they had originally perished. They had been brought here, assembled.

"Whose funhouse am I playing in?" I asked aloud.

"Schlar… vrrk," moaned a handsome stack of flesh next to me. He looked as if he were responding to the pitchfork he was holding upside down.

I tried to make a mental map of whatever structure I was in. The realization that I could have searched the various bodies, animated or otherwise, for parchment came far later than I'd care to admit, which only strengthened my resolve to do without. As I fumbled around labyrinthine corridors for what seemed like hours but could have been days or mere minutes, I noticed something had changed.

"Am I feeling… a breeze? How am I even feeling anything?" I looked around expecting an unintelligible soup of syllables, but there were no mobile bodies in this part of the dungeon. What I heard instead was the faint chirping of crickets. That's when I spotted faint rays of moonlight.

Twenty feet ahead of me was an ancient, wrought iron door that some kind soul had left partially open. I approached it slowly, suddenly stagnated by the realization that I had no frame of reference for how long I had been down here. My previous vocation in life left me little in the way of mathematical or biological knowledge, so I knew it had been long enough for me to have lost all my flesh. What that actually meant, I had no idea, and I didn't presently care, for beyond the vines and overgrowth that partially covered the threshold, I could see a meadow or forest of some kind.

"A way out, good," I muttered. I took a single step towards the door before pulling back. There was a gnawing suspicion in my bones that I just couldn't shake. Was it anxiety? Paranoia? Whatever name this particular affliction held, it compelled me to go back into the dungeon, that the answers to the question of my post-life existence might be found further within. I turned away from the threshold and began consulting the map in my mind.

As I walked on, three things gave me confidence that I was moving deeper into the dungeon. One: I was getting further away from the entrance. Two: the undead population steadily increased the further I went. And three: there were traps this way.

The first trap I noticed was by far the most traumatic, but the shock it gave me was inversely proportional to how lethal it was to me. The floor fell out beneath me in the middle of a long hallway, and I fell into a pit of spikes. I screamed as I fell, that uncanny hum interspersed throughout. Fellow skeletons lay impaled on either side of me, although I was the most lively of the bunch. The tiny spears had scratched some of my bones but otherwise left me with no sign of injury, having harmlessly passed through my ribs. My excitement subsided, and I briefly considered the idea that I was invincible, but I stifled the notion as quickly as it had appeared.

After climbing out of the pit and exploring further down the corridor, I stepped on a seemingly innocent panel which sank ominously beneath my foot. Pale green gas shot out of the walls all around me from unseen jets. While I got a general sense that things were a bit mustier, the atmosphere smelt and felt the same as before. How many of the bodies in here had suffered from this trap before me, stumbling as far as they could before the poisonous gas made their lungs collapse?

Multiple pathways crossed over and converged on one another, and after a considerable amount of mental effort (in my defense, I now literally lacked a brain) I deduced that there must be some kind of central chamber connecting all these hallways and animate bodies within. Despite believing that my efforts would no doubt prove fruitless, I continued to interview every undead I encountered in hopes that one would be like me. But my calls for friendship were met with blank stares or squelching sounds of rot; occasionally one would snarl for good measure.

At one point I felt the urge to weep, but without any tear ducts, what good would that do? I could hear a voice in my mind, possibly my father's, saying "in times of great distress it is sometimes necessary to swallow our pain." I wished the old bastard were here right now, so he could tell me how one was meant to do that with no throat.

Eventually I found the main chamber, the heart of this labyrinth, through spite if not perseverance. Infinite time with nowhere to go and nothing to do meant success was guaranteed, with enough patience. My resolve to make my way out of this place and slap senseless the person or people who put me here gave me the patience of a saint.

The entrance to the central room was sealed with a nine-foot-high double door that was flanked by two suits of armour and branded with geometric shapes that had no regard for which of the doors they occupied. Out of curiosity I touched one, and found it moved as if on some sort of invisible track.

"So I'm meant to solve this puzzle to get in, then?" The twin sets of armour gave me no response. "Spite and patience," I sighed as I began my work.

You might think it a failing of an author if they simply said 'and then they solved the puzzle,' as opposed to a detailed or even just adequate description of how the puzzle was solved. And you'd be right. But here's the thing, dear reader: as you'll come to learn in upcoming chapters, I can do some extraordinary things. I can change my appearance with virtually no limit. I can command shadows and the denizens of Hell. I can fire a beam of energy so potent and terrible that it can level mountains! But finding sufficient words to explain how I solved this puzzle? That is something I cannot do.

What I will say is that once the geometric shapes were arranged correctly, they depicted the skull of some humanoid creature. As soon as the last piece was in place, the floor and walls around me shook as the doors pulled back by themselves. A golden, relatively blinding light shone from beyond the threshold, and I recoiled for a moment before regaining my composure. I nearly collapsed again when I could see what lay before me, but this time from a panicked, wild bliss.

The inner chamber was some type of vault, definitely in a state of disrepair but significantly nicer and more intact than anything else I had seen thus far. The radiant glow was the result of a huge pile of gold and gems, haphazardly stacked nearly fifteen feet high in the middle of the room. There were also innumerable treasure chests scattered throughout with no sense of uniformity, but it was the pile that commanded the eye.

I cautiously grabbed a handful of gold and let it slip through my boney fingers, ever more fearful I was being tricked. Again there was that reduced layer of sensation in my hands, but I could still feel the coins. It was all real; I was looking at more money than I ever could have conceived of in any previous lifetime.

Seeing this collection awakened something in me, restoring some esoteric facet of humanity I hadn't realized I'd lost. I did not come from a wealthy family, and people in families like mine often say that there are more important things than money. And I'm sure many of them believe that. But there are others who lean on this virtue like a crutch, emotionally and spiritually crippled by poverty. Even they knew, logically, that money couldn't solve every problem in the planes, there was still that irrational mind gremlin whispering that with enough money, one person could conquer the gods themselves.

Remember, dear reader, that I had been avoiding the reality that I was a sentient skeleton, completely alone and underground, since I saw my reflection in that damned shield. I was, by all accounts, a monster. Even if I got outside, what would I do? I hadn't had many friends in my old life (a pang of melancholy hit when I realized I had called it that) but there was a good chance they were dead too or, if they were still alive, they certainly wouldn't remember me all these years later. And if somehow, against all odds, I had allies out there who still held a fondness for me in their hearts, would they be able to accept this pale and boney creature? They were more likely to call on a knight or an inquisitor to vanquish me for the good of the realm.

But with this fortune? There was nothing I couldn't do! I could hire bodyguards to protect me from any would-be hero or bounty hunter who thought they could destroy me. Sure, they may take issue with my lack of skin or entrails at first, but everyone has a price, and with this hoard I could pay it. How would I keep them from just stealing my liberated bounty for themselves, you may ask? I didn't care, I was too busy thinking about what kind of horses would pull my carriage that had thick, crimson curtains to keep my existence a mystery, a legend, even!

But before I could begin the painstaking chore of counting my newfound gold piece by piece, I heard a commotion from outside the vault. At first I thought I had imagined it, or subconsciously exaggerated the sound of some Zombie's shuffling. But then a piercing scream cut through the silence, sudden and intrusive enough for me to lose my footing. I caught the sight of movement and the sheen of metal just outside the door. The suits of armour, suddenly and seemingly repossessed by their previous owners, were marching away from the vault towards some unknown foe.

"Back, you soulless metal!" shouted their attacker, who I thought sounded male. I strained to see behind the animated sentries, but the perpetrator was obscured in darkness. "This is for Rowena and Duncan; they didn't deserve what they got!" I heard metal meet metal as several consecutive clangs followed the man's words, and one of the suits of armour was

thrown through the doorway before falling apart in front of me. My fear
rose anew as I regarded the unmoving pile of sheet metal, for whoever
had taken down such an automaton would surely make quick work of me.

"Hyah!" cried the man before another crash, this time outside the doorway. I held my breath, ignoring for the time being that I had no breath to
hold, and waited. There was a minute of silence, and then a figure filled up
the entrance to the vault.

I had judged him a man by his voice, but looking at him now I saw a boy.
Like everything else down here, he was without uniformity: his tunic, if
you could call it that, was just scraps of dull blue and cherry red fabric
stitched together without any sense of pattern, and his leather armor was
certainly made for a much larger, bulkier frame than his. The only things
that matched were the bracers on his arms. He had a head wound on his
left temple, wet with fresh blood. An olive green cloak was tied around his
waist, and his boots were incredibly worn and dirty.

He was also pointing a sword directly at me.

"A single Skeleton to guard all this treasure?" scoffed the adventurer. "I
must have finished three of you on the way here. What's the catch?"

"Now h-hold on —" My voice felt dry and hollow in my mouth.

"Oh, it speaks! What are you then, eh? A necromancer's corpse? A lich?
Hmm?!"

"My name is Cha—"

"Hyah!" He seemed to like making that sound. A sword came directly at
my head, and I dropped to the floor to avoid it. The felled armour was
still at my feet, and I grabbed its weapon before springing back upright. I
thought to swing at him, but the bronze mace was too heavy in my hand.
All I could do was block a series of consecutive overhead strikes. He
was relentless, and after the fourth strike my entire right arm fell to the
ground.

Somebody began to scream, and it took me a moment to realize it was me. The adventurer roared in return, thankfully not a variation of 'hyah,' and I staggered backward onto the pile of gold. He raised his weapon one more time, no doubt meant to be a killing blow, and I desperately scanned around for anything that might spare me. Thankfully I didn't need to look far; the hilt of a sword was sticking through my ribcage, and with my remaining arm I drew it from the pile just as he dealt his finisher.

A shockwave erupted from where our weapons met, accompanied by a deafening thunderclap. The boy was knocked back several feet. I stared in shock at the weapon I held. It had a crossguard shaped like two lightning bolts, and its blade was made of flawless steel with thin blue highlights throughout. The metal sizzled faintly for a few seconds as my opponent struggled to his knees.

"Fine," moaned the adventurer. "I won't walk out of here with all this treasure. But I'm owed something! I made it this far! What about Rowena and Duncan? They didn't. I need something for their families, that much I am owed!"

He held his sword in front of him before diving to the ground to collect whatever loose coins and small gems he could. The light in the room flickered with each handful, as if the incandescence of the treasure had been agitated. I was compelled to watch the intruder, but out of the corner of my eye socket I could see a black substance oozing out from either side of the massive doors. Partway between liquid and solid, the various streams flowed from between the bricks and hit the floor, pooling together before mass ballooned up and outwards. A sort of viscous cloud now sat perfectly between the man, me, and the only way out.

What happened next took approximately thirteen seconds. The black mass began to move forward, away from the doorway and towards the latest intruder. The boy turned, noticed that his demise was near and opened his mouth to scream, but he was enveloped before any sound could escape his unshaven face. The cloud hovered there, silent and still, before melting back into its individual streams, which receded back from whence they came.

The boy remained standing there, his clothing and gear untouched. His skin, though, was grey and cracked. His eyes were ugly, bloodshot white orbs and looked horribly dry. His lips were gnarled, his teeth black. I heard them chatter briefly. The newly undead creature briefly regarded me before turning around and leaving the vault, walking and behaving no differently than the countless others like him I had seen.

There was so much I wanted to say, to call out, to scream, but I didn't. I just stood there, struck dumb, as I watched that young man, that boy, shuffle off to roam those tunnels for who knows how long, an eternity maybe. No, despite the callousness he held for me and my existence, that young man didn't deserve his fate. I couldn't stop my mind from seeing his slacken face, hearing his dragging steps — was I in shock? I'd heard of people going into shock before, but had never experienced it myself. I was desperate to move forward, to do anything but stand here and think about what I had just witnessed.

To try and block out that horrid scene, I went back to my original plan and focused on the hoard around me. There was evidently a magical safeguard in place that kept someone from taking the treasure; it had activated with the mere touch from that adventurer. But I touched the gold first and nothing happened. The undead sentinels, one of whom still lay crumpled on the floor, had ignored me completely, and yet they had attacked the man on sight. Whatever this dungeon was, wherever it was, I was a part of it, so…

So it didn't register me as a threat.

I went back out into the dungeon to track down my former assailant. It didn't take long; the undead are not known for their bursts of speed. As I suspected, he had a large leather satchel with him. After emptying it out, I brought it back to the treasure room and filled it to the brim, as much as it could possibly fit. I had also grabbed the intruder's cloak on my way back, but decided (in a deranged fit of vanity) that olive green wasn't my colour, so instead I ripped a strip of the fabric and used it to affix my new sword to my pelvic bone. (The idea that I could have taken a sheath from him didn't occur to me until weeks later, at which point I promptly kicked myself).

With my newfound loot in tow and a dungeon map in my mind, I retraced my steps back through the traps and grumbling crowds of undead.

At the entrance to the dungeon, sufficiently scarred both mentally and emotionally, I pushed open the door to see what the next chapter of my life would bring me… and was immediately blinded by sunlight.

CHAPTER 2 – Find a Reliable Business Partner

Wherever you go and whatever you do, know that you are extraordinary; I promise you that. But even the most extraordinary among us are imperfect. We're not gods, and I should know, because I've met…well, perhaps I should save that for another book. The point is, despite all we are capable of, we are also allowed our failings and incompleteness. Our shortcomings are just as much a part of us as our triumphs.

And that is why the importance of a good business partner cannot be understated. Whether in literal business, the business of life or, yes, you guessed it, Skeleton Business, having someone you can trust to zig when you zag is paramount.

Like me as I ascended from that labyrinthine hellhole, for example. Bag full of money, bones void of flesh; head full of big ideas, heart currently dust. The phrase "I was in over my head" would be a regrettable underestimation on my part, to say the least.

And we haven't even gotten to the sun yet. That giant, shiny imbecile. Some postulate that the sun is a lantern carried around by Belas, a healing goddess. That's a laugh. After all that time underground, my eyes were burning in my skull, despite being demonstrably absent from said skull. That in itself could certainly be counted as a divine miracle, but it wasn't from any goddess, I can tell you that.

To be fair, I wasn't precisely blind. I could discern where the sky was, and that I was surrounded by trees (or else unusually thin and incredibly still Giants). But there was still no colour; where the dungeons were filled with black but discernible shadows, everything on the surface was a glaring white fire. And relying on my other senses was no good, either. In the dungeon, I had developed a vague understanding that the faculties I possessed which a Skeleton should not were, in some way, tied to my own perception of them. I could see even with the absence of eyes simply because I had not been blind in life. I could hear sounds through nonexistent ears because, well, I always could before.

But there were a lot more sounds out in the open than there had been underground. Birds chirped obnoxiously, and somewhere nearby a babbling brook babbled incessantly. Even the wind was insufferable when compared to the stuffy atmosphere of my dungeon.

I stopped in my tracks; I had called it 'my dungeon.' How pathetic was I, developing an affinity for a dirty underground building with no intelligent creatures anywhere within? If I hadn't been so disoriented, I would have thumped myself on the back of the head. Instead, I found what I hoped was a large tree and sat down for a rest.

As an experiment, I wiggled my toes to see if I could feel anything. I definitely felt something, which I had to assume was grass, but the sensation was even more dulled than it was in my hands. I reached down beside me and grabbed at whatever there was, just to see what would happen. I came up with a clump of dirt, and was amazed to discover I could actually feel blades of grass falling through my stark white phalanges.

My followup test was less successful, however. I thought I could pretend to close my eyes, and whatever arcane mechanism that let me speak and hear and feel would then also close them for me. But I had forgotten how, and it made no sense. Basic logic would demand that the natural state of eyes should be closed, but reality scoffed at the notion, apparently, and put the conscious effort on closing one's eyes and not the other way around. I wanted to cry, and I couldn't and I knew it, which only made me want to cry more.

I think at some point I must have slept. It didn't feel like sleep; I didn't dream, not even a little. But my awareness dipped out from under me, like the ground had suddenly disappeared, and I was left with a vague sense that time had passed. The light seemed… different, like the sun had changed positions but still shone just as bright. Had I made it to midday?

"Lunchtime!" I prattled. "Oh, what's the point? I haven't got the stomach for it anymore, ha! Oh, my comedy is wasted out here. Is all humour gallows humour when you're a Skeleton?"

"I thought it was pretty funny," said another voice. I must have given some visible sign of panic because he added "Relax, friend. Hail and well met. A bit bright out, eh?"

"It is a tad intense, yes…"

"See if this helps," he said.

I strained my vision for signs of motion, and found one blob presenting me with a larger, longer blob. I hesitated but took it, partially out of intrigue and an inescapable need for social interaction. My sight immediately cleared, I could even decipher tones and colours! It was not what one typically expects when looking away from a bright lightsource, where a fleeting, radiant scar dances across your retina, but I attributed this to the fact that I no longer had retinas. Before it had simply been too bright, and now it was not. In my hands was a beautiful black umbrella, with a pale bone handle and tipped in something that looked like gold.

I marveled at my new gift the way a drowning man might marvel at a flotation device. It felt right in my hand, as if it were meant to be there. When I turned to thank my rescuer, I saw only darkness and thought he had disappeared. Then I realized what I was seeing: standing no more than two feet in front of me was a figure made entirely of shadow.

When one thinks of darkness, the image that often comes to mind is often an inky, sprawling cloud. Smoke, in other words, but that is not what this person looked like. This was a void of a man; the space where a person should be but had been unceremoniously removed. Make no mistake, I do not mean he wore clothes or dark skin; there was simply an anthropomorphic hole in the Universe who had offered me an umbrella.

"Are you… a phantom?" I asked as bravely as I could.

"You're one to talk, mister skull man."

"My name is Charles."

"Jon."

"What?"

"You can call me Jon," said the shadow man. I noted acute movements of Jon's head as he spoke, the kind anybody would make while talking. Despite my best efforts, though, I couldn't see any sign of a mouth moving to match his words.

"So you're not a phantom, then?"

"I'm not. I realize my appearance might be a little disconcerting, and I'm very sorry about that. I hope you won't mind my saying so, but you're very well spoken for a Skeleton. How did you come to be here, Charles? Are you a necromancer's familiar?"

"That's the second time I've heard that word. 'Necromancer,' what does it mean?"

"They are the black casters," he said. His tone never changed, but his body language, such as it was, shifted slightly, like he was in disbelief that this needed explanation. "Mages who manipulate the energies between life and death to achieve their ends. They aren't the only ones who can conjure undead, but one of your…articulation, well, you wouldn't expect from anyone but a specialist."

"I see." It had been the first time someone had ever called me articulate, and all it took was my death and the complete, utter decimation of my life to make it happen. Lovely. Well, small mercies and all that.

"You don't have such a person?" asked Jon, cocking his head ever so slightly to the side.

"I suppose I must," I admitted. "After all, what other logical explanation is there for my being a walking, talking Skeleton?"

"Gaiyax is a fantastical place," Jon sighed. "Lots of things are possible. But you're right, that would be the simplest answer."

Hearing that word, 'Gaiyax,' brought back a flood of half memories. Connections. Maps I had been shown as a child, stories told to me by one adult or another trying to explain the scope and name of the planet on which we crawled. It was a little thrilling, to remember all at once that there was vastly more to the world than just one dungeon in one forest.

"I was all alone when I woke up. Well, not exactly. There were dozens of other things that looked like me, maybe hundreds, but none of them acted like I did."

"I can see how that would be upsetting," Jon sympathized. "So you just left then? With no plan?"

"I had a plan. Well… part of a plan. Coming topside was, erm, a little befuddling, to say the least."

"A walk is a reliable method for clearing one's head," said Jon, holding out a shadowy hand to help me up. "Come on, you can tell me about your plan along the way."

Sitting up a speck, I reached out to grab the hand Jon offered, but it passed right through his darkness as if no one was there. The only thing that kept me from falling face-first into the dirt was my outstretched arm, empty without another's hand to hold, as the other was still holding the umbrella.

"I can encourage your progress," said Jon, a hint of sternness in his voice, "but you have to do the work yourself. Remember that, will you?"

"Right…" Positively elated with this new riddle to grapple with, I picked myself up and dusted off my bones. Standing at my full height, I noticed that Jon was about a foot taller than me, and that the shade which made up his appearance seemed to hum slightly, though I couldn't quite say what that meant. We regarded each other for several lengthy seconds before he held out an arm, gesturing for me to follow him into the woods.

We made idle chit-chat as we walked, giving me time to observe the landscape that I had been blind to earlier. The trees, tall and densely planted, were mostly hickory and elm with a few mahogany sprinkled throughout. A sudden relief washed over me, as my conscious mind caught up with my psyche and came to a realization: I recognized these trees, not just their species but from my past life. Evidently, the dungeon where I had awoken was not that far from where I had lived all my life.

"It's really quite a common practice," said Jon, interrupting my internal tangent.

"What's that now?"

"Necromancers raising a small army of undead," he explained. "And then sticking them into some abandoned mine or underground storage chamber. Cheap, easy labour."

"So my existence is economically motivated?"

"It's entirely possible. What were the other undead like?"

"Caught in a loop, wandering around aimlessly, completely oblivious to anything around them." I suddenly felt my voice catch. "They made me… sad."

"Try not to worry too much. They're likely just shells, with nothing of the original individual remaining within."

"What does that say about me?"

"Absolutely nothing. You're an outlier, Charles; the standard rules don't apply to you." He put a hand on my shoulder as he said this; physically I felt nothing, but I appreciated the gesture all the same.

"That's dangerous thinking, isn't it?"

"What were they guarding?" he asked, not bothering to hide the fact he wasn't answering my question. "Your fellow undead."

My free hand immediately went to the satchel I was carrying, but I stopped myself. This gold was the only power I had in the world, apart from a magic sword I didn't know how to wield properly. And Jon's true allegiance was still unknown to me, to say nothing of his nature; I may be newly undead, but I was not yet arrogant enough to believe either trait was aligned with my own.

Still, he had shown me considerable kindness in our short time together. I could see the world around me because of him, and he was currently the closest thing to an ally I had. My chances of surviving, let alone thriving, were as slim as the width of a hair. And deep down in the core of my being there was a sliver of nihilism (or was it hope?) whispering that if the risk was the same regardless, it was better to expire having gambled on the benevolence of a stranger.

I opened the bag to reveal my loot.

"That's certainly impressive," Jon surmised. "I assume there was more of it, if that many undead were left to stand guard?"

"Significantly more," I admitted with no reservation. "My time down in that dungeon was… traumatic; I wasn't thinking clearly. At the time I thought I could use the gold to make my way in the world. It sounds foolish, now that I say it out loud."

"Why is it foolish?"

"I don't even know why I'm telling you all this," I continued, the momentum of my thoughts preventing me from acknowledging his question. "You're a scary shadow man, who very well might want to rob me."

Jon chuckled. "Maybe you recognize a bit of yourself in me. Both a little broken, and ambitious. Not quite the men we used to be, but trying regardless."

"It's possible."

"Answer my question, Charles. Why do you say your plan is foolish?"

"What exactly am I supposed to do?" I blurted out. "Walk to the nearest bank and say 'Hello, I'm a foul creature of the night, but please ignore that. I'd like to open an account, please'? I'll be run out of there with torches and pitchforks, and that's a best-case scenario!"

"Maybe you're getting too far ahead of yourself."

"What do you mean?"

"What do you want right now, Charles?"

"I don't—?"

"Ignore who and what you are for a minute," he told me, crossing his shadowy arms in appraisal. "Imagine that money can buy anything and everything. If you had that power, what would you want at this very moment?"

I thought hard, staring off into the distance as I contemplated the query. "A drink," I said after I turned back.

"A drink?"

"Not an alcoholic drink, mind you, though that wouldn't be half bad either. No, I mean a drink of water. Isn't that funny? I lack a tongue, or a throat, but the knowledge that I'll never be able to take a simple drink of water ever again has left me feeling… down, and more than a little dry. What's this exercise supposed to accomplish, Jon? Besides depressing me, that is."

"Follow me," he said, and he walked on without another word.

We didn't end up going far. Past a clearing was a river about five feet wide, with water bluer and clearer than illustrations in a children's book. He gestured to it as if it were a dagger, and I had just recently indicated my unwavering desire to stab myself as quickly as possible.

"It's a lovely river," I observed, trying to convey without conveying that I had no clue what the game was.

"Take a drink, Charles."

"I… I can't." We stood there staring at each other, myself dumbfounded and Jon impossible to read.

"How are you seeing me, right now?" he demanded. "How are you hearing me? How are your bones moving with no muscles to carry them?"

"I don't know!"

"Haven't you ever thought about it?"

"Of course I've thought about it!"

"And what have you concluded?"

"I suppose it's all pantomime? I can't help but act the way I always have?"

"Exactly," he gestured to the river again. "So you should be able to drink this water."

"But—"

"Just try."

I mumbled some incomprehensible protest about being told what to do, but down to the water I went. I knelt down on bony knees and tried to scoop some liquid in my hand, but it slipped through exceedingly slender fingers. Wearing my best expression of annoyance without the use of a face, I looked at Jon and groaned.

Seeing as I already felt ridiculous, I saw no harm in leaning down and putting my mouth directly in the river. At the time, it didn't occur to me that I had no lips to sip with, or a throat to carry the water, or even anywhere for a throat to carry it to. But that didn't matter. There was no logic then, or biology. I was just thirsty, and so…

"Jon… I can taste this. I can feel it." As soon as I stood up, water spilled down my spine and ribcage. Without thinking I tried to wipe my lips dry, but my hand made an awful scraping sound against my teeth.

"And how do you feel?"

"Better," I admitted after a pause. "A little closer to normal, yes. Head is clearer, too."

"I'm glad." Even though I couldn't see it, a smile radiated off of Jon as he spoke. "Would you like to continue our walk?"

"I would."

By then it was the middle of the afternoon. We were joined briefly by a family of deer, who shared no prejudice towards either of our appearances. Jon said they were strange creatures, but when I asked him to elaborate, he declined.

"So what will you do now, Charles?" he asked, simultaneously changing the subject while getting straight to the point. "What's next for you?"

"Oh, I don't know if I want to think about that," I laughed.

"Maybe you should." There was that sternness again. "You've been lucky so far, but there are settlements around here. Sooner or later you are going to run into someone, and the chances that they're the kind of person who will take umbrage with the fact that you're a Skeleton are high, higher than you should be comfortable with."

"What exactly can I do, Jon? I must be richer than some kings, but with no way to safely spend it. To get anywhere in this world, I'd require power that cannot be bought."

"True, but what if it could be taught?"

"Jon, I'm afraid you've lost me yet again."

He leaned in, which was incredibly unsettling for a shadow man, before uttering a single word: "Magic."

"Magic?"

"Magic. There are so many advantages that spellcraft could offer you. Even an inexperienced mage could accomplish wonders with your resources."

"I'm no mage, though!"

"You could become one."

"That could take years," I whined. "Besides, I know about mages. You need scholarships to special schools to do that sort of thing, and somehow I doubt I'd be welcome among their alumni."

"Though the secrets to magic lie behind a single door, it may be opened with many keys."

"Ok, now you're just speaking in riddles."

I swear I saw the tiniest twinge of annoyed fury in his demeanour after I said that. "I'm saying I can teach you magic, Charles," he explained, giving up on the implied cryptic reverence. "If you'll have me, I mean."

"You can do that?"

"I'm a being of some power, and you wouldn't be the first I'd have educated. I can teach you just enough to get you started, and then once you're on your way to everything you've ever wanted, we can do regular lessons."

"I'm not stupid, you know." I waited for him to question what I meant or raise some kind of objection, and when none came I continued. "Nothing in this world or any other is free, especially 'everything I've ever wanted.' So what do you want in exchange?"

"You're clever, I'll give you that." Jon began. "But since you brought it up I'll be straight with you. Yes, I might occasionally ask you to help me with some errands. I don't know if you can tell from looking at me, but I'm…"

"Not all there?" I posited.

"Exactly. My presence on this plane is a bit tenuous, so I'm unable to accomplish everything I want to do."

"And I'd just have to do these tasks for you without question?"

"I wouldn't ask you to do anything you'd object to, on that you have my word."

So many things flew through my mind; thoughts and fears and hypothetical scenarios I knew would likely never come to pass. It was a hurricane, but every hurricane had an eye. That thought I'd had before, about gambling on the benevolence of a stranger; I found it in that storm and held onto it, and my mind was suddenly calm. My better judgment was telling me to run, to see how far I could get on my own and to just be grateful for this victory lap of existence. But that was just it; I was already dead, so how much did I really have to lose?

"What do you say?" Jon asked me. "Partners?"

"Partners," I said with just a moment's hesitation. He held out his hand for me to shake, and instinctively I offered mine in return. To my surprise, we actually made contact, and we shook on our freshly made deal. I was awed by the brief moment of connection where there had been none before.

I didn't feel any different at the time, but little did I know that nothing would ever be the same.

CHAPTER 3 – Cultivate a List of Marketable Skills

"**H**ow much do you know about magic, Charles?" Jon asked me after we had found a secluded spot in the woods for magic practice.

"A fair bit," I lied. There was a tug-of-war going on inside me; I trusted Jon (whether or not I should was a different matter) so I was caught at a point between insecurity and sincerity. "Umm, not much. I know mages exist, though I've never seen one. They can command magic, right?"

"Yes, but they can just as easily be commanded by it. Magic, or 'mana' to the more technically minded, is energy, and like all energy it comes from the planes. But unlike most energy, it isn't tied to any one specific plane, and it is more alive than any other variety.

"Casters are those who call magic forth to achieve wonders. Some are naturally born with it, or receive it through their interactions with arcane phenomena, while others train their whole lives to cast spells.

"A spell, simply put, is the crossroads of magic and intention. There is magic all around us, so a caster, with proper training, needs only to harness it to their will. And after we're done, you'll be able to do this too."

"So I'm going to be one of these necromancers?"

"You might someday," said Jon. "If that's where your exploration takes you. But I lack the power to make you one. You heard me refer to necromancers as 'black casters.' Here in Gaiyax, the different types of magic users are identified with colours."

"That seems a little childish." Images of strange people in brightly-coloured robes flashed in my mind.

"But effective. We've made a covenant, you and I, through our agreement as tutor and student. Whenever you use magic, you'll be borrowing a fraction of my power. That makes me your benefactor, to use the technical term, and mages who gain their powers from a benefactor are known as 'yellow casters.'"

"Yellow?" I sneered.

"Is something wrong?"

"Yellow is just so… I don't know, it seems ugly."

"It's the colour you have an issue with?" he asked, crossing his arms incredulously.

"The name could use some work too."

"Yellow casters are also referred to as 'thaumaturges,' 'warlocks,' 'negotiators,' and 'enchanters.'"

"Oh, any of those will do. I withdraw my objection."

"As I was saying," he continued. "While the variations between the disparate types of casters are many, there are similarities, as well. Many of the core casters use objects called 'conduits' to channel their spells. In fact, it's typically a requirement for those under a certain skill level to use a conduit when practicing magic. If you've ever seen artwork of a mage, you've likely seen their conduit; wands, staffs, rings. Anything they can hold and draw power from."

"Where am I going to get something like that? We're in the bloody woods." Jon only laughed at my distress. "What's so funny?" I demanded.

"You're already holding one."

My gaze slowly drifted to the umbrella Jon had given me when we first met. It had been hours since then, and in truth I had forgotten it was there. Looking at it now, there was definitely something more… lively about it. It wasn't brighter or more colourful, but the shade it cast seemed to shimmer around me.

"This thing?" I pointed conspicuously at the open umbrella above my head.

"That's the one," Jon said proudly. "I made it myself, a long time ago. It was something I thought could help you, and now it can serve a further purpose." The thought crossed my mind that he was lying. Not about having made it; the satisfaction in his voice was enough to convince me of that. But the idea that he had somehow scouted me, always with the intent to make me his warlock, that was a worry I couldn't seem to shake. I wanted these spells, though, so I merely filed it away in the backlog of my anxieties.

"So what am I learning first?" I asked eagerly, fencing with the umbrella as if I were skewering butterflies out of midair. "Lead into gold? Commanding a legion of dragons?[1] Blowing up mountains?!"

Jon chuckled. "I admire your spirit, but it's better if we start with something a little simpler."

"Oh, you're no fun," I pouted. It wouldn't be until later that I realized I had closed the umbrella, and yet the sun no longer impeded my vision. You could say that my eyes adjusted, if I had any eyes in my head at all.

"This first spell is called 'Magic Blast.'"

"Oh, you have got to be joking."

"What's the problem now?"

"Honestly. 'Magic Blast'? It sounds made-up!"

"All spells are made-up, Charles." The smug grin he wore was as clear as

---

1   Lowercase 'd' for Lesser Dragons, no more than animals. Uppercase 'D' for Greater Dragons, intelligent and cataclysmic magic users. Knowing the difference could save your life!

day, regardless of how his face was devoid of detail at all times.

"I mean, it sounds like you asked a non-magic person to name a spell and they just blurted out the first words that popped into their head."

"It is pretty basic," Jon admitted. "But that's why we're starting with it. There were a few non-combat spells I had considered, but it is easier to destroy than to build, and even easier to hurt than to heal. This will give you a framework to build from. Now face that tree."

"Yes sir," I mocked. He pointed to a tree that appeared more dead than its neighbours. 'How environmental,' I thought.

"Magic Blast allows you to fire a beam of energy towards your intended target, whether that be a person or an object."

"Pretty self-explanatory," I shrugged.

"I want you to visualize it. Can you do that, Charles?"

"What, want me to close my eyes?" I laughed. The silence I got in response was worse than any reprimand, and so I simply added "I'm visualizing it."

"So you have your intention," Jon continued. "And as we've established, magic is everywhere. To bring them together and make a spell, you'll need components. Significant gestures and specific words, these are how we signal our intent to the Universe. Just about every spell requires one of these, and some require both. More advanced spells may require other tangible materials as well, like plants or crystals."

"Will there be a shopping list?"

"You're hilarious," Jon said vacantly. "Now I want you to visualize a clock face in front of you, a massive one, with twelve o'clock at the top of the tree."

"There's a lot of visualizing going on."

"Do it!"

"Alright, alright. I've got it."

"I want you to hold up your umbrella and point it toward the base of the tree at six o'clock. Now smoothly, but carefully, I want you to move the tip of the umbrella towards twelve. No, not in a straight line, but around the clock. Counter-clockwise, not clockwise!"

His slightly muddled instructions aside, I did as he said, and repeated the motion when he told me to. This went on for quite a long time, or at least I thought it did. Time is a strange entity when you're deeply focused, even more so when you lack the usual biological faculties that had previously kept you in check. I didn't get hungry, or need to relieve myself at any point. I had already proven to myself that I could sleep, but I didn't feel tired at all. I suppose I could have used the sun to note the day's progression, but Jon kept me so focused on my exercises that everything else around me seemed to melt away.

He always had a note to add to every one of my performances. Not angry enough. Too angry. At one point I had switched to going between seven o'clock and one o'clock on my clock face, which simply wasn't right. Another instance he said my eyes were crossed, and before I could finish explaining how that was technically impossible, I was met with a sharp and sudden "Again!"

Eventually the process began to wear on me. The light was different when I came out of my reverie, like it was suddenly morning. I sincerely doubted I had become a capable enough magician so quickly and with so little awareness that I had managed to reverse time, so the more reasonable conclusion was that I had been at this a lot longer than I thought, doing the same rigid motions and thinking the same mental attack commands on repeat.

"Jon, I'm starting to feel ridiculous."

"That's good," he said from behind me. "Feel ridiculous; kill your ego." I hadn't realized that I had completely lost track of Jon; apparently, my peripheral vision did not fall under the same category as my tasting the river or feeling grass between my fingers, perhaps because these were tied to memories of my previous life. Or maybe we are all used to having a shadow behind us, and mine was just a little more autonomous than the rest.

"Raise your ego from the dead, stronger than before," I continued, parroting his tone.

"Despite what you might think," he said sternly, "you actually are making progress. I want you to try it one more time. This time, though, try to block out everything but you and the tree. Picture a blank, black void around you. There is only you, the umbrella, and the tree. Again."

With efficient movement I stabbed the umbrella forward, allowing everything else to fall away as Jon had described. I envisioned a mighty bolt of energy, and the tree splitting in half straight up the middle. As I brought the tip of the umbrella up from six to twelve, as perfect a semicircle as I could, I amplified these thoughts, letting them blend and bleed together until it was a soup of conscious thought. I screamed internally, or so I thought, as I realized I was externalizing once again. But there was no sound beyond my voice, no flash of light as wood splintered and cracked.

"Open your eyes," Jon said, another smug smile oozing off his words.

"I don't have—" I began to correct him, before I actually noticed what he was referring to. The dead tree stood tall and unexploded as before, which was a disappointment, but my umbrella was…different; its brass tip was glowing bright white, like the end of a fire poker pulled straight from the hearth. The light faded within seconds, and I was back to square one.

"That's wonderful, Charles," encouraged Jon.

"How?"

"It's the most you've done thus far!"

"I feel like I should be further by now." I examined the umbrella, caressing the point with my thumb and forefinger. Even with my limited capacity for touch, I could tell it wouldn't harm me.

"If you think you could learn a beginner's syllabus of spells in a single day,

I'm afraid you'll need to readjust your expectations. Now let's begin your exercises again."

Three days went by before anything changed. I was able to make the tip glow several more times, but the lack of further progress robbed me of any sense of pride. Jon was reassuring to a point, but he made it clear it was not his vocation to coddle me, or give undue credit if I was feeling particularly low.

On the third day, I pointed towards six o'clock as I had countless times already. Before proceeding I paused, hoping to gather whatever secret mental ingredients were necessary to advance, even though I had no idea what those might be.

"If it really comes down to it," Jon whispered in my ear. "Think about what you really want to be attacking. What saddens you? What angers you? What makes you afraid for your life? Find that, and make the tree become it."

So I tried. Same as before: black void, nothing else but me, the umbrella, and… something else. Someone else. A warrior, at least seven feet tall. Indigo skin, tusks, and a mohawk of maroon hair. He carried a battle-axe adorned with decorations I couldn't completely make out. There was something… familiar about this person. This wasn't merely a vision, or something I had created just for the spell to work. This was real. I was seeing a memory. I think…I think I was seeing the face of my killer.

The Orc, for that is indeed what he was, charged at me, weapon drawn, mouth open, eyes wet with tears. I brought the point of my umbrella up to twelve, a perfect semicircle, as natural as breathing. No, more than that; I no longer drew breath. The tip of my umbrella glowed, and then a beam of crackling energy shot forth, bright green, hitting the Orc square in the chest. But they did not register the fatal hit, and instead faded along with the rest of my void. But I heard the snapping sound of impact, and I was in the world again.

"Congratulations!" beamed my benefactor. "Charles, you've just cast your first spell!"

"What happened?" I mumbled, faltering slightly with a sudden wave of fatigue. "Where did it go, my spell?"

"You didn't see?" laughed Jon. "Look here."

He made his way past me towards the tree, gesturing at a mark on its trunk. I hobbled over to it, and saw there was a black space there, not just scorched but utterly pulverized.

It was about the size of an apple.

"All that effort for this?!" I was incredulous, but also so drained that yelling made me feel lightheaded. "I could hit harder than that!"

"You can't," Jon said flatly. "You have no muscles. But trust me, you hit a monster with a few of those and they won't be bothering you anymore."

"It just seems so anticlimactic…"

"It's a starter spell," Jon reminded me. "But Magic Blast is unique, one of only a few spells which actually grows in power along with its caster. What you're looking at is an assessment of your current abilities. Keep at it, and you could take down the Walking Calamity[2] with that spell."

That was the last thing I remembered Jon saying; apparently I had slid my spine down the trunk of the tree and fell asleep before my tailbone hit the ground. I had no memory of this, of course, but Jon filled me in later while assuring me that as I improved, so too would my stamina. In time, my weaker spells would be ones I could do repeatedly with little drain, whereas more robust magic could be performed once or twice before I needed a
recharge.

Just to be sure it wasn't a fluke, we spent the next day making sure I had truly mastered Magic Blast. Once it was clear to both of us that I had, Jon wasted no time in telling me about the next spell I would be learning.

"It's called 'Lesser Telekinesis,'" he explained.

---

2   A legendary, colossal beast. A titan fabled to destroy Gaiyax upon waking from its slumber.

"Really?" I asked in disbelief. "Couldn't we start with 'Greater Telekinesis'? Hell, I'd settle for just 'Telekinesis,' nice and neutral."

"You need to be able to walk before you can run. Besides, do you even know what telekinesis is?"

"Is that the one where I'm in one place, but then suddenly I'm somewhere else?"

"That's teleportation."

"Oh, I'm such a fool," I guffawed. "Will I ever be free of this shame born from ignorance?!"

"You're ridiculous."

"Thank you."

"Moving on," Jon groaned. "You've made an important first step by learning to channel magical energy through your conduit. Now we want to take it a step further. Lesser Telekinesis isn't just expelling raw energy, it's creating a controlled effect on the environment around you."

"So how do we begin?" I asked. "Another clock face?"

"Actually, yes."

"Oh, for crying out loud; I was kidding."

"They won't all be clock faces," he promised. "Now point your umbrella in front of you. Aim for seven o'clock, and move counterclockwise to five. Now go back to seven, and again to five. Back and forth, quick but smooth motions."

"Seems simple enough," I noted, somewhat optimistically.

"The motions are to establish a connection with whatever you're trying to manipulate, which you'll want to keep as close to six o'clock as you can."

"So what will I be moving today? Rocks? Fruit from some unwary tree?"

"Actually, I want you to look in the river." He gestured to the same water I had taken a drink from all those days ago, though we were further upriver. "I want you to try to pluck a fish from the water."

"But…they're moving." My mouth hung open, which embarrassed me a little afterwards.

"Exactly. If you learn the spell on a moving target, you'll have no problem on immobile ones."

"I sense this isn't up for debate, is it?"

"It's not," Jon chuckled. "Now let's begin."

He hadn't been lying when he said this would be different from Magic Blast. With that spell, I just needed to get it out and it was over. This was doing the motions continuously, even if it was only for a short time. But despite the added complexity, I managed to master Lesser Telekinesis in half the time. It took me less than two days of repeated umbrella swinging before I managed to pulled a largemouth bass out of its migratory path.

"Jon, I'm doing it!" I squealed like a child as I held my aquatic abductee over the river, its slick scaly body flopping inelegantly in the air.

"I see that," Jon beamed proudly. "You're progressing nicely. Now put that fish back before you drown it."

We were mutually eager to get to the next spell. Jon made a point of saying it was most likely to be the most popular choice in my magical repertoire.

"That's quite the introduction," I noted.

"As we discussed previously," Jon recapped. "One of the most glaring obstacles to your goal is the fact that you are a Skeleton."

"My singular character flaw," I moaned sarcastically.

"You need a way to combat people's hang-ups and prejudices. That's why you're going to learn how to cast 'Tailored Illusion.'"

"And what exactly is a 'Tailored Illusion'?"

"Illusions are expressions of magic which fool the senses. Images and sounds and smells that simply aren't there."

"I like where this is going."

"Tailored Illusion changes your appearance, and the change clings to you. You can give yourself splendid new clothes, alter the way your body is seen by others. Give yourself a different eye colour, or appear as an Orc where once you were an Elf. Or —"

"Give myself skin?" I teased.

"Exactly. For this one, keep your back straight." I straightened my posture. "Next, hold your umbrella in front of you — no, so that it lines up with the horizon." I did.

"The motion is very simple. Hold your arm above your head as high as you can. Then lower your arm until it is nearly slack at your side, keeping the umbrella level at all times. Now, do you have the motion down?"

"It's child's play."

"As you do it, you'll want to say the word 'presto.'"

"Okay, now I know you're playing a prank on me."

"What's the issue?" Jon asked innocently.

"'Presto' is a word children use when they are playing magic. What's next, 'abracadabra'?"

"Magic words are old, Charles. They find their way into all facets of life and every corner of this planet."

"Fine. Anything else I need?"

"A clear image in your mind of your new appearance. We should start with something basic and familiar. Let's try what you looked like in life?"

"Right, okay." I took my stance and readied the umbrella. "Presto!" I exclaimed as I ran the umbrella down the length of my torso. A faint shimmer covered me for a few seconds, flowing down my body before dissipating.

"That's ok," Jon consoled. "It's just because it's your first time. You'll—"

"No," I interrupted, partially lost in thought. "It's not that." I attempted the spell again. My words were clear; my form was perfect. There was another shimmer, and this time it stayed. I looked at my hands…and I couldn't see bone! It still wasn't right, though. Jon muttered something to get my attention, but I ignored him and ran to the river.

"Oh! Well that's not right, is it?" I said to my reflection. It wasn't that I looked deformed. No, it was more complicated than that, like there were half a dozen faces existing and overlapping in the same space, all vying to represent my countenance. This monstrous medley gazed up at me from within the mirror image, and I caught every blink and twitch that matched my own. "Jon, how do I stop this? How do I get it off me?!"

"You say 'Change-O,'" he said plainly.

"Change-O, Change-O, bloody Change-o!" I shrieked. The malformed vision melted away and was replaced with a familiar, garden-variety skeleton; one monster exchanged for another.

"What the hell was that?" I looked at Jon, hopelessly trying to read expression on his blank head.

"You tell me, Charles. Did you look quite so… exotic, when you were alive?

"Obviously not! I don't understand. I-I remember who I am. My name is Charles Miller. I'm forty-one years old. Or… I was. I've lived here all my life. I know who I am… so why can't I remember my own face?" I was caught off guard, this was a devastating blow. Sure, a face was a relative thing to a Skeleton but… I wanted mine. "Give it back…" I said to no one in particular. "Give me back my face!"

"Charles," Jon tried to calm me. "Just breathe."

"How?!"

"Alright, fair point. Just listen, then." He approached me slowly and put weightless hands on my shoulders. "I don't know why you've lost these memories. Necromancy isn't an exact science. It's possible they may return to you someday. Or they could be gone forever. It may be hard to believe, but I'm uniquely qualified to understand how disconcerting it can be to not have a face."

"Ha!"

"So, I'm sorry. I can't give you back your face, but do you know what I can give you? Any other face you want." There was kindness in his voice, like a mother's calming tone to a crying child, and I felt comforted for the moment.

We took a short break after that, going for a walk to clear my head and find another suitable training spot. When we got back to practicing Tailored Illusion, we took six full days to explore a wide array of potential appearances. Existential crisis aside, it was actually a lot of fun experimenting with the spell. I was able to tap hitherto unrealized recesses of my imagination to craft strange and bizarre looks for myself.

One minute I was a man, and another I was a woman. I could be a Human or an Elf, a Dragonkind[3] or a Dwarf. As a Hellborn[4] dressed like a highwayman I gave an address to the few birds that had yet to be scared away by my antics. The loss of my face, both physically and in memory, had left me feeling trapped, but this new ability freed me in equal measure.

"Well, Jon?" I said through the guise of a Dwarf beggar I called Roder-

---

3   When a person has Draconic ancestry, there's a chance their offspring might possess a Dragon's head, scales, unique breath attack, and other traits.

4   Same as a Dragonkind, but involving the denizens of Hell instead of Dragons. Typically has some combination of scarlet skin, horns, unique eyes, and fangs.

ick — (yes, I knew it was a slippery slope creating dozens of personas but caution be damned, I was having fun!) "You said you were going to teach me four spells. By my count, I have learned three."

"If you don't make it as a warlock, you'd make a superb mathematician," Jon sniped cheekily.

"I'd make a better mathematician than you would a comedian," I chirped back, hand indignantly placed on my hip. "What is this spell, then?"

"You'll need to get a few things." Jon held out his hand, and shapes began to manifest above it, all made from the same shadowy material as his non-corporeal body. He explained what each symbol meant before sending me on my way.

Some things were harder to find than others. I was to find a leaf that was neither green, nor orange, nor brown. This proved to be considerably difficult since, as far as I could tell, we were in the middle of a balmy summer. Eventually, I found a tree branch which appeared to have been severed by a bolt of lightning, its leaves in a state of decay. Feeling there might be some significance in it, I snapped off a whole branch and took it with me.

Next there was a requirement of grave dirt. How fortuitous was it, then, that I had resisted the urge to bathe as soon as I had attained my freedom from the underground. I could always feel some grime in the corner of my eye socket; the compulsion to wipe it away, as one wipes sleep from their eye upon waking, was ever-maddening. But like a good Skeleton, I saved it and moved on.

Water was also required, but not just any water. It had to be taken from a source of water which was significant to me. This was by far the easiest part of my scavenger hunt, since the river nearby was both the site of my first drink since I died, as well as the location of my first major existential crisis. The loot I had taken from the dungeon (it seemed like that little adventure was a lifetime ago) included a jewel-encrusted silver bowl, complete with a lid. I scooped up as much water as possible and headed back to Jon.

"It looks like you have everything," he observed. "Except…"

"The bone of a Human," I said. "Already taken care of." I bent down and snapped off the tip of my right pinky toe. The ease with which I performed the task shocked me; was I already so used to being a dead man walking?

"Half-Human, on my mother's side. Will that work?"

"It might," Jon said impassively.

"Maybe we'll get lucky and it will be the right side," I joked.

Jon instructed me on how to go about combining my ingredients. My leaf had to be ground into a paste, which I accomplished with the help of two rocks. When I explained that I took the branch due to its connection with a lightning bolt, Jon said to include that as well, though it took me considerable time and effort to grind the wood. Once it was sufficiently mashed, I scooped it into the bejeweled bowl, and used a discarded stick to mix it with the water. As I stirred I added the grave dirt, liberated from my skull with great relief.

"Next the bone?"

"Next the bone," Jon confirmed. "Grind it up as you did the branch."

I let out a groan as I went through the tedious effort of pulverizing solid bone. Once I added the powdered remains of my pinky toe, Jon approached the bowl slowly and skimmed the surface of the water with his left hand. The murky water turned inky black and began to boil.

"Sit in front of the receptacle, Charles. Get comfortable," Jon instructed. "Situate yourself so that the length of your umbrella fits comfortably between you and the bowl. Keep a firm grip on the handle, and point your umbrella towards this concoction you've made." I did as he told me.

"Amic Arcanus," he continued. "I want you to repeat these words steadily, over and over again. Don't stop, regardless of what I say."

"Amic Arcanus," I annunciated. "Amic Arcanus. Amic Arcanus."

"Magic is a great tool, Charles. I have taught you how to defend yourself with it. I have guided you to use it constructively. And I have shown you how you may change your form to suit any environment. But there is more it can do for you. Infinitely more, if you have the wisdom, patience, and courage to see it through."

"Amic Arcanus."

"I'll always be on your side, Charles, but I cannot always be by your side. I want you to have an ally, a stalwart companion to see you through difficult times when no one else can."

"Amic Arcanus."

"This spell is called 'Arcane Companion', a deeply intimate and personal evocation. It will provide you with a magical familiar, a creature loyal only to you and can act on your behalf."

"Amic Arcanus."

"Your essence. My power. Your will to make it manifest. On the other side of this moment sits your familiar, waiting for you to cross the breach and bring it through."

"Amic Arcanus."

"Do it, Charles. Reach into the aether and bring forth they who are waiting for you! Do it now!"

"Amic Arcanus!"

As Jon spoke and I incanted, the black liquid bubbled out and upward, taking an oblong and unnatural geometric shape. The sky had become darker since we began the ritual, but faint traces of light caught in the froth, revealing dozens of writhing shapes inside. At the last 'Amic Arcanus' the mass shattered like a crystal if it were struck with a hammer.

A great wind blasted forth from the epicenter of the strike, and I instinctively shielded my face. When I looked back, I was slightly dispirited; the bowl had been devastated, its silver twisted and burned, its jewels faded and crumbling. A breathing mass lay next to the smoking vessel. It was made up of a dozen different shades of grey, and it was small enough to fit in both my hands. It looked weak, or possibly scared. I reached out to pick it up, but quickly pulled back, and I looked to Jon for confirmation.

"It isn't a baby," he laughed. "But do be gentle. First impressions, and all that."

I scooped my hands under the familiar's body, digging into the dirt slightly so as not to disturb it needlessly. Raising the tiny bundle towards my face, I offered a soft and unassuming "Hello?"

Bat-like wings unfurled from around a slender, translucent body. Its legs bent at the knee as a person's did, but bent again the opposite way, ending in clawed feet which matched a tinier pair of hands at the end of spindly arms. Its head was very round, possessing a miniscule pair of horns and two beady, obsidian eyes that looked up at me. The tiny creature yawned, and from the dark material of its jaw a tiny mouth appeared, filled with the tiniest teeth I have ever seen.

"Well hello, indeed! Are you my familiar?"

"Ehh," it said after regarding me for a few seconds. "Who's asking, bone-head?"

CHAPTER 4 – Establish a Business Model

Regardless of the type of business you may find yourself in, a good business model is paramount to success. For those looking to profit from fighting or, perhaps more accurately, from starting fights, your business model may resemble a military plan of attack. If you're a lover, not a fighter, a more creative model will help potential investors envision your plans before you even start the creation process, and so on.

Even magic requires certain existential boundaries, especially when your studies have only just begun. You cannot simply open yourself up to the Multiverse, arms out and mouth agape, and expect the arcane to happen. You have to visualize your intent before you can make it a reality.

Sadly, all I could visualize in my present circumstances was my vexatious new employee…

"Who are you calling a cretin, bonehead?" demanded the Imp.

"I-I didn't say anything," I stammered defensively. "And quit calling me a bonehead!"

"I heard you loud and clear." The creature folded its arms and turned its head away derisively. "I wasn't born yesterday; I know what 'cretin' means!"

"You were born today! Waitaminute… can you read my thoughts?"

"Just the ones you think at me." His head turned back towards me. "Bone-head."

"What does that even mean?!"

"It means you have more bones than brains."

"Not that!"

"I don't know what I expected," Jon laughed. "But this is so much better than I could've dreamt."

"What does he mean, Jon?" I wrenched my head to look at him hard enough that I felt my neck pop, which might have been pleasant if I wasn't so agitated. "Thoughts I think 'at' him?"

"You two can communicate without speaking. But it isn't a constant connection, you need to consciously maintain it."

"Oh," I voiced quizzically. "You'll be an efficient little spy, then, won't you?"

"Hey, I ain't no snitch," hissed the Imp.

"You have the right idea," said Jon approvingly, ignoring the familiar's objection. "Emery, could you please show Charles what else you can do?"

"Sure thing, sir."

"Hold on," I challenged. "You're supposed to be my companion, so why is Jon 'sir' but I'm 'bonehead'?"

Emery shrugged. "I call 'em like I see 'em." He floated a couple of paces back, holding himself aloft with a few flaps of his wings, before his body began to twist and contort. In a few seconds he had become a raven, jet black eyes with matching glossy feathers and huge wings, which he used to fly circles around us before plunging to the ground. Moments before impact, his form changed again, taking the shape of a charcoal grey rat. It looked from me to Jon before rolling onto its back and burst into a swarm of spiders.

"Different forms for different needs," Jon explained. "He can even become invisible in relative darkness. Emery should prove extraordinarily useful in intelligence gathering."

"And from the looks of ya," said Emery as he returned to his original form, "you'll need me to gather a lot of it." I glared at him, but Jon interjected before our bickering could begin anew.

"He also has two other abilities which will be helpful to you and your goals specifically. As a familiar, Emery is capable of 'borrowing' spells from his conjurer, meaning you. Not all spells, just the simpler ones. But this can still be a great boon to you, Charles. Try giving him a Tailored Illusion."

I aimed my umbrella and said "Presto!" The Imp disappeared, replaced with the image of a classic garden gnome, complete with a pointy red hat, white beard, and blue overalls. For a brief moment I wondered if this caricature was offensive to actual Gnomes, and I resolved to ask about it if I ever met one.

"The indignity…" Emery seethed.

"Crude," Jon surmised. "But serviceable for demonstrating my point. You see, Emery is a familiar, but he is also a Shadow Imp."

As if on cue, numerous 'poink' sounds went off one after the other, and it took me a moment to connect the noise to its source. There were now a dozen garden gnomes staring at me, all with contemptuous eyes.

"Duplication?" I asked, dumbfounded.

"More like shadow copies. They're weaker and less durable than Emery himself, but they can perform basic tasks for you. Now, knowing all this, what do you suppose Emery would be good for?"

It was clear that Jon was giving me some kind of riddle, not a random rhetorical question.

"Shadow copies…" I began.

"Yes," Jon encouraged.

"Armed with Lesser Telekinesis…"

"Very good."

"Oh gods!" I exclaimed. "The treasure! I could do in hours what might take days, even weeks to do!"

"Look at you," said Jon, his voice beaming with pride. "Learning more than just magic."

"I've had a good teacher."

"And I've had about all that I can take," Emery groaned. The squad of lawn ornaments had reduced back to a single Imp.

"On the topic of your gold," said Jon, his tone shifting ever so slightly towards grave. "We should discuss what you're going to do next, establish a plan."

"We've got plenty of time," I said optimistically.

"That's just it, I'm afraid. We don't." Something changed in Jon just then, and I had to rub my nonexistent eyes to get a good grasp of what I was looking at: my friend, my only friend in the world (present familiars excluded until further review) was disappearing.

Even as I try to remember now, it's difficult to describe. Because Jon's form had a strange, umbral pitch to its nature, he wasn't so much ceasing to be there, as the absence in the Universe created by his presence was being filled in with the rest of the world. He… came in and out, and I got the sense that this had been happening for some time. I had merely failed to notice until this condition had intensified past the point of 'normal'.

"Are you ill?" was all I could think to say, and he immediately put up a hand to steady my resolve.

"It's as you said before, my friend. 'Not all there.' Usually that means a person's mind isn't entirely composed, but it's a tad more literal in my case."

"Jon, I'm worried."

"Don't be. I'm perfectly fine, just… becoming slightly untethered from your plane of reality. You see, I don't originate from here. Well," he stopped himself, evidently reconsidering what he was saying. "I guess that's not completely accurate either. But the point is, I'm something of a guest on this plane. Staying here requires a lot of energy and effort, and I seem to be running out of both."

"So what happens then, if you run out completely?"

"I'll have to return to my plane of origin. Err, again not entirely correct, but you get the idea."

"I really don't," I said blankly.

"This isn't goodbye, if that's what you're worried about." He approached me and grabbed the umbrella, not disarming me of it but raising it so it was horizontal between us. "You can still contact me with this. You and I are linked by it."

"It's just, I assumed you were going to help me start my enterprise." I could hear the glumness in my own voice, and I regretted speaking at all.

"I am. I have two further instructions for you, and if you heed them you will find success."

"Alright, I'm listening."

"Northwest of here is a small town by the name of Humble Corners. Go there and look for a man named Raeden Lockwood. He's a short fellow with hair the colour of rust. Tell him Jon sent you, and he's calling in his favour from Duzt. Say it like that exactly, he'll know what it means. After that, he should be able to help you with whatever you require."

"I don't suppose I should ask any follow-up questions about this Lock-wood person?"

"You could, but our time is already limited. Are you ready for your second task?"

"I suppose."

"Throw away the Storm Sword."

I felt the urge to blink as I so often did when I didn't fully comprehend what I'd just heard. 'Storm Sword' was what Jon had said. I looked to my waist, and sure enough there was the weapon I had taken from the dungeon, the one apparently imbued with the properties of thunder and lightning. It sat awkwardly on my side due to being tied to my pelvic bone.

"Why?" I asked, a little more defensively than I intended. "It's mine."

"You have Magic Blast now, isn't that enough?"

"Frankly, it isn't." I was getting away from myself. Inside my skull I chided myself for my own feelings and actions; if Jon was telling me to do it, there must be a good reason. I couldn't help but take the idea personally, though.

"Tailored Illusion will enchant you and your umbrella, but anything else that's removed from your person will be exposed for what it is. That sword is far too rare and powerful, and the first town guard or lawman to check your possessions will ruin everything. At best they'll start asking questions you don't want to answer, and at worst you'll be found out for what you truly are."

"Isn't that something we all fear?"

"I'm serious, Charles. I know you're excited to have a weapon which can figuratively split the heavens, but it's more trouble than it's worth right now. There will be other swords."

I sighed. "You're right, you're absolutely right. I'm sorry, Jon, I don't know what came over me." I immediately untied the sword and regarded it intently. Jon nodded, and before I had the chance to reconsider, I threw it into the river. The water's surface crackled fleetingly on impact, but smoothed within moments of the blade sinking into its depths. Even now, the flowing waters continued to aid in my character development.

"I know that must not have been easy," Jon said, not without some sympathy.

"I don't much care to dwell on it. Are you going to be alright, friend?"

"I should be," he replied. "By and by."

"Then I'll wish you luck." If I had possessed tear ducts, I surely would have shed a tear or two at that moment. Jon put a ghostly hand on my shoulder.

"I wish you the same, my friend," said Jon, his form continuing to flicker almost excessively, but his calming tone coming through all the same.

"Just tell me one thing before you go." I let the words hang in an effort to build suspense, and sure enough the flickering slowed, as though Jon were clenching some metaphysical muscle to stay a moment longer. "Which way is northwest?"

Jon howled with laughter for several appreciated moments, then pointed. His laughter echoed as he faded from view, back to whatever shadow realm he may or may not have originated from. What a mysterious friend I had made.

"Well, Imp," I said to my only remaining companion. "I believe northwest is this way."

For the first time since making my egress from the dungeon, there was a proper rainstorm. However, I was surprisingly neutral to the whole affair; the horrid things about existing in the rain typically came from sopping wet hair and clothes that chilled one to the skin. Since I lacked all these things I found myself no more uncomfortable in rain than in sunshine. I did, however, have a satchel full of gold around my shoulder, but it was of a sturdy make, and I had no reason to assume my wealth was in any danger. To avoid any suspicion that may fall upon me, I cast Tailored Illusion for a new persona, a modest Elf ranger named Galen who looked sufficiently drenched.

"So your name is Emery?" I asked, trying to sound sincere. The Imp was currently perched on my shoulder in the form of a raven. If the rain bothered him he gave no clear sign of it.

"So what if it is?" His face pointed away from mine, gazing out at some vague point in space.

"Well I didn't give it to you, and I didn't hear Jon name you. Where did it come from?"

"It's just my name. I don't really think about it."

"Strange, given how you're only a day or so old." At this he turned towards me.

"You got some kind of issue with what I'm called?"

"It just reminds me of… nevermind. I don't suppose you could fly up and scout ahead to make sure we're still on the right path?"

"Beats making conversation down here, I guess." He pushed off from my shoulder and took flight, his ebon wings disappearing over the treeline.

I had to admit I was a little nervous about being around people again. Had my time in isolation made me strange, undesirable? Or was I just afraid that I was always that way, and pretending like my death had anything to do with it would only highlight that fact?

Of course there was Jon; we had gotten along just fine, but he was hardly 'people,' or was he? I had so little frame of reference (the uncertainty was actually a tad disquieting) but I had the persistent feeling that the rules didn't apply to him. But what rules? What game, for that matter? The answers evaded me for the time being, though I would consider them deeply during my quiet moments in the months ahead.

(We still have about an hour's walk ahead of us.)

I looked around, startled by the sudden voice. A blackbird appeared out of the sky and perched on my shoulder, wings dripping. I recognized it as Emery, and that he had spoken telepathically.

"This non-verbal thing will take some getting used to," I mumbled out loud.

(For you, maybe,) said Emery, again without words.

The rest of our walk consisted of sparse conversation. By the time we had found a dirt road, with a town just visible in the distance, the storm had broken. A pale grey light dominated the day, and the few others who shared the road looked particularly miserable, likely having been traveling for longer than we had.

"Anything to trade?" asked an unfamiliar voice. My first instinct was that someone was talking in my head as Emery did, but I quickly saw that a cart had pulled up beside me, strangely silent despite its lumbering shape.

"Excuse me?" was the only socially agreeable response I could think of.

"Going to do business in the Corners," said the Gnome driving upfront. "Wanted to see if you had anything good on you before I made it in."

My hand tightened around the satchel. "Nothing, I'm afraid. Practically a beggar, actually!" I laughed in an attempt to punctuate my point, but I kept it going too long and likely wound up looking quite mad.

"Ah, that's alright, then." He bid the two mules pulling him to pick up speed, and without thinking I began to jog alongside to keep pace.

"Excuse me, sir?" I called.

"Yes?" said the cart driver, polite enough but not stopping either.

"Begging your pardon, but I've been wondering. Garden gnomes, are they offensive? Assuming it isn't rude to ask, of course."

"Ha!" chortled the Gnome. "The only thing offensive about them is how much I charge for the little buggers." He slammed his fist into the cart wall directly behind him, and the entire side panel opened up, revealing a huge assortment of goods. Nestled between kitchen implements and farming tools was a row of garden gnomes, their faces lacking enough detail to make out a proper expression. The driver slammed his fist twice more, and the panel closed just as quickly as it had opened.

As the gates of Humble Corners grew closer, traffic was divided into two lines: those who had a vehicle, and those who did not. We moved briskly, which gave me hope that getting in would not be all that complicated.

"Name?" asked a city guard. He was Human, or at least looked Human. Couldn't have been older than twenty judging by his voice and size. He wore a barbute helmet and matching steel chainmail, apparently standard issue for local law enforcement in these parts, though his seemed a little big for him.

"Ch—" I began, before overthinking muddied my speech. Should I be giving my real name? I wasn't technically myself, but how much subterfuge was warranted? "Galen," I added, faking a cough to justify my pause.

"Chigalen?" he repeated back to me.

"...yes?"

(Dumb kid probably thinks that's just how Elf names sound,) laughed Emery.

"And what's your business in Humble Corners, Mister Chigalen?"

"I have business with a contact here," I answered honestly, contradicting my earlier thoughts of deception entirely.

"And do you have any weapons on you, sir?"

"No." I silently cursed Jon for his foresight. "Just my walking staff here, but I doubt I could hurt anything larger than, oh, an Imp with it." The raven on my shoulder chirped irately. I presented the disguised umbrella as though I had nothing to hide.

"Hmm…" said the guard, taking it from me and weighing it in his hand. At that moment I was thankful I lacked the ability to sweat. After a few seconds the guard handed the staff back to me. "Should be fine. Move along."

As I finally stepped through the threshold, I committed to the idea of not pressing my luck and immediately got to work. I'm not too proud of a Skeleton to admit that I was a little out of my depth. Trying to formulate a plan with my minimal resources felt like a waste of time, so I approached the problem head-on and simply began asking people if they knew Raeden Lockwood.

Most regarded me strangely, like I was some bizarre thing which had turned up at their doorstep. Did they have some sense of my true nature? Could they intune the skeletal form that sat beneath the deception of my custom Elven face?

Eventually one woman, a mother haggard by a day out shopping with three young children, told me she knew of no such individual, but had heard of a shop called 'Lockwood's Luxuries' that was in the next district. I bowed profusely in thanks, while one of the toddlers who was wrapped around her neck waved passionately at Emery, who remained indifferent and aloof.

The shop in question was a strange one. It was located around a corner and down an alley, a considerable distance from the main thoroughfare; it would be difficult to find unless one was specifically looking for it. And at a glance, the business seemed aimed towards people of a higher social status than the average citizen of Humble Corners, which only made it more of a delicious enigma.

A bell jingled pleasantly as I opened the door. Sunlight was shining brightly through the front window, and its rays shattered and bounced off the racks of jewelry in countless directions and colours. Finely dressed mannequins in suits and dresses alike were bathed in anarchistic rain- bows, not beholden to any particular set of chroma.

"Can I help you?" The voice came from a man standing behind a counter in the back corner, the bottom half of his body obscured. He wore a suit of khaki, which incidentally was the exact shade of the shelving unit behind him. I admired his sense of camouflage, but the effect was made moot as my eyes went straight to the mop of orange hair on his head.

"That depends," I said, trying to sound stoic. "Are you Raeden Lock- wood?"

"Who's asking?" The man walked forward and seemed to bisect his body on the countertop. Before I could fully register the horrific scene, I real- ized what I was looking at. His lower half was not, in fact, hidden behind the desk, but his entire body was actually on top of it. The man I suspected of being Raeden Lockwood was roughly three feet tall.

"Goodness, you're short," I blurted out, immediately regretting my own stupidity.

"Nothing gets by you," the man said flatly, and he hopped onto the floor to approach me. "What's the matter, never seen a Halfling before?"

"I… what exactly are you half of?"

"Depends on who you ask. Gnomes and Dwarves call us that because we're half of each of them, give or take a few drops in the gene pool. Hu- mans, though, think we look like pint-sized versions of them, thus 'Hal- flings'. Now once again I ask you, who wants to know?"

"Uhm, the wording you used before was 'Who's asking?', not 'Who wants to know?'"

"I'm calling the constable."

"Wait!" I shrieked. "Jon sent me."

"Jon? Jon who?"

"He…" I knocked my skull trying to recall his instructions. "He's calling in his favour from Duzt? He said you'd know what that means."

The Halfling's eyes went wide. His skin blanched, and I swear I saw a visible chill go up his body. He hurried past me with surprising speed and flipped the 'Open' sign on the door to 'Closed.' As he hastened back to the middle of the room, he clapped his hands three times, and every bit of glass on the exterior of the building tinted, giving the room a dark, muted look. By this point I was pretty confident I had found Raeden.

"Alright," he sighed, his breathing ragged from the sudden exertion. "I need your whole story."

"All of it?" I was a little taken aback by the bluntness of his request. "I just met you."

"Do you trust Jon?"

"I… I believe I do, yes."

"Then you can trust me. You'll have to, or else I can't help you."

"Alight. Can anyone see us through your window enchantment?"

"No one," he promised.

"Then… I suppose I should start from the beginning. Change-o!"

Raeden's reaction to my being a Skeleton was, to put it mildly, not what I expected. There was initial surprise, of course, but as he listened to my tale, from the dungeon and treasure to my learning of magic from our mutual acquaintance, there was this subdued, curious look of awe on his face. I could see the gears turning in his head, perhaps recognition that there was more to the world of magic and Skeletons than he had previously believed. But there was something else, another thought process growing behind the gears; there was cunning at work.

"That's quite the story," he said at last, examining the satchel of loot I had refused to take off throughout my tale. "And Jon was right, if anyone can help you, I can. But there's one thing I don't get."

"And what's that?"

"What exactly do you want me to do?"

"I don't understand."

"I get you have all this wealth, but what do you want to do with it? What does a better life look like to you?"

The question was surprisingly easy to answer. "Without a way to spend my treasure, my gold and jewels are just metal and rocks. I need power, security clout! I want to be someone who commands great influence in the world. I'm not a Dragon, and I refuse to sit in a cave richer than a king with no means of enjoying what I have. I'm a Skeleton, these bones have self-respect.

"You want to be a king? I can make you a king."

"...really? Just like that?"

"Well it would take some time, and a lot of shuffling of resources. But it's possible."

"King Charles…" I ruminated.

"Want my advice, though? Being a king isn't all it's cracked up to be. You could do a lot more with a lot less so-called 'power.' Royalty may be beneath you."

"What do you suggest, then?"

"How do you feel about nobility?" he smirked.

"I could do with some nobility."

"Alright." Raeden clapped his hands and rubbed his palms together. "We'll make you a noble. It will be tricky, but I can do it. I'll need you to trust me, though. Also half of what's in this bag of yours."

"Half?!" I spat. I could hear Emery's impassioned, derisive laughter rollicking in my head.

"Before you freak out," Raeden cautioned, holding up his hands as one would to try and calm a startled bull. "Keep in mind that with half I can get you everything; the keys to the kingdom. Figurative keys, since we've established an actual kingdom isn't the goal. After that, you'll only be making money. In fact, keep me on your payroll and I'll make your current holdings look like a handful of coppers."

It should come as no surprise to you, dear reader, that I eventually agreed to Raeden's proposal. It was difficult parting with so much gold; his share alone could have bought and sold my old life a hundred times over. But I'd learn very quickly that Raeden Lockwood was an exceptional promise keeper. Truth be told, I liked Raeden; initial impressions aside, he came off as someone I could depend on, and he'd wind up being gratifying company on the days I felt like I couldn't be myself.

What a shame, then, that he'd be dead by the end of this book.

CHAPTER 5 – Learn to Operate Within High Society

While Raeden saw to the necessary deeds, I procured a room above the local tavern, a watering hole with the charming name of 'Tumble Corners.' There were nicer inns I could have stayed at, but Raeden said this was the time to be penny-pinching. Until plans were underway, my holdings were finite and could easily dwindle if I wasn't careful.

I was left to my own devices for two days, and the boredom was merciless. Exploring the town should have been an easy answer, but I feared I had been removed from society for too long; I was rusty, and did not want to jeopardize the entire mission by bumbling around town getting lost, or worse. I knew that I would eventually need to be among people again; the notion gnawed at the back of my skull, but I chose to ignore it and settled down to practice my spells instead.

Magic Blast wasn't an option; while Tumble Corners was by no means a high-end establishment, I somehow doubted that holes in the wall would endear me to the management. But I could make my bed with Lesser Tele-kinesis; not like I was sleeping much, anyways. Just like back in the forest, there were times when I simply stopped functioning - I saw this as a kind of rest cycle, but they came and went sporadically and could happen anywhere, even while I was standing up. Just for fun, I once tried to do it consciously, and sure enough there was a noticeable passage of time once I came to my senses again.

"What strange abilities we Skeletons have," I mused to Emery.

"Calling it an 'ability' implies it's something useful," chuffed the Imp, who had taken his natural form whilst we were concealed from the world.

"Surely it will be useful!" I whined defensively. "I just haven't encountered a scenario yet in which it could be useful. But while we're on the subject, make yourself useful and go scout around. Find out interesting things about this town and report back to me."

"Me and my big mouth," Emery groaned. As he took off, his form shifted into that of a raven once again, leaving behind a handful of black feathers. After he left I tried to pick one up, but they melted into black vapor at my touch.

Raeden returned before my familiar did. He was dressed nicer than he had been at our first meeting. His cheap khaki business suit was replaced with a smooth, charcoal grey number, and his red hair was combed and tied into a smooth bun behind his head. Under his arm he had two brief-cases, both chocolate brown but one was longer than the other.

"Say what you will about mages," he panted. "But I'm the real miracle worker in these parts."
"Were you successful?" I prompted him eagerly.

"'Was I successful?' he asks me!" He dragged a small end table into the middle of the room and placed the smaller briefcase upon it, all the while giving me a dramatically pained look as if I had dishonored his mother's prized chili recipe by calling it 'adequate'.

"These," he began, referring to a stack of papers he had pulled out. "Will identify you irrefutably as a lord of these lands, the last heir of an obscure bloodline which still holds certain claims and titles. And this," he said, removing a gilded ring from the briefcase, "is your signet ring. It's a forgery, yes, but a good one. Remember these aren't actual magic. If someone did enough digging they could discover your true identity, or lack thereof, but by the time anyone would think to put in the effort, we'll have the resources necessary to make those problems go away."

"Impressive," I assessed.

"You gave me a lot of money," laughed Raeden. "You get what you pay for. Which brings me to my next point. Your birth certificate, complete with your new name. Now, there's still time to change it if you weren't completely—"

"You're the one who said I needed something fancy!" I objected. "I would have been fine remaining plain old Charles Miller, but apparently that's too blasé for high society."

"Yes, but 'Chadwick Bonesbury'… isn't it a little obvious?"

"Think of it like hiding in plain sight," I said optimistically. "And if anyone questions it, I can just say I'm descended from morticians."

"Fine," Raeden sighed. "I dub thee, Sir Chadwick Bonesbury the first, lord of the realm." He handed me a rolled up scroll as he spoke, and I was briefly caught up in the prestige of the moment.

"What realm am I the lord of, then?"

"We'll get to that. You should put these on, our carriage will be here in an hour and I don't want to be late." From the longer briefcase he produced several large bags, enough to make me wonder if the outer shell was somehow enchanted. He laid them out in a line before me and prompted me to open them. The first contained a pair of tall walking boots, the same charcoal grey as Raeden's suit.

"The best in form and function," he assured me.

In the next bag was a black velvet tailcoat, complete with matching pants, and a crisp white shirt with a heavily starched collar and cuffs. The third bag, the smallest, contained a pair of chalk white gloves, a navy blue bow tie made of the smoothest silk I'd ever seen, and a strange gold circle with a crystal lens inside.

"What's this, then?" I asked.

"That's a monocle," Raeden said, a hint of condescension in his tone. "You wear it over one eye, a lot of rich people have them."

"You'd think rich people could afford a whole pair of eyeglasses," I grumbled, struggling to get my pants on.
"You'd think," Raeden agreed.

"I don't see how all this is necessary," I told him plainly after I got the outfit on. "I could just whip up an illusion that does all this."

"Real is better in this case." Raeden walked over to stand between me and the mirror in the corner of the room, fussing with my bow tie and smoothing out any wrinkles in the fine fabric of my suit. "People will be able to tell, even if they wouldn't know it was an illusion specifically. Real clothes carry better, see, and that affects your poise. Plus, if you're stuck in a situation without magic, a skull face is easier to explain away than a skull body."

"I suppose you're right. I think I could get used to this look. But it's missing something…"

"Oh!" shouted Raeden, loud and sudden enough to make me jump in my new boots. "I can't believe I almost forgot. Here, take this." From out of the larger briefcase came a rounded, oblong box with a simple pop-off lid - now I knew that those briefcases were enchanted. Inside was the most beautiful hat I had ever seen: a jet black top hat with a shiny band of silk wrapped just above the brim, and fit my skull perfectly.

"Well?" asked my co-conspirator. "How do you feel, Chadwick?"

"In a word? Grand."

We rode in a modest carriage. I reasoned it could have fit about five adult Humans inside, or twice as many Gnomes, but other than myself, Raeden, and the Half-Elf coachman he hired (and Emery napping inside my hat, of course) we were alone.

I had chosen the guise of a Human man with high cheekbones, a strong chin, and eyes that were pale blue and a little misty. My hair was on the cusp between brown and blonde, and I wore it short. I was advised by Raeden to remember this arrangement of features well, since they were what the world would know as Chadwick Bonesbury. Emery refused to comment on my look, content to nap comfortably inside my spacious hat.

"Raeden?" I beckoned to my traveling companion, whose feet were dangling off the cushioned bench seat in front of me.

"Yes, Chadwick?"

"I have some concerns."

"And what would those be?"

"Well for starters, you haven't told me where we're going."

"I can see how that would be concerning," he said casually before taking a sip from a flask he pulled from inside his jacket.

"Where the hell are you taking me?"

"You are a lord without a castle, Chadwick, so first you need to acquire an estate. And less urgent but still important, you need to familiarize yourself with the elite. After all, you're one of them now. Lucky for us, both of these issues can be solved by attending an auction. There's one happening today a few miles northeast of here, so I took the liberty of securing you an invitation."

"I've never been to an auction before."

"I'm not surprised by that. It'll make good practice for you. But there's one important thing you need to keep in mind, not just when interacting with those of means, but anybody. You need to develop an underlying sense of superiority."

"I'm not sure I follow."

"People with wealth, especially those who are used to having wealth, naturally feel they exist above everything. To them, the world operates on a different level, a lesser one. In every conversation you have, you need to have one foot outside of it, as if the very act of interaction isn't worth your time.

"Be subdued but consistent in how you present your accomplishments. You're an important man, but a truly important man doesn't need to be brash or boastful. Your gravitas should be enough to tell people that."

"My gravitas?"

"The way you carry yourself. Rich people possess a certain aura, you know."

"Well where are we going to get one of those?!"

"This might be harder than I thought…"

Thanks to Raeden, I received numerous (and frustratingly vague) lessons on how to be a rich person. However, as our journey continued I was finding it more and more difficult to focus on his tips and tricks, and instead spent most of the trip gazing out the window. Memories of my old life were fuzzy, made up of half-true recollections and a distinct lack of divide between dreams and facts, but I was fairly certain I had owned a cart of some kind. Whatever it had been, it wasn't nearly as fast as this vehicle, where the landscape seemed to pass us by as if we were flying.

Eventually we reached the grounds of Hanging Gardens, an estate whose name, Raeden told me, could be morbidly traced back to its original use: a gallows complex where criminals could be hanged en masse. It was eventually bought and converted into a sort of country club, and to legitimize the name, they erected elaborate hanging basket displays of flowers as a permanent fixture.

Our credentials were checked by a sentryman at the front gate. His entire face creased when we told him my name, as if he was attempting to calculate the degree to which he should be impressed. Raeden assured me later it wasn't his job to know every house and family that held prominence in this land, only to keep out the riff raff. A flash of my signet ring was enough to get us through without the least bit of fuss.

A valet relieved us of our carriage, while a well-dressed Human man with slicked-back hair told us to follow him. We were led through the front doors of a grand building, evidently the main structure of Hanging Gardens. We found ourselves inside a huge ballroom, at least three stories high. The floors and walls were all made from polished marble, with a crystal chandelier swaying ever so slightly above the room, both emanating light and reflecting it around the room with equal gusto. The whole area had a clean yet artificial feel to it; there wasn't a single bit of wood or stone in sight.

"Presenting Sir Chadwick Bonesbury, and concomitant," our escort announced to the room. For a brief moment, all conversation stopped as every head and eye turned our way. Just then it occurred to me how woefully unprepared I was for this moment. Was I supposed to say something? Wave? Bow? I was teetering on a needle, where even the slightest incorrect action or inaction could ruin me. I wracked my brain for anything Raeden had said which might guide me. The best I could manage was to turn up my illusory nose and strut forward, trying my damndest to look like I was too good to be here.

To my surprise, the sashay served its purpose. Conversation resumed, and I received no more than an occasional side-eye from the other guests.

"Care for a refreshment, m'lord?" asked a waiter. He carried a silver tray full of appetizers and drinks that was far too big to be carried on the single hand he was using; the only thing keeping it from the consequences of gravity was some kind of mechanism attached to his forearm. I helped myself to a cup of tea and sipped it gingerly.

"Go easy on that stuff," Raeden reminded me. "The padding we put in your ribcage is only so absorbent."

"I remember. What exactly are we supposed to be doing?"

"The main event doesn't start for almost an hour. So you should be mingling, meeting your fellow attendees."

"Like who?"

"I can only offer so much input, 'm'lord.' Don't let all the pomp and circumstance fool you, these things are no different than schoolhouse social circles. Just pick a coterie and insert yourself into their dynamic."

I looked around the room, scanning for potential people of interest. One table was occupied entirely by a group dressed in similar attire: dull coloured suits with wide-brimmed hats, elegant leather gloves, and modest capes. While I appreciated their fashion sense, they seemed a miserable lot. The man in the middle, an older-looking Elf, spoke calmly while the others nodded. A few were vigorously taking notes on small reams of paper, flipping pages with a sharp 'phifft'.

"Tell me about them, Raeden."

"That's the D'Graszia family," he said with reverence. "Very important, and powerful. The amount of business they deal in is astronomical. Almost assuredly involved in organized crime. Hell, they are organized crime. The law never seems to catch up with them, though."

"When you've got money, I guess you're able to pull further ahead than the rest of us," I sighed, already looking for a better target. "Tell me about that short fellow, the one dressed like me."

"The Dwarf?" Raeden seemed surprised when I gestured towards a large group which was congregating by a table in the corner. At its epicenter was a man a little over four feet tall, with a massive dark beard tied up in braids. He had on a stovepipe hat — its height rivaled mine significantly - and he wore a dark suit similar to my wardrobe but with particular nuances I couldn't quite fathom. He was smoking a cigar and laughing, a deep and vigorous sound that could only come from a full belly laugh; he was apparently in the middle of telling an amusing story.

"That would be Sunder Blackstone," Raeden reported. "Heir to a massive fortune. His family owns a coal mine across the sea, in the far north. It's fabled to be bottomless."

"What's he doing all the way over here?"

"Probably on vacation. Either that or his family couldn't stand his obnoxious antics and needed to send him away for a while. Likely a bit of both. He's known for being… eccentric."

"That's something we'll have in common soon enough, I reckon." Before my companion had a chance to approve of or veto my decision, I made my way over to the corner with as much of a confident strut as I could muster.

"…and it turned out those rare stones he was trying to barter with were, in fact, Dragon eggs!" Sunder bellowed to the assembly. "No idea how the merchant got the damn things, or how he had evaded their parents for so long. But just then those lizards arrived and I tell you, it was a sight! We had just replenished the coal reserves, you see, so the whole town was especially flammable. I've met master wizards who couldn't cast a fireball that big!"

There were laughs from the group, some more hesitant than others.

"Was there no helping the people?" asked a finely-dressed woman sitting next to Sunder. She wore an emerald ring and a silk dress to match.

"The thing you must understand about Dragons, princess," spouted Sunder between puffs on his cigar. "They are creatures of passion. If they wanted that town destroyed, it would be destroyed one way or the other. It just so happened that my family's coal, sold at a charitable rate I'll have you know, hastened the inferno. Tragic, really."

"How did you survive?" I asked. There were worse ways to implant myself into the conversation, at least that's what I told myself. And the question was honest enough.

"Finally!" the Dwarf shouted. "Someone else who knows how to dress. What's your name, man?"

"Err, Chadwick—" I mumbled. The name would take some getting used to, but I reminded myself that it was necessary to keep up this lofty facade if I was to make a worthwhile impression. "Sir Chadwick Bonesbury. Charmed, I'm sure."

"Quite," Sunder retorted. "To answer your question, Bonesbury, it just so happened that my coachman was an expert tunneler. His father had dug tunnels in the war, you know. He managed to direct my entire entourage to dig, and these tunnels were beauties, mind you, a sight to behold if we weren't digging for our lives. He led us so deep and so far underground that not even a cinder followed us down that hole. Saved my life, he did."

"How brave of you," said the woman in the green dress. Did I sense a bit of sarcasm in her voice? Sunder had referred to her as 'princess'; what kind of relationship did they have that would warrant that kind of pet name? "What sort of business are you in, Mister Bonesbury?" she asked me suddenly.

"Me?" I looked around for Raeden, but he was across the room with a plate full of sandwiches, chatting up one of the men from the D'Graszia table. "What businesses aren't I in? 'A wide net yields a big catch,' I always say." I laughed nervously, hoping none of them realized I had just made-up the expression.

"Ha! I like this one," Sunder laughed. "Many pots, but too few hands, eh? Are you local, Chadwick?"

"Oh, that's a complicated question," I tittered. "I am, but I've been away for some time. Hoping to… reinvent myself, I suppose."

"That sounds lovely," said the mystery woman. "I hope you won't find me rude, but I have to find my party before the auction begins. Much to discuss, still. We'll get properly acquainted another time, I'm sure. Gentleman." She gave a gesture somewhere between a bow and a curtsy before leaving, followed by three men from the crowd who seemed to be attendants of some kind. As Sunder's audience thinned, many gave respectful bows before moving on, while others stood awkwardly, unsure of whether they should stay or go, before leaving with no goodbye at all.

"What a magnificent woman," Sunder sighed. "Can I offer you a cigar, Chadwick? My own special brand."

"Oh, that's mighty generous, my friend, but I don't think I have the lungs for it. I'll stick with my tea." Sunder nodded, unoffended, before gesturing for me to sit with him. "Tell me, though; who is that woman you were speaking with?"

"Oh, that was Valeria Mercy, the princess of Mot."[5]

I deeply regretted taking a sip of tea just then, because I immediately and involuntarily spit it back out all over Sunder Blackstone.

Shame altered my perception of time after that. Raeden hurried over, followed by multiple staff armed with towels. He tried to stammer some hasty explanation as to why I had just dealt Sunder this grievous offense, before the Dwarf held up a hand to silence him. Shockingly, he began to laugh.

"Don't worry, lad! I remember my first princess. No harm done." One of the stewards waved a small wand over Sunder, who became relatively cleaner and dryer than before my spraying incident. "And I'll count my doused cigar as the one you would have taken had you not refused." He winked at me, then set off for some other circle of bluebloods.

To his credit, Raeden waited until Sunder was out of earshot before scolding me for my lack of decorum. I nodded, not really listening to what he had to say. He then led me around the room to meet with various other important people. They smiled and laughed and said all kinds of things. I smiled back and bobbed my head up and down, oblivious to what they were saying.

The only ones who called my mind back to some kind of attention were the D'Graszias. There was something about the way they presented themselves that unsettled me. They emanated all the power of royalty, but were nothing like what I imagined royalty to be. They moved uniformly, and whenever one of them spoke they did it quickly, not wasting words and cutting straight to the point. Accentuating their presence was a young Elven girl with silver hair, a servant judging by her comparatively drab attire, who played the violin beautifully but was clearly in some kind of daze.

The older Elf, one Metrion D'Graszia (whom I came to understand was

_____
5   The continent that Humans hail from. Across the sea to the southeast from Elarden, I would later learn it is divided into three kingdoms. Valeria's family rules the south kingdom. I hope to visit it someday.

the family patriarch) was the only one who looked me in the eye while speaking. He too asked what business I was in, but with more interest in specifics than Valeria. Raeden covered for me, saying we were currently in the process of restructuring and looking for new pursuits in the region. I approved of the deceit; it was the truth, technically, though shaped to our purpose. Metrion narrowed his eyes but wished us luck in our endeavours.

Then it was time for the auction to begin.

We were led out in groups to the garden area, where dozens of chairs had been arranged in front of a large bandstand. Stewards tried to direct traffic, but most of the guests just sat wherever they wanted. Raeden fetched us a numbered sign, a vermilion paddle with '32' written in bold sky blue print, and I happily followed his lead to available chairs.

"Patrons hold these up to make a bid," Raeden explained.

"I know that!" I hissed.

"No you didn't," huffed the Halfling. "Now isn't the time to be making extravagant purchases. You want random crap? Buy it on your own time. We're here to get you an estate."

The auctioneer was another Halfling. This one wore burgundy suspenders and a bowler hat the shade of an eggplant that seemed to glow in the sunlight. He thanked everyone for coming and then immediately began the proceedings. I was amazed by the speed with which he spoke, somehow listing off item descriptions and asking for starting bids all in the same breath.

To be honest, there were very few items that I didn't want. A collection of swords once owned by a master swordsman by the name of Lituin. An emerald necklace which could protect one from certain magic assaults. Paintings and statues of great heroes of legend and royalty whose names I didn't know. It broke my heart when I saw my old Storm Sword being brought to the front of the stage; according to the auctioneer, it had been recovered by a fisherman from a nearby river. Raeden saw me eying it, and encouraged me to sit on my paddle before I did something stupid.

That strategy worked for a while, until I found myself bidding on a one-of-a-kind firearm known as a Ripple Gun. Only fired once by the grey caster[6] who made it, the auctioneer explained, its body made from electrum, with segments of the most striking shades of cobalt blue and violet. Its exterior had electric coils, crystals, and containers of vibrantly coloured liquids, all of which came together to make one of the gaudiest weapons to ever see the light of day. I bid five hundred gold pieces over the other bidder, and actually won it. I was thrilled.

"You're an idiot, Chadwick."

"That may or may not be true, but now I'm an idiot with the finest mantlepiece on Elarden."

There was only one other item before the one we were waiting for: the last shield used by the Elven prince Nuemin, which bore the image of a swan facing forward with outstretched wings. Raeden whispered that this was

good luck for us, since the more robust bidders were likely to exhaust their coin purses on such a piece. Finally, there was the announcement of an estate, located only a few miles from Hanging Gardens.

"Once home to the famous Gnome bard, Coglio Magella!" the auctioneer announced enthusiastically. "Violin Heights is fifty acres of beautiful local real estate! Shall we start the bidding at one hundred platinum?"

There were murmurs from the crowd. All the starting bids up until now had been in gold, and even with this more potent currency, as Raeden explained to me, one hundred platinum wasn't much for a property like this.

"Why so low, then?" someone shouted.

"I'll tell you why!" Turning in my seat, I saw it was Sunder, who was standing on his chair to be better seen and heard by everyone. "Coglio Magella was a mad genius! Plenty of genius, yes, but with twice as much of the madness! He took his own life last winter. It was in his own house, wasn't it?"

---

6   Artificers who blend magic with technological innovation and engineering. One of my dearest friends in the world happens to be a grey caster, but do forgive me if you don't meet them in this book…

"Shall…" the auctioneer trailed off, visibly sweating and showing signs of subdued rage. "Shall we start the bidding at one hundred platinum?" The fine print was evidently not up for discussion right now.

"One hundred platinum!" called one of the D'Graszias, their group taking up a section of seats somewhere between Sunder and I.

"Two hundred!" roared Sunder.

"Bid now, you skeletal dolt," Raeden whispered to me out of the corner of his mouth.

"Five hundred!" There was something admittedly addictive about this exercise.

"One thousand platinum!" It was the D'Graszias again. A few of their members were looking my way with icy stares. Metrion did not, merely stewing in his seat while a vein throbbed fiercely on his temple.

"Twelve hundred!" I put forward. I looked to Raeden for a sign in case I was overextending, but he was incredibly still in his seat. That's when I caught on that something was wrong, but what? I jabbed his bicep with my finger to no reaction whatsoever. Suddenly, everything seemed far too quiet, save for the dulcet tones of a stringed instrument. I observed that everyone around us was frozen in place - everyone save for Metrion D'Graszia, who had stood up and turned towards me.

"I suggest you reevaluate your course of action, Mister Bonesbury."

"Are… are you freezing time right now?" The thought was enough to make my blood run cold. Wherever my blood had gone, I wished it well.

"Please," he said contemptuously. "Only gods can stop time. This little trick is just to give us some privacy. My son is a talented enough mage, and my bard has her uses." My sight drifted to Metrion's flank, where one of the younger men was muttering and making arcane hand gestures, and the silver-haired musician I had spotted before was playing her violin. "It's an easy enough feat with the Power of Three."

"The Power of Three?"

"I didn't come here to teach neophytes about the rules of magic. I came here to acquire Violin Heights. The property presents a… very desirable investment for my company. So my recommendation to you is that when the auction resumes, you keep your paddle down and your mouth shut."

"Are you threatening me, sir?"

"Just a bit of friendly advice. I would hate for our professional relationship to be soiled before it can even begin. I hold a lot of influence in this region, it can be hard for an enterprise to thrive here without me as their advocate. And Mister Bonesbury?"

"Hmm?"

"That was a threat."

There was an abrupt snapping sound, and suddenly everyone around us was moving and speaking once more. Metrion's son looked around worriedly, as if this was happening earlier than planned. The patriarch shot a death glare towards the bard girl, who was nervously inspecting the string which had come undone on her violin.

"Are you placing a bid, Lord D'Graszia?" questioned the auctioneer.

Metrion looked around, befuddled but only momentarily, before taking his seat again and proclaiming "Fifteen hundred platinum!"

Raeden swirled his index finger around the side of his head and smirked at me. I had a quiet giggle about the context my friend was missing, but decided to let him go on believing Metrion D'Graszia was a madman. I considered the gravity of our clandestine discussion for just a moment, but my mind and heart were already decided when the auction resumed.

"Twenty-five hundred platinum!" I shouted, making a point to slowly turn my head towards the D'Graszias. My coy smile almost faltered when I saw that the musician had been crying, but the daggers I saw in Metrion's eyes cemented my grin rather than enfeebled it. Chadwick Bonesbury was a new man, and I decided he didn't much care for bullies or scoundrels.

"Going once, going twice, sold! Congratulations to Mister Bonesbury on his new home!"

CHAPTER 6 – Stand Out

I had to spend two more nights at Tumble Corners while my new home was made ready for our arrival. A skeleton crew (pun not intended but appreciated) of former staff had agreed to stay on for sixteen weeks for a set wage, after which we were expected to either make them an offer or hire replacements. Apparently, the method by which their previous employer had vacated the premises had left many of them quite distressed, if not a little disturbed, so the realtor advised I not get too attached.

While affairs were being settled, I wasted no time and directed Emery to retrieve the rest of my treasure. He and his shadow copies, of which he could safely maintain about ten, were to delve into the dungeon I had awoken in, armed with leather sacks. I could hear the Imp's whinging inside my mind the whole time he was gone, but in between bouts of complaining he kept me up to date on his mission, reporting that none of the dungeon's undead defenses were giving him any trouble. It may have only been step one of the plan, but to say its success was a load off my mind would have been an understatement.

Step two involved the group filling their sacks with as much treasure as they could carry; they would then bring it outside, under the cover of night, to a waiting armoured carriage procured by Raeden. Carriages would come every hour on the hour — the task might take longer than necessary, but it would also be less noticeable. The loot would be transported to Violin Heights, which conveniently already came equipped with a massive safe. The handoffs had begun one hour after dusk, and ended just over an hour before dawn.

"I did it," I said aloud to no one. "I can't believe I actually did it."

(You mean I did it,) Emery spoke into my mind from miles away. (Now if you'll excuse me, I'm going to sleep for a week. If you need me for anything, I suggest you don't.)

A carriage came for me the next morning, with Raeden waiting for me inside. Once we were on our way, he asked me how I was feeling.

"Good, I suppose. I'm excited to see the house."

"I'll warn you now," he said neutrally. "The place needs a lot of work. That old bard was a bit of a recluse. Not many people outside his staff saw him in the flesh during the last few years of his life. Home upkeep was probably the last thing on his mind."

"You do realize my last home was a dank hole in the ground, right? And before that… well, nothing as nice as where we're going, I'm sure."

"Fair enough," Raeden shrugged. "I had a grey caster come by to reinforce your safe from physical and magical tampering. His credentials are good; he knows his stuff. Nothing short of an Elder Dragon is getting in there."

"Then let's hope to never encounter an Elder Dragon, then. I quite enjoy being rich, I'd like to keep it up for at least a little while."

 "Oh, I wouldn't worry about that. Dragon slaying is a pretty popular profession these days."

"Really?" I put down the newspaper I had been aimlessly flipping through.

"Dragons have been pretty feisty for the last few years. Some of the more radical ones have been making trouble in the north and overseas. A lot of kingdoms are sponsoring guilds to train dragonslayers. It pays well, and comes with a lot of glory. Hell, I might even try it if this little experiment goes belly up."

"'Little experiment'?" I scoffed. "You mean my life?"

"Easy, now. Just a little teasing between friends. Speaking of, look and see what an excellent friend I've been. Behold!" Raeden opened a briefcase that had been sitting on the carriage floor and produced a series of coloured file folders. I opened one to find a multi-page contract, which I attempted to decipher, but the print was small and densely packed on the pages. I put it away and opened another, but my perception of this one was not much different from the first.

"What are these, then?"

"They're contracts, Chadwick."

"I can see that!"

"They're from people who want us to invest in them. Your business, Bonesbury Holdings, is already growing!"

"That's wonderful! So we have all these contracts?"

"Well, no," Raeden said in a cadence one might use with a child who asked if it was possible to eat the sun. "We can't invest in everything. We'll spread ourselves too thin, or risk diminishing returns. I'm just showing you these as samples, ideas of where we'd like the company to go."

"I see…" I thumbed through the remaining folders, feeling more and more ignorant of such matters with every page, followed by a growing sense of shame for my ignorance. "I'll be honest, Raeden… I don't have much of an eye for this sort of thing. I think I'm fine with giving you creative control on this one. Just so long as you make me money, I don't really care what you do with the company."

"Wow," Raeden sighed, his smile gleaming. "I appreciate the confidence."

"Just not the D'Graszias," I punctuated. "Anyone but them." His smile disappeared so quickly I started to wonder if it had ever been there.

"Why not just say you actually don't want to be rich, Chadwick? It could save us a lot of time and effort."

"Surely aligning ourselves with that dreadful family can't be the only way to turn a profit."

"But it would help!" squawked Raeden. "Ugh, your mind's made up, isn't it?"

"I'm afraid it is."

"Fine." To emphasize his frustration, Raeden separated half the contracts from the pile and threw them out the window. "They'll be more useful to the birds for their nests. You're lucky I'm good. Good at my job, and a good friend. Okay, this will be interesting…"

We reached Violin Heights by lunchtime. The first thing that amazed me about it was how long it took us to get to the front door even after the coachman had announced that we'd arrived. Realizing how much land there was between my home and the borders of the estate made me feel big in a way I'd never experienced before.

Light born from an overcast sky did little to illuminate the house, which was nevertheless framed nicely by a wall of green trees on the far end of the property. It brought to mind the forest that encompassed my family's cottage when I was a boy, and I felt more at home than I had in ages.

Three figures stood waiting for us as we pulled up to the front door. Raeden explained that these were the remaining heads of staff, each of whom would be overseeing a team of less than half a dozen people. When we exited the carriage they each bowed with varying levels of enthusiasm. Raeden introduced them from right to left.

"Fred Avalon," he said, referring to a Human man with atrocious posture and a large forehead. "Groundskeeper and custodial services. In want of more staff, he'll also be the substitute maintenance man and head architect of Violin Heights."

"How do you do, Mister Avalon?"

"Before I was hired, Master Magella said a Human wouldn't make a good groundskeeper because our lifespans aren't long enough to see the long term impact of our work."

"I see…"

"Sorry, sir," Fred sputtered. "I'm trying to say I'm good at my job… because he hired me anyway despite his preconceived notions. I've put a lot of work into this place, I'd like to stay on if it's at all possible."

"I'm sure we can work something out." I noticed a complete shift in Fred's body language afterwards, as though the simplest assurance was enough to put him at ease. Never made eye contact with me once, though.

"This is Hayra Bloomkin," Raeden gestured to the Halfling woman standing in the middle of the trio. Her hair, as if informed by her name, was the colour of dried grass, and I could see that she had bags under her eyes. "She's the head gardener around here, one of the finest on Elarden. During this transitionary period I've been told she's taken on culinary duties, as well."

"And housekeeping!" she added. Her voice was unusually high-pitched, and she had a sing-song way of speaking. "I'm a woman of many hats, you know."

"That's splendid," I said uneasily, not sure what to make of her tone. As if she sensed my discontent, her smile suddenly melted. After sniffling once, she began to blubber as tears poured passionately from her eyes.

"Oh, Mister Bonesbury!" she wailed, grabbing one of my hands with both of hers and pulling me closer; from her grip I could tell she pulled weeds all day long. "The gardens here mean everything to me! Coglio was so supportive of my creative pursuits, that poor man. I can't bear the thought of anyone else tending to my babies. I'll be fine no matter what happens, but they need me."

"Miss Bloomkin, was it?" I tried to sound sympathetic, but made sure to pull my hand away just the same.

"Please, call me Hayra," she whimpered.

"Hayra. I've only just arrived, but I can tell you right now I haven't come here with the intention of firing anybody."

"Oh, really? That's wonderful news! Bless you, sir!" she exclaimed through her tears, which hadn't ceased throughout our interaction.

"Pull yourself together, Bloomkin," chastised the third and final staff-member, an Elf in a chestnut-coloured suit. His hair was neatly trimmed and stark white, which made him look older but with a distinct and distinguished air. I had to remind myself that this gentleman could easily be over two hundred years old, though he looked not a day over thirty by Human standards.

"And who might you be?" I asked, trying to sound authoritative.

"Pontius Breadalbane, sir," he said, standing at attention with his arms straight as boards at his side, his eyeline just above the horizon. "Or simply Breadalbane, if you like. When the Heights is operating at full capacity, I am the butler and head of staff, as well as the guest director. I've since taken on partial housekeeping duties, as well as assisting Miss Bloomkin in the kitchen when necessary."

"Fantastic," I smiled. "And I take it you also wish to tell me how much you like your job and want to stay on?"

He hesitated for a moment before leaning ever so slightly towards me, whispering, "May I speak plainly, sir?"

"I insist on it." I failed to match his secretive tone, but lowered my voice a tad all the same.

"While some staff," he began, pausing to side-eye Hayra and Fred, "are eager for confirmation that they will be rehired, many of us are just here to finish the last four months of our contracts, after which we'll be happy to never see this place again."

"That's quite the statement." One thing I enjoyed about my Tailored Illusion was knowing that I now had eyebrows to adequately express my astonishment in times like this. "Is there a particular reason why?"

"I'm not sure it's my place to say, sir." It was only now his posture loosened, and his talent for eye-contact began to align with Fred's.

"Oh, now I must know," I said, equally with my eyebrows as with my words.

"It's the belief of some of the staff that the Heights is haunted…by the ghost of Coglio Magella."

I looked to Raeden, who shrugged nonchalantly. Hayra whimpered and put a hand over her mouth. Fred had his head bowed, not looking at anyone.

"What fostered this belief?" I asked Breadalbane.

"There's been phenomena…"

"Oh, we just miss him, that's all!" argued Hayra.

"My hair wasn't white a week ago!" the butler shot back.

"You're scared of your own shadow!"

"Maybe if you actually set foot in the house once in a while instead of playing outside in the dirt-!"

"Well I have to admit I'm intrigued," I interjected loudly, trying to lighten the tone. "Ghosts, strange affairs. But if you're eager to leave, I won't impede your exit. We'll just have to get you training your replacement sooner than expected."

"That being said, sir." Breadalbane adjusted his lapels; he seemed to have regained his composure. "It is also part of my function to serve as concierge. Anything you need, whether it be internal or external, you need merely come to me and I will make it happen. If you have a particular request for lunch, I can alert the kitchen to it. If you wish to have a portrait painted, I will summon an artist here forthwith."

"I imagine you'll be remarkably useful, then. I'll be sorry to see you go."

"Is there anything I can do for you at the present time, sir?"

I surveyed the massive house before me, with its boring, even paint job and boring, uniform windows, and smiled. "I have a few ideas."

When Breadalbane made me his offer, I suspect his intention was something in the vein of preparing afternoon tea. Little did he know that I had been almost immediately inspired by the mansion before me. After giving me a compulsory tour (I promise to give you one as well in the coming chapters, dear reader) the butler showed me to a study in the northeast corner of the building, accommodating my request for a private space to discuss my ideas.

Producing an inkwell and quill seemingly from thin air, Breadalbane readied himself to take notes while I dictated. In no short order, I instructed him to find the finest architects, artists, and artificers that this country had to offer and bring them all to Violin Heights. No, not the finest. The most extreme ones. I told Breadalbane to find me artisans who were so dedicated to their craft and so capable in their ambitions that they have soiled their own reputations by virtue of innovation. This property was now owned by a man like no other; it should have an appearance to match.

Raeden stood towards the back of the room, observing the scene with his arms crossed and an incredulous smile on his face. He would ask me later where this sudden creative surge had come from.

"All this could be gone tomorrow," I would tell him. "For this brief moment in history, I am an obscenely wealthy Skeleton. I'd like to leave my mark while I have the opportunity. And besides, if I'm not rich enough to indulge whatever stupid idea or impulse that bursts forth from my skull, what's the point of any of this?"

He would look on during the meeting while I turned my attention to Hayra. She had seemed flustered since meeting us outside, but her mood improved dramatically when I told her I wished to expand the gardens.

"I want huge floral displays, creeping vines. What do you think about a hedge maze?"

"I've got just the thing!" she squawked, and ran out of the room. She was gone for several minutes, but before anyone could suggest going to check on her she rushed back into the room with a large scrapbook. Inside was a number of sketches and designs for elaborate garden arrangements. Walls covered with ivy and flowering vines that would depict living mosaics, the scenes changing as they transitioned from buds to open blooms to faded seed heads. Exact plans for how to grow and trim hedges to look like fantastic monsters and animals. The ideas went on and on.

"Did you do these yourself, Hayra? You're some kind of genius," I raved as I flipped through her drawings that filled every page.

"Oh, you're too kind, sir."

The next few weeks saw very little rest. A team of artisans had been assembled to almost my exact, inane specifications. Many esteemed engineers and builders were hired to be mere general laborers, jobs they were grossly overqualified for, while the renovation project was overseen by a single man: a Gnome artificer by the name of Glyph Bonben. Though architecture and interior design were far from his expertise, he was a great inventor who had been banned from most major guilds on the continent for either the number of workplace injuries or the extent of property damage caused by his inventions — sometimes both.

"Science and artifice require sacrifice!" he told me during his interview. He was very reluctant to work on a job like the one I had described to him, but when he received his first commission (in advance) he started to come around to the idea. His involvement was solidified by the assurance that he would be in charge of a group of people who were required to listen to every word he had to say.

Under Bonben's guidance and near-total artistic control, the Heights received numerous new additions and architectural angles to give it that otherworldly visage I had envisioned. His team of engineers and builders were opposed, at first, with taking orders from an untested supervisor such as Glyph, but his passion and personality quickly won their hearts for the most part. Content with his leadership skills, I spent my time working directly with a second team composed of artists and craftspeople to ensure that the smaller details would also reflect my sensibilities.

We hit our first hurdle early in the project, when I was told flat out that there was a shortage of materials. Apparently, there was a war going on across the sea which was slowing imports - how inconsiderate. So with limited options for immediate commissions, I asked my artisans what was readily available.

"Glasswork, m'lord," a young Elf told me. "We can make you glass sculptures in azure blue or ruby red."

"I think that will do nicely!" I agreed.

"Which colour, m'lord?"

"Oh, I don't like making decisions. It'll have to be both, I suppose." The team all shared unsure looks between them, but I figure I must have seemed imposing, because not a single one raised an objection or concern.

So thanks to some tiff across the sea, a number of paintings and statues were bought secondhand. Some depicted great heroes or epic battles, while others were loud and abstract. I made sure to include one tasteful depiction of an Elven Skeleton, which was hung with pride in the library. In addition to these, over a dozen blue and red glass art fixtures were installed throughout the estate and all over the grounds. On the sunnier days, with which we were blessed many, they would cast the most wonderful purple light. As a result, many of the workers and merchants bringing supplies would mistakenly use the name 'Violet Heights.' The name stuck, as people would quickly use this moniker instead of the correct 'Violin Heights,' including myself. Hayra was particularly fond of the name, and started growing petunias, lilacs, and hydrangeas to match the aesthetic.

At the end of a particularly long day, I retreated to my bedroom, a monument to excess in itself, and laid back on my bed. I had given explicit instructions that I was not to be disturbed for any reason, and so…

"Change-o," I whispered. Without getting up, I turned my head towards a looking glass hung on the far wall. There I was, a Skeleton who had somehow found himself in finery and silk sheets. My experience had been lovely thus far, for the most part, but it was still a relief to exist just as myself for a moment, and not the curated persona of an eccentric aristocrat that I was becoming. Had the lines blurred? Were there even lines anymore?

My mind struggled for answers for half an hour, a fruitless endeavour with no clear answer in sight. I reached for my umbrella, bringing it close and feeling the silky fabric between my bony fingers without my gloves on. For weeks I had been too busy, literally building this new life of mine. Maybe I was just distracting myself with pretty projects to keep from opening myself up to disappointment. What if it didn't work? My heart (lack of an actual heart aside) knew I could delay no longer. I held the umbrella aloft and opened it.

A shade cast down from its underside, unnatural for the level of light which filled the room. I gazed into it, that dark outpouring, and caught signs of movement. Stepping into the threshold between that black abyss and my bedroom, was a Human-shaped shadow.

"Jon!" I cheered.

"Hello, Charles," he replied, smiling with his words if not his face, of which he had none. "It's good to see you."

"Likewise! And it's Chadwick, now. I've accomplished quite a lot since we parted ways."

"I can see that. Look at you, all fancy dress, no illusions. You're quite the made man."

"I'm glad you're here."

"So, shall we get started?" he asked me plainly.

"Started on what?"

"Why," he smiled again. "Learning more spells, of course."

CHAPTER 7 – Find the Right Balance Between Yes Men and Effective Personnel

Greetings, dear reader! Welcome to chapter seven — that's a third of the way through this book, for those of you who neglected to read the table of contents. I'll be honest and admit that I didn't think I'd get this far, but I'm so happy you have. Let's celebrate our mutual accomplishment by diving further into the story, shall we?

Violet Heights was becoming a truly remarkable place. Did it not make sense, then, to fill it with a remarkable staff? I had so many straightforward options ahead of me, the best money could buy and all that. But 'straightforward' wasn't in my vocabulary. I wanted the best — the 'best of the best' if you will - but oh, so much more than that.

Transferable skills, for example, are some of the most overlooked talents in the world. Why, consider Glyph Bonben! Here is a man with not a single day of architectural experience in his life, let alone on his résumé. His talent for design is wanting, and his knowledge of the finer methods of construction is spotty, at best. Nevertheless, he is the one I selected to refurbish my house. His background as a grey caster gave him an eye for blending magic and science in a way that no 'straightforward' designer ever would. I was confident he would help me turn my home into a do-main of majesty and whimsy, and I would use this same logic to fill the remaining staff positions at Violet Heights.

I'm especially fond of how I went about appointing our chief of security. There was a particular name that had been tickling the back of my skull since the auction, a proverbial thread which compelled me to pull it so I may witness the outcome.

"Lituin, my lord?" I had caught Breadalbane in the middle of preparing iced tea for the workers, but he dutifully put down his tray and stood at attention. I must admit, sometimes he made me feel like a schoolmarm constantly quizzing him on algebra.

"Yes, Lituin, I believe he's some sort of master swordsman. What else do you know of him?"

"His father was a known legend," Breadalbane recited, as if I was indeed quizzing him, "who died well into old age, even for an Elf. Served in the military for many years, then left Elarden to train overseas in Gielran."

"Gielran…?" I questioned. Breadalbane had named it so casually, like it was any other country or island, but I had never heard of it. Was it simply that my knowledge of geography was greatly lacking, or had I miscalculated how much time had passed between my death and reawakening in that dungeon? (One day, while we were going over documents I needed to sign, Raeden mentioned that the year was 223 AFG. Those numbers and letters meant nothing to me, but I was too embarrassed to ask for an explanation).

"Yes, sir. Gielran. That's where Lituin was born. He's supposed to be a renowned fighter, very accomplished despite his young age."

"I think I'd like him brought here, if at all possible."

"Sir…?"

"His swords were sold in the same auction where I acquired Violet Heights. I bet he's not that far from here, wouldn't you agree?"

"His family does hail from this region originally," Breadalbane conceded. "I could make some inquiries. But sir-,"

"You can call me Chadwick, Breadalbane. Or 'Mister Bonesbury,' if Chadwick is too informal."

"Mister Bonesbury. Lituin is a figure of some acclaim, and furthermore, he is someone with no permanent residence or homestead. These factors will make locating him difficult at best."

"I'm not asking you to perform miracles, Breadalbane, just to do your best."

"As you wish, sir."

It was almost a week before I received any update on my request. It was becoming clear to me just how seriously Breadalbane took his duties as concierge. With some light prompting I convinced him to tell me a bit about himself, and apparently his family went back many generations in this area. His family tree possessed members from all four varieties of Elf: those of the forest in the east, those of the cities in the west, those of the cold tundras in the north, and those of the deserts in the south. With a social profile like that, Breadalbane had cultivated a long list of contacts and informants over his two hundred years on this world.

And it was this very network that found Lituin.

In the last four months, the Elven celebrity had been spotted by several people in the region. The head record-keeper of Hanging Gardens had confirmed that the collection of swords had been sold to them directly by Lituin, who gave no reason as to why he was parting with such an impressive arsenal, only that he was in need of coin. This left me hopeful that, with a little monetary compensation, he could be persuaded towards my way of thinking.

From there, it only took some rudimentary detective work to find the swordsman. He was just an hour away by horseback, and thanks to my forethought of sending along a personally addressed letter which politely summoned Lituin to Violet Heights, he was alerted with no unnecessary delay.

In hindsight, perhaps a little delay would have been nice, as Lituin's response reached our door a mere four hours ahead of his arrival. With so little time to prepare, and priority of course given to the transient warrior, my business dealings for the day were immediately canceled. I'm sure this came as a great annoyance to Jacob Ryker, the man Raeden had recently hired as our director of finance, who was already seated with a cup of tea and paperwork in front of him. I wasn't particularly fond of the man, but he was exceptional when it came to numbers; Raeden insisted that we needed him, that Ryker considered money above all else to be holy. Ergo, he saw me as a saintly man, which meant I could bet on his forgiveness.

Lituin arrived with no fanfare. As far as we could tell, he had walked the entire way. Breadalbane showed him to the lounge and offered him refreshments, which the swordsman accepted with humble gratitude. He took one sip of tea before setting down the cup on its saucer and did not touch it again. I showed myself in just minutes after Lituin, who politely acknowledged his list of feats as I prattled on, before asking me why he had been summoned.

"Did my letter not explain?" I laughed. "We're building something here, something grand and wonderful. I'll have no one but the best for my head of security."

"Yes, that much was clear. But I am not a security operative. I study the blade."

"You're an expert, I appreciate that."

"While your offer is most gracious, Mister Bonesbury," he said with what seemed like a great deal of trepidation. "I'm afraid I must decline."

"If it's a matter of money-" I began, but he shook his head.

"Respectfully, that is not the issue, Mister Bonesbury. I crossed the seas to come here so that I could pursue my Great Work."

"'Great Work'?"

"If I may," Breadalbane chimed in from his corner of the lounge. "Some Elves choose to spend our long lifespans perfecting a particular skill or profession. It is our 'Kula-Vay,' which loosely translates in the Human tongue to 'Great Work.'" Lituin smiled warmly, seemingly grateful someone else had defined it so succinctly.

"I see," I said after a short pause. "May I ask what your 'Kula-Vay' is, Lituin? Swordsmanship?"

"I can see why you might assume that," the Elf chuckled. "But no, that was my father's task. He was unparalleled in his day, but he was already quite old and past his prime when I was born. Before he died, I observed him at his happiest when he was teaching his art to others. And so, my chosen goal is to become a great teacher."

"How admirable!" I cheered.

"It is my intention to open a school. This is why I sold my swords to the auction, to gain the necessary funds, and it is why I cannot commit to a position here."

"So you've already founded the school?" I asked, with a heightened tone of innocence so as not to betray my true plan. I held no malicious intent towards this man, I assure you, but he was imperative to my vision and I could not risk him leaving the grounds, regardless of his noble dream. Besides, there was a certain satisfaction in circling around his wishes while, in reality, achieving mine; I believed my verbal opponent was none the wiser, which sweetened the entire plot.

"This I have not done," he said softly, bowing his head. "I underestimated the amount of money and work that was necessary to do such a thing. There is a long road ahead of me."

"What if I could shorten it for you?" I smirked. This was almost too easy.

"I don't understand your meaning, Mister Bonesbury."

"Open your school here!" I shouted, as I leapt to my feet with enough force that it knocked my armchair over. "At Violet Heights! Let me fund the entire thing. You could pay me back by becoming my head of security, so we both get what we want!"

"You would do that for me, sir?" Lituin stood now as well, meeting me on my level both figuratively and literally.

"Of course! Instead of tuition, simply require that all your students spend a set amount of time protecting my estate. Say, one year? Gods, it's so simple! Every student would be trained to your impeccable standards, and Violet Heights would have an endless supply of guards for her protection!"

"This would be a great service to me, sir!"

"The honour would be mine, I assure you," I grinned, barely containing the giddiness building inside me. "I'll make all the arrangements and do more for you, on one condition."

"Anything."

"Make me your first student."

"You wish to learn the blade?" Lituin gasped.

"Well, I'm already so accomplished." I winked an illusory eye to convey that I was merely joking. "I have wealth, looks, magic, a dizzying intellect. I could use something a bit more somatic to round out the list, don't you think?"

"That sounds wonderful, Mister Bonesbury!"

"Call me Chadwick."

And that was how I became a swordsman.

Other staff acquisitions had more mundane origins, but some led to interesting results. Breadalbane had put out notices for a head housekeeper, as well as a permanent on-site cook. True, I couldn't taste any of the dinners Hayra made, but there had been murmurs among the staff that her meals were a little too… grassy.

We had dozens of applicants, all with impressive bios from a wide range of backgrounds and specialties. But remember, I desired only the most extraordinary staff for my estate. So while Breadalbane would make a note of all promising individuals, he was instructed to alert me personally about any strange or unconventional cases.

It didn't take long. One woman, a Dwarf, applied with no résumé to speak of. When asked whether she was inquiring about the housekeeper or cook position, she seemed confused, telling Breadalbane that she assumed both were part of a single ad. When he tried to turn her away, she insisted on doing an interview with me directly. I imagine he scoffed at her as he left her standing in the foyer; of course, I accepted.

Calliope Baines. Ninety-three years old, which was just south of middle aged as far as Dwarves went. She wore her auburn hair in a messy bee-hive, and her blue eyes were as dark as the night sky. I met her in the same lounge where I had acquired Lituin, and asked her directly why she felt she was qualified to fill not one, but two important positions here at Violet Heights.

"Well, I'm from Dorovan, you see. Husband dragged me and the little ones here across the ocean some decades ago."

"How many children do you have, Mrs. Baines?"

"Twelve."

"Gods above!" I cried, momentarily losing my composure. "Erm, please allow me to apologize for my outburst. I realize that was rude."

"Never you worry. Now, back to it. I'm a capable housekeeper and cook because I spent nearly thirty years taking care of all those little buggers, and all by myself to boot. I don't need a résumé to tell anyone that."

"What about your husband?"

"Left 'im. Good riddance, too. The whole reason he brought us here was because of some damn pyramid scheme."

"Oh dear. Selling something?"

"No!" she declared. "Some awful man convinced him there were actual pyramids! Here, in Elarden! What a ridiculous notion. The idiot thought

he was going to become some great treasure hunter, feed us with sacred rubies
and cursed amulets. But he was a worthless clod even before all that, so I was
better off for it."

"I admire your resolve," I told her honestly.

"Thank you. All the kids are grown now. Some are in school, a lot are working.
A couple went off to look for their father, the ungrateful lumps. So I need something to do with my time, and the fights are starting to wear on me."

"The fights?"

"How do you think I kept all those mouths fed? Not by slavin' away in some
mine or workhouse, no sir! I was in the pugilist league, a real tough as dirt fighting guild."

"Goodness. That's quite the claim."

"Don't push me and you won't have to see me prove it," she said sternly.

"Understood. Simply put, Mrs. Baines, I like your moxie."

"Thank you. So do I have the job or not?"

"Right to the point, you are."

"No point being any other way, I reckon."

"Quite right." I stood up and extended a hand to my interviewee. "Welcome to
the team, Calliope."

"Nice to be welcomed," she concurred, clasping my arm past the wrist and shaking it firmly.

Other staff members merit some explanation, and I won't spend too much time on them, but Felsha the Pursuer is certainly someone of note. While Hayra and I were developing the new layout for Violet Heights, she affectionately referred to me as a peacock on account of my penchant for fancy clothing. This immediately sent my mind racing, and I set out to acquire a great number of exotic birds for the grounds. These mainly consisted of peacocks (obviously), as well as flamingos for no other reason than they amused me.

This attracted the attention of Felsha, a semi-infamous Half-Elf beastmaster. Evidently, she had spent the last two years obsessively tracking a bird of mythic ancestry, one which possessed a certain amount of phoenix blood in its physiology. As it turned out, said bird was one of my flamingos, which had been unknowingly swept up with the flock.

This realization was a surprise to all of us, though not as surprising as having a 6-foot tall wild woman show up on my doorstep, hammering on the heavy oak door with her fist and demanding my bird. The woman was quite obstinate about the matter, refusing to leave until she got her prize. Lituin managed to get her away from the house, but she could often be spotted lurking on the periphery of the forest. After three days I had finally had enough, so I marched out to those woods single-handedly (Lituin was only fifteen feet behind me; I'm brave, not stupid!) and demanded a parley.

"Speak, whelp."

"Lovely…" I cringed. "Look, we are clearly two fantastic, exceptional individuals. We possess comparable levels of passion and similar thickness of skulls. I appreciate the fact that I can see a little bit of myself in you."

"Your words are cheap, aristocrat." She spat that last word with palpable disgust. "Insulting for one of such wealth, but expected. I will not sit idly by while you hoard animals the way a Dragon hoards gold."

"Oh, I have plenty of gold, too."

"Feh!"

"Alright, alright. Consider this, then. If I own these animals, that prevents others from owning them. Or worse, hunting them. My menagerie could be a service to the beasts of this world, under the right supervision, of course. I assure you, no living thing is a bauble at Violet Heights. Everyone in my home and on my land will be cared for."

Before responding, Felsha reached into her blouse and retrieved an opalescent pendant, made from some kind of stone or crystal that I could not discern. She considered it briefly before saying "You speak of supervision. Even if I believed your words, how am I to believe you will do right by these animals and find someone worthy of them?"

"Because it should be you." I registered the faintest twitch in Felsha's eyebrow, the only tell she gave away of her surprise. "Come work for me. Care for my animals, and protect them from those beasties which stalk these woods and prowl this world." I neglected to share my notion that building a fence would have been simpler and more effective in the long run. "I'll even pay you more than your wild little heart can dream of."

"Do you think you can sway me with the promise of coin?"

"No, I think I can sway you with the allure of the job. I'm offering to pay you merely as a courtesy. You could even go out in the world and find other specimens, equally in need of protection and admiration, if you don't want to stay cooped up here all year."

She narrowed her eyes but said nothing. In place of a response, she retreated backwards into the trees, never taking her gaze off me, until she disappeared. I silently applauded her flair for the dramatic, yet another trait we had in common. She never formally accepted a job position at Violet Heights, but after our meeting I would often find her tending the animals lovingly, sometimes with a smile, and she in turn would often find a pouch of gold tied around the ankles of one of my flamingos.

At the start of this passage, I said I would not spend too much time on Felsha. Looking back, I see I have gotten carried away…I detest editing, so I'll simply tell you about one more staff member, this time with no fanfare or clever transition.

The subject of Breadalbane's replacement was hotly anticipated around Violet Heights. This was the case because I let slip to the biggest gossips among the staff (Calliope and Fred, for the curious among you) that an interesting character was being interviewed for the position, and no other applicants were being considered at this time. I adore drama and suspense (at least when I'm the one supplying it) so this was just my way of making a little fun.

On the day the interview was to occur, a carriage arrived which appeared to move on its own power. After releasing its passenger, it turned around and left the grounds entirely, disappearing shortly after it passed through the front gate. Either our guest was starkly confident that he would have no need to leave after today, or he possessed some secret means of summoning the vehicle as needed.

The man in question was Human, very slender, and looked to be in his late twenties. His raven hair was relatively short, ending just past his ears, and he had an equally dark goatee which he kept well-groomed. He wore an expensive-looking dark blue suit. Raeden would later comment that it was something I would wear if I weren't, and I quote, an "aesthetic maniac."

"You picked these clothes out for me!" I would protest.

"Yes, Chadwick," Raeden sighed." To make an impression at your first public appearance. But you refuse to wear anything else, so now you've made an impression on the entire world of fashion. You know, the way a rock makes an impression on someone's head."

Ahem, anyway…

I wanted Breadalbane to wait with me in the lounge, since it was his position being filled. However, this led to the question of who would meet the applicant at the front door in his stead. There were a lot of enthusiastic offers from various staff members, but the job ultimately went to Felsha, primarily because I knew she was the only one with zero interest in the whole affair.

"May I return to the animals, now?" she asked after showing him in.

"Yes, Felsha. Please begone," I affectionately commanded. She nodded and lef
paying no more mind to our visitor. "Come in, sit down. Did you have any tr
ble finding the place?"

"None," said the man as he sat down. "I just followed the purple glow emanat
across the countryside."

"It's really quite lovely, isn't it? Tea?"

"I'm fine, thank you." He surveyed the room, commenting on a painting of a
sailboat on choppy waters hung above my chesterfield.

"Sadly, I cannot take credit for that choice," I lamented. "It predates me here.
fine enough piece, I'm sure. It's just so…"

"Ordinary?" he put forth.

"Yes, exactly! I knew I liked you."

"You'd have to, in order to pay a complete stranger what you're offering." He
leaned forward and arched his fingers like a steeple; up close, I could see a pe
ring on his right index finger. "I'm fascinated by your logic, Mister Bonesbur

"Well, my headhunters said you were a promising candidate." Breadalbane sid
eyed me, knowing full well that was a bold-faced lie. "And your credentials
speak for themselves. The latest graduate of the Wizards' Guild, colour me im
pressed!"

"I'm hardly the only one. Besides, I feel I'm simultaneously overqualified for t
job and painfully underprepared. Why me?"

"We've been having this same conversation a lot this past week, haven't we,
Breadalbane?"

"Yes, sir."

"Call it a hunch," I admitted, turning back to face the Violet Heights hopeful.
like the idea of a talented young wizard helping to run things around here. W
not you? Plus, I'm absurdly rich, I can afford to go all in on a hunch."

"I don't know what to say." I could see confusion in his eyes, but his mouth betrayed a smile.

"Say you'll do it. If you don't like it, retire in a couple years on the small fortune you'll amass from your salary."

"That is a compelling argument. Alright, I guess I'll do it," he said cheerily.

"Wonderful!" I shouted. We both stood and shook hands. "Breadalbane, please welcome Alan Miller to Violet Heights."

(I sense some context may be required, dear reader, as I just laid upon you a shocking revelation. Did you catch it? Maybe you did, maybe you didn't. For my own sake, or perhaps my own ego, I'll elaborate).

Around the time Glyph had begun renovations on the house, I tasked Breadalbane with an important mission, one which was to be treated with the utmost secrecy. He was already busy looking into Lituin's availability and undertaking about five other ongoing tasks, but he said he would do his best regardless. If he despised me for the workload, he showed no sign of it.

I provided Breadalbane with only a name. The name was not one of note. The person in question came from no noble family, nor did they do any famous deeds; to make it even more challenging, they lived over two hundred years ago. Despite these hurdles, I needed information on this person, as much as Breadalbane could find.

The name was Sterling Miller. They were the child of farmers, an Elf father and a Human mother. When Sterling was just an infant, their only brother was married off to the daughter of a family who owned a great swathe of land across the countryside, so the two siblings had no relationship or further contact. When Sterling came of age, they took a wife and had at least four children; many years later the father died, and Sterling inherited the family farm.

Breadalbane could only find information on one of Sterling's children: Abraham Miller. Abraham was a rambunctious kid, as stated in the personal journal of the town's librarian. Farming and mercantile pursuits were apparently beneath his interests, and when he reached the age of sixteen he set out on a pilgrimage to find adventure. Sadly, he only made it two towns over before offending a local warlord and having one of his legs emancipated from his body.

As it turned out, had he arrived just a day later he might have joined forces with a small band of heroes who eventually managed to overthrow said warlord. But fate is rarely so clear-cut. Instead, Abraham fell madly in love with the town's healer, who had been tending to his grievous wound while the other heroes found glory and began on their path towards becoming legends. They married quickly and had one child together, Alan Miller. Unlike his father, Alan was a mild-mannered boy who was well-known, even from a young age, for offering aid to anyone he met.

A good deed done for a passing stranger with no thought of a reward earned thirteen-year-old Alan a lesser spellbook, which he carefully studied over the next few years. As it turned out, he had an innate talent for minor spellcraft; nothing too fantastical, just enough to lend aid and comfort to those in need, as was his nature. This talent led to him being scouted by the Wizards' Guild, an institution for blue casters, from which he had only just recently graduated. Alumni are given a grace period, during which time they can decide whether they wish to join the guild permanently or pursue academia or other exploits elsewhere. It was during this small window that Breadalbane was able to track him down and offer him the job, upon my request.

But why, then, did I go out of my way, wasting both my time and resources, and those of my employee, just to track down this one person who was in no way suited for stewardship? Well, dear reader, it's quite simple, really. You see, Sterling's older brother was me.

Alan is, therefore, my great nephew and, as far as I am aware, my only living relative.

CHAPTER 8 – Actually Start a Business

There came a time, nearly four months into my residency at Violet Heights, that Raeden saw fit to educate me on the very basics of our business. Apparently, I had embarrassed him more than once with my ignorance during the few meetings that required my physical attendance. Raeden may be the one making all the relevant decisions in this company, but I was still its figurehead, and as such I was expected to keep up a certain appearance of competency if we were to be successful.

While we did have some international interests, Bonesbury Holdings was primarily focused on Elarden, so my instruction began there. Elarden was a massive continent in Gaiyax's northern hemisphere. Its highest territory touched the north pole, and its bottommost edge came close to the equator. Massive forests covered its eastern half, domain ruled over by the aptly named Forest Elves. Very tribal, generally peaceful; if no one bothered them, they were the furthest thing from a bother to others. Their neighbours who controlled the central and northern portions of the continent were the Grey Elves: wardens of the north who were said to hold back the coldest winds.

To the west were the City Elves, the quintessential example that often springs to mind when one thinks of Elves. Posh, sophisticated, elitist; they see themselves as paragons of culture and intelligence, dedicating their long lives to the pursuit of great talents and accomplishments. And finally, to the south were the Dry Elves, so named because they lived in the most arid, dusty deserts Elarden had to offer. They lacked much of the decorum that graced the other tribes, living out their innumerable days as humble workers and warriors.

The country we resided in — which I was shocked to learn had no official name — began in the southeast where the forests and the deserts canceled each other out, and extended across a great peninsula which stuck out into the sea. This land had been ceded some time ago to those in need, the immigrants and the exiles and anyone without a place to call home. However, there was a thinly-veiled and dark purpose behind this ostensibly charitable decree: the peninsula was the most vulnerable domain in the War of the Ardens, and so no tribe wanted to endanger their own people by settling there.

What was the War of the Ardens, you ask? Well you see, to the south of Elarden was another massive continent called Ardennor, home of the Orcs. Some ancient territorial dispute which long-predated even the oldest living Elves, had led to a conflict between the Dry Elves and the Orcs, which spread like wildfire into a blaze which burns on to this day. Each year, both sides would hurl thousands of soldiers at one another, and nobody ever gained much ground.

The sea which surrounded our little peninsula seemed to impede both parties, as neither side possessed much in the way of naval capabilities. Raeden told me that the Elves had one of the smallest navies of all the major races, second only to the Dwarves, who sank like rocks and generally avoided large bodies of water when they could help it. So most of the fighting happened on land. But, if an attack did come by sea, our country would be the first to suffer, thanks to the 'ideal' landing sites along our miles of coastline. Supposedly, Raeden said, it had happened once before, a long time ago.

"I know it has," I seethed, quietly fuming with a rage I hadn't expected. My entire life, and the lives of my entire family, had been nothing more than fodder for Elves who would never know or care about us. And I had been ignorant to it, limited by my narrow awareness of the world. But how was I to process this information? Assume all Elf tribes were unfeeling, wretched bastards who personally sanctioned our suffering? I couldn't, and I knew I couldn't because it wasn't true, and that aggravated me in re ways than I have room to describe in these pages.

to distract myself from this glut of emotions I did something uncharacter-
:: I actually focused on the task at hand. Raeden expounded about how the
erent tribes had different relationships with one another, and different sub-
ups within the tribes had even more complex ones. What our company did,
imple terms, was pay existing manufacturers across the continent to make
ir goods, which they would be making regardless of our involvement (I am
uncertain of how Raeden managed to finagle such a deal). In exchange, we
l a level of control over which groups those goods were sold to, with every-
receiving a share in the profits.

turally, we get a little more profit than everyone else," Raeden added with a
k.

turally," I winked back. The motion still felt strange, conjuring my illuso-
ace to wink when I had none of the actual physical components. I glanced
mery, who was busy napping on the desk between us, today in the form of
rge black rat. "I assume, if you're giving me this crash course now, we have
ne sort of important meeting today that I need to be ready for?"

e do."

ho with?"

he D'Graszias."

hat?!" On the bright side, my indignant rage was gone. However, it was re-
ced with blind, petty fury.

ow don't overreact-"

u went behind my back!"

adwick, I run your company for you. Everything I do for you is done behind
ir back, you bonehead." I thought Emery had been asleep, but I heard him
gh inside my head when Raeden used his favorite insult.

lon't want to do business with those people," I said petulantly, using my
brella like a pool cue to knock my familiar onto the floor. "I thought you

said you were good at your job, that you could make me money without them?"

"I am, I can, and I have been. But it would be so much easier if you let go of this childish animosity. And, I can't stress this enough, so much more profitable!"

"I'm already wealthier than I could possibly fathom. I don't want to be greedy."

"Ha!" howled the Halfling. "The ship has sailed on that one, my friend."

"Careful, Raeden."

"Just do the meeting, you impossible pile of bones. Our business has a strong foundation now, and plenty of clout. We can hold our own against the D'Graszias."

"I won't do it."

A few hours later I was waiting for the D'Graszias to arrive.

I was positively stewing in the front hall. Raeden, Jacob, Breadalbane, and Alan stood with me and, to their credit, they gave my rage a wide berth. It had become a habit for me to wear my rapier on my hip at all times, so I imagined I must have looked a tad intimidating.

I gave special instructions to the entire staff. Hayra was given just a few hours to make the most breathtaking and flamboyant floral displays; to the surprise of no one, they were spectacular. Fred worked overtime making sure every blade of grass was uniform and every tree was trimmed to code. On one half of the lawn, Lituin was teaching a small class of beginners rudimentary fencing exercises, with free license to show off once our guests arrived. On the other half, Felsha had brought out the most vibrant and exceptional-looking animals, purely for their afternoon exercise and no ulterior purpose.

A gilded carriage appeared on the drive, along with a retinue of knights on horseback, two in front and two behind. Everything about the procession was immediately offensive to me; even the dust it kicked up seemed especially maniacal. When Metrion finally stepped out, I started to approach but Raeden put a hand in front of me.

"Don't. Let him make the first move," he whispered. "On the surface it comes off as being polite, but it also gives you the opportunity to react. We control the conversation, we win the day."

"Hello, Mister Bonesbury," said Metrion, followed by three men dressed in the same ugly suits from the auction. Behind them, the silver-haired Elf girl tripped on her way out of the carriage. Metrion gave her an open look of disgust, then nodded at one of his men who I thought I recognized as the one he called his son. The junior D'Graszia helped the bard to her feet before giving her a swift, decisive smack on the back of the head.

"We're happy to be here," the patriarch grinned once the pair caught up to their party.

"Metrion!" I cheered. "You old gargoyle, you." Raeden immediately cleared his throat to curb my cattier impulses. "So good to have you with us today."

"Violin Heights looks… quite different from the last time I saw it."

"People have taken to calling it 'Violet Heights,' actually. I'm probably going to make the name official. Why not? After all, I do own it."

"Mister D'Graszia!" Raeden interjected. "My name is Raeden Lockwood, business manager for Bonesbury Holdings. If you and your entourage would like to come inside for refreshments, I'm sure we can discuss our affairs in a more comfortable setting."

"Nonsense!" Everyone turned to me as if I had just emphatically belched. "There will be plenty of time for business later. Let me treat you to a personal tour of my abode."

"I have seen the interior of Violin Heights before," sneered Metrion.

"Ahh, but you have yet to witness Violet Heights. Violin Heights was merely a building, one which has since gone through a metamorphosis like no other! Come, it will be a grand time. Breadalbane and Alan will take your drink orders."

(Did I not promise you a tour, dear reader? Don't say I've never been good to you.)

As I led the D'Graszias into the main hall, I caught glimpses of a frustrated Raeden, who was trying to signal me with his eyes. I decided to gamble a bit and ignored him, wagering that he'd eventually forgive me for playing with my food.

"I really do love the main hall," I announced. "Look at all this marble. Have you seen this much marble before, Metrion? Of course you have." He had stopped to inspect the statue I had procured to fill the empty space in the middle of the room. "Ah, a fellow admirer of dragons, are you?"

"This monstrosity is atrocious," he said with open disgust. "What's it made from, blue jade?"

"Carved azurite. I think it holds a certain charm, like a part of the ocean that's been frozen solid."

"Let's just get this ridiculous tour over with."

If one were to look left upon entering Violet Heights, they would be greeted by a set of double doors which led into the lounge, complete with comfortable seating for relaxing and receiving guests. The opposing wall was made of the clearest glass and thinnest iron rails, so as not to disrupt the views of Hayra's impressive gardens and the distant hills surrounding the estate. Even the door handles that led out onto the patio beyond were hidden within the ingenious design.

Continuing past the lounge was the dining hall, sure to be the site of many dinner parties. And those parties would require food and drink, all of which would be prepared in the ample kitchen that lay in the back corner of the building, accessible through a hidden door in the dining room's back wall. Who wants to see where the chickens are cooked, am I right?

The rear of the house, which lay facing north, was where the heaviest

modifications had occurred. A modest servants' quarters had been converted into a large and state-of-the art dormitory for all my colorful and
treasured employees. A door at the very back of the room led to what
had once been Fred Avalon's storage shed, which was also upscaled to be
of better use. Somehow, Glyph had managed to fit his workshop in there
alongside Fred's yard tools, which to me sounded cramped and far from
ideal, but I was told the pair got along like a house on fire.

A seldom-used fitness room was converted into a full dojo where Lituin
hosted his training sessions. Should students want to train their minds
as well as their bodies, next door in the northeast corner was a two-story
library where I had already spent a lot of my time. For more private study
was the…study, a cozy space which continued down the east wall. Before
completing the full circuit you'd hit the games room near the front of the
house. Nothing too elaborate; billiards, darts, a card table, and a wonderfully chaotic Gnomish game known as "foosball."

The second floor, accessed by a dramatic spiral staircase behind my azurite dragon, was half unused rooms and half peacocking, with an art gal-
lery next to the library and a room for baubles and "treasures" next to
that. These last two were sparsely decorated, but I intended on filling them
over the course of this new life I had made for myself.

Metrion took it all in with unenthused tolerance. If you have yet to notice,
reader, I find certain social situations, especially those with a heightened
degree of expectation, to be a tad overwhelming. As such, I admit that I'm
prone to, sometimes, not picking up on obvious details until much later.
In this case, it was the fact that Metrion's bard had been playing sweet,
dulcet tones on her violin since we had brought them all in here. I asked
him about it on our way back down to the lounge.

"The girl has some use," he said with all the love and tenderness of a
sleep-deprived honey badger. Her playing had faltered when I referred
to her directly, but a stern look from Metrion kept her in tune. "I am often plagued by headaches, and bardic magic is one of the few things that
keeps them at bay. I wouldn't keep her in my employ otherwise. Good
help is so hard to find."

"Really? That hasn't been my experience." I allowed myself a quick smile
at Breadalbane and Alan, who had been dutifully following us with trays

of drinks and little sandwiches. Breadalbane stayed as stone-faced and respectable as ever, but Alan gave me a little smirk when he caught my meaning.

Back downstairs, Raeden expressed his delight that business could finally commence. I could tell from his tone and his body language that he was uneasy, desperate for this to go well. For his sake I hoped it would, but I had no idea what I might do should things take a turn. I considered there to be two Chadwicks: there was the me that existed in the current moment, the one I consciously inhabited, but there was also the Chadwick composed entirely of impulse and instinct. And of course, there was poor old Charles Miller, who crouched beneath both of them.

None of the prior owners of this house had been particularly business-minded, so there was no official boardroom. Instead, a spare dining room table was brought into the lounge, placed just a few feet from the Ripple Gun in its place of honour on the fireplace mantle. The couches had been removed during our little house tour, by whom and to where I neither knew nor cared about at that moment, as the meeting was about to begin.

The D'Graszias took the far side of the table, with Metrion in the middle and his people on either side of him. Everyone sat but the bard, who continued to play inconspicuously behind her benefactor. I mirrored their intent and placed myself across from Metrion, with Raeden and Jacob around me; Alan and Breadalbane stood at attention behind us; ready to serve as needed.

I didn't have to do much talking at first. We were informed, succinctly, of all the ways in which the D'Graszias could help us. Primarily, it seemed, they would give us access to certain high-profile clients who were sure to provide a lot of business, along with proprietary use of a number of factories across the continent that would exponentially increase our output of goods.

"That doesn't sound half-bad," I posited.

"Wait for it," Raeden warned under his breath.

In exchange, we were expected to turn over a percentage of Bonesbury Holdings every quarter, starting today. Within two years, the D'Graszias would own fifty-one percent of our business. In five years, Bonesbury Holdings would no longer exist.

"And in exchange for this generous offer," Metrion added. "We will take possession of Violin Heights. Immediately, of course, but you can have a month to get your affairs in order."

"Are you joking?" I scoffed.

"Chadwick…" cautioned Raeden.

"No, I really want to know." I stood up forcefully. My chair would have fallen over had Breadalbane not deftly caught it with his foot. "Who the hell do you think you are, suggesting a deal like that? 'Gracious offer,' ha!"

"Mister Bonesbury," said the head of the D'Graszia clan. "If you could put aside your bluster and stop caterwauling for just a few minutes, you'd be able to see that this offer is really the best thing for your… little operation." He smugly folded his hands in front of him to emphasize his point. "Maybe your little friend can explain it to you."

"Well, I think—" Raeden started to say before I cut him off.

"Don't be ridiculous! Tell me how no business is supposed to be good for our business?"

"With our help, you'll make more in those five years than you would in ten on your own. And selling to me now is better than letting your company fester and die, at which point you'll be lucky to get a handful of coppers for it."

"Bonesbury Holdings is doing great!"

"Chadwick. May I call you Chadwick?"

"No."

"Chadwick. While it's true that your company has made a few economic accomplishments, it doesn't change what you are."

"And what am I?" I asked incredulously.

"A foppish buffoon playing businessman the same way that children play house. The truth is, you need us. We will always be a client's first choice. We're older, better respected and well-established. And that isn't even factoring in what will happen if we blacklist you. I warned you before, I hold a lot of influence in this region. You do not want to test how far my power goes."

"Ooo, I'm rattling in my silk boots." Metrion sighed, evidently not an appreciator of my sarcasm.

"Charming. Here is the contract listing all our terms." He slid a small stack of papers across the table. "Read it, don't read it, frankly I don't care. This is your last and only hope, so you just need to sign it."

I snatched up the document with as much intense, visible animosity as I could conjure, not allowing myself to break eye contact with Metrion as I did so. I flipped through the pages, observing neatly-written gobbledygook not unlike the contracts Raeden had first presented to me on our arrival at Violet Heights. I turned to my friend, and he was looking at me with large, pleading eyes.

"Well…I suppose we should at least discuss it," I declared, sinking back into my chair and hunching over the table. "Alan, could you give us some privacy, please?" Alan took a step forward and pointed his index finger towards the ceiling, drawing messy circles in the air with it. His pearl ring glowed a baby blue colour, which spread out from its source to the ceiling and cascaded like a waterfall over our side of the table.

"You're in a Zone of Silence now, Mister Bonesbury. No one outside of this bubble can hear what we say."

"Thank you, Alan. Raeden, I believe you were about to tell me not to do something stupid?"

"Chadwick, please don't do anything stupid!"

"Alan, I think your spell is broken, there seems to be an echo in here."

"Listen," Raeden implored. "This guy's a scumbag, I know that." I gave Metrion a toothy, insincere smile when he said that. "But he's offering us a lot here. We can haggle, get something better out of it. Dissolve the company in ten years, maybe even twenty. By then you'll be rich enough to do whatever you want in the world."

"I like my company, though…"

"You don't know the first thing about our company."

"I'm not giving up this house! I won it at that auction fair and square. And…" I looked back at Breadalbane and Alan, and I caught a glimpse of shadows moving under the door; surely Calliope and the others listening in. "I've put a lot of work into this place."

"Yeah, I'll admit that's weird." Raeden rubbed his chin. "This place is valuable, sure, but what's its value to him?"

"Likely it's all my superb, post-modern additions to the house."

"I guarantee you it isn't that. But regardless, we should make some kind of counter-offer. Go on the offensive, you know?"

"I couldn't agree more," I admitted happily. "Alan, please drop the Zone of Silence."

"Waitaminute—"

"Of course, Mister Bonesbury." The butler-in-training spun his finger again in the opposite direction, and the blue tint disappeared.

"After much deliberation," I announced in an authoritative voice. "We've decided to make you a counter-offer." With the elegance and grace of a newborn giraffe, I reached across the table for an inkwell and quill. The first page of the contract had no writing on the back, so I flipped it over as if it were a cocktail napkin and scribbled a quick note. Using Lesser Telekinesis, I floated the page over until it fell right in front of Metrion.

He glared at me with an exhausted sort of annoyance on his face, but he did pick up the paper. "'Slurp… ink'?" he read off the page. "What the devil is that supposed to—?" His words were halted when a full inkwell inverted over his head, floated there by a second casting of Lesser Telekinesis. Black liquid stained his fancy hat and dripped into his face and onto his lap.

"Whoops!" I cried mischievously. "Sorry, Metrion. Spellcraft, so tricky, right? At least it is for, oh, how did you describe me? A foppish buffoon?"

"Gaah!" cried my soon-to-be ex-houseguest. He shot out his chair and whipped his hat to the ground. His seat drove the bard into the wall, her playing cut mid-note as her violin and bow fell from her hands.

"This is not a game!" roared Metrion. "You loathsome worm! I offer you kindness and you spit in my face?! Of all the—" Whatever tirade he was about to unload was cut short as he suddenly winced in pain and put a hand to his temple. "Who told you to stop playing?!" he screamed, whipping around and delivering a backhand to the musician's face. She had already taken a knee to retrieve her instrument, but the smack sent her fully to the floor.

"Hold now, sir!" I exclaimed.

In my training with Lituin, I had become fascinated with the art of swashbuckling. After I convinced him that I had mastered the basics, he relented to my pleas and agreed to show me a few moves. He marveled at how light I was on my feet; I neglected to tell him this was a result of my body lacking flesh to weigh it down. Encouraged by my progress, he taught me one tactic that would utilize my natural strengths: to literally leap into action.

Conjuring forth my training, I leapt from my seat across the table, landing between Metrion and his battered employee, knocking Metrion aside with a hip check. On instinct I drew my sword and took a defensive stance. (Later on I would giddily retell this feat to Lituin, sure that he would be pleased that my training was paying off).

"Listen here, now," roared the old man, who had been caught and steadied by one of the men who had been sitting next to him.

"No, you listen!" I amplified my voice with one of the new spells Jon had taught me, a simple one only called 'Trick': it accomplished very minimal acts of prestidigitation and showmanship, which served no practical purpose beyond being as dramatic as possible. Jon said the spell and I were made for each other.

"I don't care if she is your employee, Metrion! You are under my roof, do you understand? As much as you'd like the fact to be anything but, this is my home! And while you are in my home, you will not show undue violence to anyone undeserving! No amount of money or power in the world earns you that right!"

I turned to the felled girl and offered her a hand up, making sure to disperse my Trick. "Are you alright, miss?" I asked as gently as I could. She recoiled from my touch briefly, before taking my hand and rising.

"I...I think so," she mewled. "Thank you, sir, you're very kind."

"You dare speak to one of my people?" Metrion hissed.

"I dare to do a lot of things, you old vulture," I spat back. Turning back to the girl, I said "Miss, what did you say your name was?"

"C-Cassandra. Cassandra Lemos."

"Cassandra Lemos," I repeated. "Beautiful name, makes me think of citrus by the seaside. Cassandra, do you have any moral or sentimental obligations towards the man who just hit you?"

"I'm not sure I understand the question, sir?"

"I'm guessing this isn't the first time you've been mistreated. Come work for me, Cassandra. You don't need to leave with this man."

"What?!" Metrion guffawed.

"Whatever he's paying you, I'll double it," I continued. "You'll also have your own room, free meals, and unconditional respect. No one will ever hurt you at Violet Heights."

"Sir, I-I—" she stuttered, eyes wider than a deer's in fairy lights.

"I've had enough of this!" Metrion screamed. "You've made a powerful enemy today, Chadwick Bonesbury. When we're finished crushing you, you'll be underground, do you hear me?!"

"I've risen from the underground before. I'll do it again."

"Cassandra, we're leaving." Metrion D'Graszia dripped ink over my carpet as he stomped towards the door. "Now!" he punctuated when he saw her hesitate.

"You have a choice," I pleaded with her. "I don't know you or the minutiae of your situation, but I can't see the appeal of walking out that door right now, not if I were you." Cassandra pondered for a moment before taking a sidestep behind me, clutching her instrument close to her chest.

His face beet red but his words suddenly calm, Metrion uttered "you'll all live to regret this" before storming out with his people, sans one bard.

(He's going to feel really stupid when he finds out I'm already dead,) I thought at Emery, who was currently nestled snugly inside my hat. The Imp responded in kind by laughing, which I considered to be my second accomplishment of the day and patted myself on the back.

CHAPTER 9 – Become a Compelling Leader

We began the next morning with a duel!

Well, that's not precisely true. As we watched the D'Graszia carriage speed off down the drive, Raeden and several others asked me, repeatedly, if I was absolutely certain that bringing this strange girl into our operation was a good idea. I chose to ignore their warnings that a former employee of our biggest competitor may prove to be trouble, and instead gave instructions that Cassandra was to be assigned a room of her own and given paperwork to fill out. Of course, I had one of my underlings do it for her (gods above, I would need to find another word for that tier of employee) and we got on with our day.

After assessing her list of abilities, Breadalbane determined Miss Lemos would best be suited to train for the master of ceremonies position at Violet Heights. In time, she would arrange all parties, celebrations, festivities, galas, and soirees which happened in or in-relation to Violet Heights. Naturally, the girl was modest and insisted she wasn't up to the task.

"Cassandra, allow me to share with you an important lesson I myself have only learned recently. You're capable of far more than you realize, especially when you accept help from others."

"You give me a lot of credit, sir. Thank you, I promise to do my best."

"I know you will."

So, about that duel.

I've found that there is much that needs doing in a day, and that the amount of time left to do the doing is often inversely proportional to the number of things that need to be done. Therefore, Lituin and I have our private lessons in the morning, typically first thing as he was an early riser by nature, but that day it would be delayed to just before lunch on account of all the hullabaloo.

Lituin didn't mind the change in schedule, even though it interfered with his students' training, but then I was his patron and therefore I had first dibs. He had worked out a system with his students where, should their daily roster be disrupted, they would assist the house staff with any physically demanding work as needed. So I made a game out of it with them. When I arrived I would bark "secure the perimeter!" as if that actually meant something, and then they would scatter to their self-appointed posts, stifling snickers born from my attempt at sounding authoritarian.

Cassandra watched all this unfold with patient obedience from the corner of the room. I assured her that she could join Lituin's class if she wished to learn the blade, although she didn't seem terribly interested. As she was wont to do, the girl just smiled and nodded politely.

And now, at last, it was time to duel.

"At last it's time to duel!" I announced dramatically, pointing my sword towards Lituin from across the dojo.

"Only a fool rushes towards a blade," he bantered.

"Only a fool would challenge me." There was lightning in my bones; I felt as if I could challenge a god. "Now en garde!"

"Sorry, dears," came the tender voice of Calliope Baines, pausing us in mid-charge. "Just popping in to collect the laundry, won't be a minute."

"Gods above, woman. You could not have picked a worse time!"

"Oh, you can still do your fancy dancing with me pitter-pattering in the background."

"'Fancy dancing'? I'll have you know I'm in training to be the greatest swordsman in the world! I figure I have a decent shot, since I'm being trained by the current greatest swordsman in the world."

"You flatter me, sir."

"We've been over this, Lituin, it isn't flattery if it's a fact."

"Yeah, yeah, greatest swordsman," Calliope continued. "But it isn't real fighting, is it?"

"In what possible way is it not real fighting?"

"The blade does most of the work, don't it? Real fighting is hand-to-hand, I say."

"Do you hear her, Lituin? She's diminishing your craft!"

"Miss Baines is entitled to her opinion, sir," Lituin said pleasantly. "And I am confident in my abilities. The opinions of others could never lessen me."

"Good lad," Calliope said with a satisfied grin. "Some blaggard comes at me with a sharp stick, I'd break his nose and then his blade, in that order."

"I don't know, Lituin says my skills have drastically improved."

"I never used the word 'drastically,' sir." There was something charming about Lituin attempting to tease me and failing entirely to hide it.

"I'll say to you what I said to any of my children when they announced that they had successfully done a cartwheel: that's nice, dear."

"Are you suggesting I couldn't take you?"

"I don't need to suggest anything, Mister Bonesbury. Just like I don't need to suggest that birds fly, or that the sky is blue. People just sort of get it."

"Do you let all your servants talk to you this way?" asked Cassandra, who had been watching our conversation unfold with a growing look of bewildered horror.

"Just me," Calliope giggled while pressing the lid of her laundry hamper closed. "And that's only because he knows what's good for him. Oh, close your mouth, dearie. I'm just taking a bit of piss out of the boss, no harm done."

"Yes, harm done!" I wailed, grasping my chest flamboyantly in a show of mock pain (I didn't want anyone to think I was actually wrathful). "My pride, madame! I think a duel is warranted."

"Fight my boss?" she laughed. "Do I dare live out every working-class person's dream? Oh, I can't fight you, Chadwick, I'd feel bad! You always look so frail and malnourished. I thought rich guys were supposed to be husky."

"Tomorrow, after lunch. We'll make it an event, the first Violet Heights celebration of staff talent!"

"I don't know…"

"I'll make it worth your while. Name your wager."

"Well," she hummed. The smile on her face told me I had been baited, but it was too late. "If I win, I get to set my own schedule for a year."

"I suppose that's reasonable. And if I win?"

"You can keep my salary for a month. Make that wee Raeden fella happy, he's always going off about how much money you pay us."

"Agreed!" We shook hands and parted ways to attend to our respective duties. Lituin and I opted to cancel our daily spar, given how much time we had already lost.

"What strategy do you plan to employ in the coming fight, sir?"

"I was hoping you could offer your expertise, Lituin. You've been teaching me for a while now, what are my strengths and weaknesses?"

"Well, your skeletal body is certainly an advantage." I had been putting away my sword when he said that, but his use of the word 'skeletal' caused me to miss the loop on my hip, and the sword clattered loudly on the floor.

"Cassandra, could you leave us for a moment?" Once she had gone, I pulled Lituin to the middle of the room, having once read something about both spies and devils making their homes in corners.

"Surely you were meaning to imply I'm malnourished," I said in a hushed tone. It wasn't a question.

"I don't know about that, sir," he said, matching my volume but looking confused as to why it was necessary. "I only meant that your physical form as a living dead man comes with advantages a mere mortal could not possess."

"You know I'm a Skeleton?!" I shrieked, in what could only be described as scream-whispering.

"Yes, Mister Bonesbury."

"How?!"

"Simple," he began plainly, as if I had asked him how he failed to harm himself while cutting a piece of meat. "You are incredibly light on your feet, more so than someone your age, race, and build should be. I have also cut you numerous times which you have either failed to notice or you reacted in such a way that did not match the blow. I have also witnessed your face shimmer when you exert yourself in combat, specifically the first time you managed to parry one of my attacks."

"Why haven't you said anything yet? Are you not afraid of me?" My voice had returned to its typical pitch but with a sadness I did not expect; the thought of Lituin being the one to expose me would be the most devastating blow to my spirits ever.

"It is not my secret to tell, sir. And I do not fear you because you are not a wicked man. Growing up, I heard many of my father's stories, about the terrors that the Orcs inflicted on his people during the War of the Ardens, terrors they still inflict to this day. But we lived in Gielran, where Orcs were our neighbours. I once asked my father how we could live amongst monsters, and he told me not all Orcs were monsters. He believed it was not what you are, but who you are, that defined you."

"He sounds like a decent man, your father."

"He was the best of us. And you need not worry about me, Mister Bonesbury. I have only discussed your true nature once before, but I did not initiate the conversation."

"Who else knows?!" I scream-whispered, this time with more scream than whisper.

"Your beastmaster, Felsha the Pursuer."

That caught me off guard. In the short time I had employed Felsha, I've never been able to get an accurate impression of where I stood with her; I had assumed she thought little of me, but tolerated my eccentric ways because it gave her free rein with her animals. But knowing that she knew about me, had known for who knows how long… I had to know. I bid Lituin farewell, with plans to see him again soon to talk strategy for the fight, and made for the door.

"One more thing, sir?" called my head of security. "There is something I wished to discuss with you. You see, many of my students and I agree that it would be beneficial to have a forge at Violet Heights, somewhere we can craft our own swords and armour. Equipment we make ourselves would enable us to be better warriors and better defenders. I spoke to Mr. Raeden about it, but he said it was an unnecessary luxury. We were hoping you would still consider the proposal."

"I'll see what I can do, friend."

The sky was overcast, but it was an otherwise perfectly splendid spring day. Things had quieted down outside, as my vision of turning Violet Heights into an otherworldly cathedral was nearing its final stages. And it was breathtaking, if I'm being honest, with its uneven paint job, chaotic angles, and extensions that went nowhere and served no functional purpose other than to make me smile. I had found Cassandra out on the lawn, just beyond the front steps, and asked her to walk with me. My mind was reeling from my talk with Lituin, but I still felt protective of my newest employee and hated the thought of her wandering the grounds alone. As we made our way across the manicured lawn, I asked Cassandra what she thought of her new home.

"It's certainly… unique, Mister Bonesbury."

"Unique is one word for it," laughed Fred Avalon, who startled us both as he appeared from behind a tree. "It's not my taste, but I can't say my take would have been any better when I was the acting 'architect' here. What a scary, ridiculous week that was."

"Hello, Fred. How are you?" I tried to pass off my surprise with a chuckle, but I don't know if it landed.

"I've been better, sir. It would be lovely if these clouds would provide us with a little rain, but I have my doubts. It's been a horribly dry month, you know."

"Is my humour that bad?" I teased, hoping to get a laugh. He smiled, but continued on like I hadn't said anything.

"It's made the grass and hedges around here awfully parched."

"Hayra's garden seems to be doing fine?"

"Aye, sir, but that's because her green magics keep them lush and respectable. Some trapiches would help with that."

"Some what?"

"Trapiche emeralds, they're enchanted to spread the range of magic like the kind Hayra uses. It would make maintaining the grounds a lot easier."

"Where does one find trapiche emeralds?" I had to admit, the idea was intriguing, and I didn't want Violet Heights to look sloppy.

"A merchant, probably, but they're terribly expensive. I can't afford one, let alone the two or three I would need to do the job properly. I put in a request for them to Mr. Lockwood, but he just laughed at me. Short little bugger."

I snorted at that final comment, but quickly composed myself when Cassandra and Fred looked at me strangely. After a moment's deliberation, I gave Fred my word that I would look into it before announcing our leave.

"Is it true you're fighting Calliope tomorrow, boss?" asked the groundskeeper.

"She told you?"

"She's telling everybody," he chuckled. "'I get to beat up the boss, I have permission!' is how she's been putting it."

"The staff weren't too envious, I hope?"

"Some. Others, present company included, are sort of confused as to why it's even happening?"

"How do you mean?"

"Well," Fred furrowed his brow slightly. "Why are you fighting the maid, sir?"

"She's also the cook," I pointed out, looking to Cassandra to back me up. The poor girl just stared at me. "But, point taken. I'm engaging in a duel with Calliope because she insulted my honour."

"That doesn't sound like Calliope to me."

"I also think it will be a good show for the staff."

"I suppose, sir." Fred's smile had diminished, although not to a scornful degree. "If you'll pardon me, I have to see to my work."

Felsha wasn't difficult to find after that. She tended to move around the grounds a lot, and I got the impression this was some kind of hunter's habit; never stay in one place and you'll never become easy prey. Currently, though, she was stationary, engaged in an apparently hilarious conversation with my gardener, if Hayra's rapturous laughter was any indicator.

"Afternoon, ladies!" I greeted them.

"Good afternoon, Mister Bonesbury," Hayra chimed back.

"Hello," said Felsha, polite but unenthusiastic.

"I'm just showing Cassandra here the lay of the land. How goes it with you both?"

"Felsha was just," the gardener began, but she stopped herself suddenly with a hand to her flushed and rosy cheek. "I mean Miss Felsha, she was telling me about how one of the peacocks has apparently fallen in love with a shrubbery I grew in their likeness!"

"You're kidding!" I laughed. There was something different about these two, something I had missed amidst the chaos I chose to surround myself with. I could see it in Hayra's smile, which had always been there, but it was brighter and more steadfast than before. It was the way in which Felsha, normally confident and restrained, would shift her weight from one leg to the other whenever Hayra looked at her.

"Ladies," I announced, desperately wishing I could pry into their blossoming tryst. But Lituin's troubling words were playing on a loop in my mind, and I was brought to my senses. "I was hoping someone could give Cassandra a tour of the gardens, as there might be a garden party on the horizon. Hayra, would you do the honours?"

"Of course! Come along, dear. You have to tell me all about yourself. Oh, I just love musicians." Felsha and I regarded one another silently until Hayra's voice trailed off into the distance.

"I'm guessing there's not actually going to be a garden party," the Pursuer said stiffly.

"Oh, there is now, it sounds like a splendid idea. But if you're suggesting I just made it up to get rid of our companions, then you'd be right."

"What do you want, Chadwick?"

"This is difficult for me to bring up. I've heard some troubling talk, as of late. It has me, well, troubled."

"Am I being fired?"

"What? No!" I found her casual civility most perturbing; how can one person knock me for a loop twice in as many hours?

"Please be direct with me, Mister Bonesbury. I don't like dancing around topics, especially 'troubling' ones."

"Very well." I cleared my throat, which was an easy task, given that I had no throat in which to accumulate phlegm. "I'm concerned you know a secret about me, a pretty damning one. Specifically one you've discussed with Lituin before. Ringing any bells?"

"About how you're a talking Skeleton?"

"I… yes. When did you find out?"

"Less than two minutes before accepting your offer of employment."

"How did you know?" I crossed my arms in an attempt to seem aloof, but deep down I knew I just looked ridiculous.

"Thanks to this," said Felsha, pulling out the pendant I had seen once before. "This opal is enchanted, it lets me 'read the heart of a creature' by interpreting minute changes in its colour. It was given to me as a gift when I conceded to the fate of being a beastmaster."

"Why would you need such a thing?"

"I… was not born usual. Elves call it, ah, in common tongue it would be 'the disparity of knowing.' Humans call it a 'social disorder.' I don't think as many do, so what may be obvious about the behaviour of others is a mystery to me. The pendant helps."

"So you read me that day," I surmised, replaying that first meeting in my mind with new context. "Gods, I'm a fool."

"On that we agree." To my surprise, I thought I saw the faint beginnings of a smile on her lips. "But I've read you several times now. I had to be certain."

"And of what are you certain?"

"That you're undead, and steadily growing in power." I allowed myself a certain amount of pride when she said that. "And you're not quite good, but you're not malignant either. It was a confounding read, to say the least."

"Thank you."

"Not a compliment. But I chose to observe you, decide for myself what sort of creature you are."

"And?"

"You're an idiot, a boastful lout with more gold than sense."

"Thank y—"

"And if you thank me for that, Gaiyax help me, I will loose your skull from your spine. Now, despite your faults, and there are many, I've also seen you help people, ones who can do little for you. That is enough for me to tolerate your existence."

"And keep my secret?"

"Yes, Chadwick. Sadly, your ruin would spread to those around you, some of whom are dear to me."

"Like Hayra?" I teased, the corners of my illusory mouth and one of my illusory eyebrows raising in unison.

"Silence yourself and begone from my sight!" roared Felsha, though she was unable to keep her face from flushing.

"Alright, I'm gone. Before I go, I don't suppose you also have some kind of expensive request for me?"

Felsha's eyes went wide. "How did you know?"

"It seems to be a running theme today. And let me guess, you already spoke to Raeden and he said no?"

"Your powers are strange, Skeleton. I would have you teach me, someday."

"It can't be done, Chadwick," Raeden said sternly when I confronted him in his office later that day. "None of those things they want are necessary for them to do their jobs. We would just be hemorrhaging money on needless luxuries."

"Surely Bonesbury Holdings is—"

"Over budget. And I'm still doing damage control after you rebuked our best shot at making a fortune. The cash flow will pick up, but until it does we'll have to tighten our belts."

"Then I'll pay for everything myself with my own money."

"I wouldn't do that." Raeden had been mulling over paperwork while we spoke, but for this he looked straight at me. "I know you think you're simply doing a nice thing, because you just want people to like you, but actions have consequences. If you show favouritism to certain staff, even if it's for a good reason, it will sow dissent among the ranks. People will start to resent you, and then they'll start to leave. I'm fine with replacing staff, but I don't think you are."

"...I don't just want people to like me," I pouted.

"Yes you do. Trust me, Chadwick, this isn't a good idea."

"Fine," was all I said before marching out, enunciating as though I had lips and a tongue with which to lace the word with venom.

Late that night, the need for rest had still not seized me so I sparred alone in the dojo. While I parried away one intrusive thought after another, I was interrupted by a knock at the door.

"Cassandra," I said, pleasantly surprised. "I thought you retired an hour ago."

"Second night in a new house," she shrugged. "Couldn't sleep."

"Ahh." I sat down on a bench and gestured for her to join me. "I sympathize. It's been months now and I'm still no stranger to sleepless nights. Plus there's the ghost."

"Ghost?" Despite her timid demeanor, she didn't seem all that shocked or aghast.

"Yes. Several staff seem to be under the impression that our Violet Heights is haunted, although I've never seen so much as a levitating book. Well, one that wasn't perpetrated by me, that is."

"Maybe he's building up to something." Her use of 'he' instead of 'it' was unusual; I told myself to make a note of it, but it would be forgotten by morning.

"Was there something you wanted, Cassandra?"

"Just one thing. I was going over it in my head, and I can't figure out why you invited me to live here and work for you. Your staff is full of extraordinary people, are there not more exciting bards that could fill my position?"

"I've been learning a lot about myself lately, Cassandra. Who I am, who I want to be, what I value. And I see the value in finding a way where everybody can get what they want. In this case, I saw an opportunity to do a great kindness to someone in need of one, which at the same time would brutally scorn an enemy. I consider that a win-win of the highest order."

"But those are all things you want."

"Well, I'm included in everybody, aren't I?"

"How does fighting Calliope benefit everybody?" Cassandra regarded me coldly, not with disdain or censure, but I disliked the lack of feeling in her eyes. "If she wins, you'll have made a fool of yourself, and if you win, then you'll have crushed the spirits of a woman whose only crime was being proud of her abilities."

"It's funny, this is the most I've ever heard you speak."

"You don't have an answer, do you? This is just about your bruised ego. Are we your staff, Mister Bonesbury, or are we your playthings?" She stood up to leave, and I mimicked the gesture; it was meant as a sign of respect, but I also wanted to meet her gaze.

"I have to believe Calliope wants to fight me as much as I want to fight her," I blurted out. "Maybe that's just what I'm telling myself to feel better about a challenge I issued impulsively, but it's the best I've got. I do care about all of you. This existence is mine, and I intend to surround myself with only the best people."

"I'm sorry for speaking out of turn, Mister Bonesbury," Cassandra said placidly.

"You can call me Chadwick, you know."

"I think I'd like to go back to bed. Goodnight… Chadwick."

(Emery), I thought as I watched her go. (Fetch me a quill and some paper. And stretch your wings, you've got some flying to do tonight.)

It was decided the fight would take place outside in order to give the staff ample room to observe. I suspected some of them were taking bets on which of us would win, but the numbers involved were confusing and unsavoury, so I washed my hands of the matter.

What came as a surprise to many, though, was the presence of so many outsiders. Word of the match had spread to the two nearest settlements from, both an equal distance from Violet Heights though in opposite directions. One was a small hamlet, mostly farmers and fisherman, and the other was a rural dwelling just outside Humble Corners. Much of the staff, who had not seen fresh faces in months, were a little awkward and reserved, although a few made fast friends. Fred had accumulated a small audience of farmers, all of whom were fascinated by his approach to landscaping.

Eventually, Calliope and I were brought out one by one. I had not seen my opponent since she accepted my challenge, and that day she bore little resemblance to the Dwarven woman who hung my bedsheets out to dry on the line. She wore a unitard the colour of basalt, and her hair was in a tight bun as opposed to her usual messy beehive. I could see that her hands were wrapped in thick bandages.

"It's not too late to back out, boss," she told me. There was only a hint of mocking in the way she spoke, baiting me with advice she knew I could never accept.

"That won't be necessary, Calliope. Let's just try to give the people a good show, hmm?"

Alan served as our referee, citing his qualifications as knowing us equally well and liking Calliope slightly more, which was evened out by the fact that I was the one who paid his salary. Having not expected a crowd, he listed out the rules for everyone so the stakes were clear: a point was scored for each knockout, physical removal from the ring, or when your opponent cried for 'mercy,' and the first to three points was the winner. I was determined to never suffer that first blow; Jon had warned me my spells might lose their effects should I be rendered unconscious against my will, and that included the Tailored Illusion which convinced everyone I wasn't a scary Skeleton man.

"Begin!" shouted my butler-nephew.

The first point was scored within six seconds. I had drawn my sword, but in the time it took me to draw my blade, Calliope had let out a primal scream, and I was momentarily caught off guard. Like a seasoned fighter she used that moment to quickly close the gap between us, delivering a series of precise punches to my midsection. They weren't the hardest she could hit, that much clear; their intent was not to damage, but to push me back until my heels touched the edge of our makeshift arena. From there, Calliope drove her palm into my chest so that I fell, landing on my rear end and landing her the first point.

We met again in the middle of the ring, my ego and bottom slightly bruised but both ready. Alan marked the start of the next round, and I drew my sword much quicker this time. Calliope's initial strategy was identical to before, screaming and running towards me at top speed. I positioned my weapon so that it guarded my front, but that seemed to be exactly what my opponent expected me to do. Rather than unleashing a flurry of blows, she dropped to a crouch and struck the side of my knee with immense force. I heard a cracking sound, and pain flew through my whole leg as I was driven down onto my opposite knee.

Calliope darted in and out, easily dodging swipes from my rapier which were entirely reactionary and not remotely planned. She evidently found her opening, because next thing I knew she slammed my temple with a right hook, and I was launched headfirst into the ground. Though I knew the expression "seeing stars" I had never experienced it until that moment, and the fear that I might be down for the count became a bit too real.

"Mercy!" I cried, stopping Calliope mid-attack.

"Point Calliope, two nothing," Alan announced.

"Do you want to throw in the towel?" asked my opponent as she helped me to my feet.

"You wish," I groaned, trying to hide my pain but failing miserably.

At the next round's start, I immediately hobbled backwards, the most I could do with my injured knee. As I expected, Calliope charged me for a third time. I waited for my moment, and once she was close enough I launched myself forward into the air (with my good leg; I'm not a masochist) just as I had done two days prior against Metrion. While I was still airborne and passing over Calliope, I drew my sword and slashed her shoulder into her bicep.

The crowd audibly winced as Calliope yelped in pain, her blood staining the ground red. Just as I anticipated, Calliope was unable to slow her momentum in time to keep from running out of bounds.

"Point Chadwick, two to one."

"Are you sure you don't want to throw in the towel?" I taunted. Calliope put a hand to her arm and looked at me with an intense determination which, while not hateful, bordered on mad hostility. She drew her hand from the wound; her palm was wet and crimson, the blood a bright stain on the gauze.

We took our positions; before the round started I tried putting weight on my bad leg, and found the pain had subsided somewhat. Alan marked round four, but Calliope just stood there, feet planted and fists up. Not wanting to miss my moment, I shot forward as fast I could, bad knee and all, blade drawn. With the point of the rapier mere inches from her body, I saw something flash in Calliope's eyes, a killer instinct unlike any I had seen before.

She moved faster than dragonfire. With her bloody hand she grabbed my sword mid-blade; there was a sharp clanging sound, like metal on metal. She yanked hard to the right and snapped off the end of my weapon. She cast the broken half aside, embedding it in the ground while never taking her eyes off me. I staggered backward just a step but that was enough. She positioned herself before me, winding up to strike, and in that moment I saw it.

In my frequent perusing of Coglio Magella's library, I had once come across a footnote on a rare form of Dwarven magic. Apparently, Dwarf blood contained incredibly high levels of iron, which a warrior could transfer to other parts of their body, thus giving them the properties of metal. At the time, I understood it as a sort of magical metal plating process.

And by cutting Calliope's arm, I had given her everything she needed to secure her victory.

With a fist of iron, she delivered a powerful right cross to my chest. That single hit was enough to knock me down, but she wasn't done. As I staggered backwards, she hit me again, and again, and then yet another time, unloading her attacks with machinelike efficiency. Each one felt like cannonfire and pushed me further back, until one last cross knocked me off my feet and almost a full yard past the ring's edge.

Raucous cheering drowned out Alan as he announced Calliope the winner. Several of her subordinate staff rushed the arena and hoisted their leader onto their shoulders. At least, that's what I was told afterwards. I, meanwhile, chose to remain lying on the grass, taking a full ten minutes to process all the different forms of pain a person could possibly experience, and how it was possible that I was feeling all of them all at once.

I would wait until the following day to reveal my secret: the reason so many civilians had shown up was because I had secured a corporate sponsor for our little event. I had promised an annual showcase of all the martial, matchless, and mystical talents Violet Heights had to offer, and thanks to Calliope's prowess in the ring, my concept was proven a success. According to the contract agreement, one that I had drawn up without Raeden's knowledge, we were to receive a generous payment of gold which was neither my money nor the company's, but could easily pay for forges and emeralds and anything else my staff might need.

And all it cost me was my pride. Oh well, some things were better done without.

CHAPTER 10 – Learn How to Deal With Competition and Ill-Wishers

Never before had I witnessed a single nervous breakdown carried out simultaneously by two distinct people, but that was the case during the committee meeting to plan my first garden party. Rather than begin with any logical step, I composed the guest list first because that was much more enjoyable than the other mundane tasks which I was choosing to ignore for the time being. Breadalbane took issue with having to send out the invitations, and Raeden took umbrage at my complete lack of understanding how the world worked.

"You want to invite Sunder Blackstone, and… an actual princess?" bemoaned the Halfling.

"Not just any princess," I reminded him. "Valeria Mercy. She was nice."

"Are you insane?!"

"I'll write the invitations," muttered Breadalbane. "And after the fury of the royal family dies down, they'll trace them back to me by my penmanship. I'll be hanged, the first man to be hanged at Hanging Gardens in over a century!"

"You're both being a tad dramatic, aren't you?"

"Chadwick," Raeden began, his condescending voice primed and ready to go. "When I said we needed high profile guests, I didn't mean… literal royalty and Sunder goddamn Blackstone."

"I don't know many people!" I defended. "Who am I supposed to invite then?"

"I think it's a good idea." Everyone turned towards Alan with varying expressions of awe. "I'll write the invitations if it's an issue. All you need to do is add 'Additional Guests Welcome.' Sunder and her Highness then bring some friends, and suddenly a couple people turn into a dozen, all probably just as important as the ones we invited."

"Brilliant!" I cheered. "That's the kind of can-do thinking we need on this."

"Even if that was a good idea," Raeden interjected. "Which it isn't," he looked directly at Alan with a steely gaze, "a dozen people still don't make a garden party. Not the kind you're trying to throw, at least."

"You have a point, Raeden." I rubbed my chin, both to stimulate ideas and to show that I was, in fact, thinking the whole matter through. "Humble Corners has a mayor, no? Invite them and their family. Same goes with the nearby towns. 'Additional Guests Welcome,' just like Alan said. Local leaders, captains of industry, all of them. Show them their neighbours are good people. Is that enough?"

"Nearly," Breadalbane assessed. "This is madness, but it could work. If the local well-to-do see you consorting with royals and aristocrats, it would do wonders for your reputation. You'd be an overnight legend."

"Why would you tell him that?" groaned Raeden. "Now there's no way we can stop him."

"He's right," I admitted. "You really shouldn't have told me. But I know who else we can invite."

"This should be good," Alan said enthusiastically.

"This should be rich," sighed Raeden.

"Get me the names of Metrion's business partners and collaborators." The room was silent. Everyone looked at me expectantly, waiting for the punchline to an obvious joke. "I'm serious, really."

"If you're serious, then you've officially lost it." Raeden didn't look angry or surprised; he just looked defeated.

"We're trying to make friends, aren't we? We don't need to turn all of them to our side. Even just one would be beneficial. We can be subtle about it, invite them under the guise of… I don't know, one of you can think of something."

"Truly your tactical wit knows no bounds," huffed the Halfling.

"Could we do it, Breadalbane? Alan?"

"Possibly," said the butler.

"Definitely," said the butler in-training.

Raeden agreed to attend the party, but he refused to help with the planning. A formal declaration of being cross with me had been issued, but it was given with such ceremony that I knew he'd get over it. Thankfully, the rest of my core staff was more than happy to contribute. Even Breadalbane, a veritable sourpuss, rounded up Alan, Calliope, and Cassandra for decorating duties. Felsha initially said she would not take part, content to stay back at the outermost perimeter as a lookout for suspicious types.

"But you have to come to the party!" Hayra protested. "You were the inspiration for at least two of my floral displays and three of the topiaries!"

"Y-you added another topiary of me?" Felsha blushed. (Dear reader, I sincerely hope you've been enjoying my story at least half as much as I enjoyed watching the unfolding romance between these two).

My first instinct was to pick multiple dates for the party, wait for confirmations, and then hold the event on the day that worked best for everybody. Breadalbane put that line of thinking to rest, insisting I set a firm date before sending out the invitations.

"Make them come to you," he said. "The idiosyncrasies of high society are that of a cat and mouse…who are playing chess. All right, the metaphor escapes me, but you don't want to make yourself too available. The key is to make them believe this party will be the social event of the season, one that cannot be missed." To the butler's credit, one hundred percent of the guest list promised to be there with bells on.

"My friends," I said during a staff meeting, which included Alan, Breadalbane, Calliope, Cassandra, Felsha, Fred, Glyph, Hayra, and Lituin. I told Raeden to come too, even if he had washed his hands of the whole affair.

"My friends, it's been a long week planning this party, but I'm so incredibly grateful to each of you. Even you, Jacob!" There was a short laugh as I addressed our director of finance; I didn't have the heart (or other organs) to openly admit I had only invited him for the sake of having the complete set present. "I don't know how you've kept the cost so low, but I thank you, sir!

"As for the lot of you, I want to make one thing very clear, because ambiguity is for poets and prophets. This party is for you. Glyph has made Violet Heights into one hell of a building, but you all have made it a home. I…I'd kill to protect you, I really mean that. Let's hope I never have to prove it, hmm?"

"Hear, hear!" cheered the assembly, toasting with champagne glasses Breadalbane and Alan had somehow provided despite never having left the room.

"You've become a superb butler, Alan."

"Just call me Breadalbane 2.0, boss!" he laughed. Breadalbane 1.0 made a point of rolling his eyes.

"What I'm trying to get at," I continued, "is that at the party tomorrow, I want you to celebrate yourselves. Can you do that for me?" After another toast, we all turned in for a night of much-needed rest.

I won't bore you with the details of how the party started, dear reader. Truth be told, I was so enraptured by my first big party that I'm barely familiar with the details myself. But I do recall welcoming politicians and lords from the neighbouring towns and hamlets, as well as the company-owners who were in business with Metrion. They were all polite and cordial, but when an actual foreign princess arrived on my doorstep, complete with a full entourage and a belated housewarming gift[7], their demeanour became far friendlier. To the surprise of very few, Sunder Blackstone made an even flashier entrance than the literal royalty.

"Chadwick, you skinny devil!" cried the opulent Dwarf, who was wearing an outfit nearly identical to mine. "It's been too long, too long! How have you been, old sport? I hope you don't mind, I brought provisions." He snapped his fingers, and several Dwarves with crates over their arms came running past us into the party. "Just some smoked meats and ale."

"Dwarven ale? Oh, you've saved the party. Sunder, I could kiss you."

"Ha! Oh, Chadwick, I'm having a grand time already. Now, I've brought more of my cigars, and I won't have you refuse this time. Now we just need-"

"Matches?" I asked, conjuring a pack from my pocket through the use of Trick. "You're too predictable, Sunder!"

As the party unfolded and I puffed away with Sunder while he loudly exclaimed about his latest conquests, I started to worry that Raeden was right, that it may have been a mistake putting 'Blackstone' on the guest list. Thankfully, within ten minutes he had become thoroughly enamored at the sight of Calliope, who was celebrating her recent victory with an especially sparkly dress. I nearly lost an arm as he dragged me across the party to make introductions.

"I suppose I could have dinner with you," Calliope sighed flirtatiously. "After all, I do make my own schedule now." The derisive smile she gave me was potent enough to make my non-existent skin crawl.

From there, I made my rounds shaking hands, saying hellos, generally being a good host while Cassandra's violin sang like a choir of nightingales in the background. I saw my staff mingling with high society, which

---

7   It was an exotic plant, for those curious.

would have been enough in and of itself, but they were genuinely enjoying themselves too. The sight brought a warmth to my chest cavity, right where my heart had once been.

But every rose, so say the bards, has its thorn. Everyone was gathered so nicely in their own little groups, and I felt awkward intruding on their conversations. The patio looked to be my salvation from the increasingly stuffy atmosphere; most of my guests were out among the gardens or in a recently-installed gazebo.

"I'm not big on parties either," said a shape in the shadows that I had failed to notice.

"Jon, is that you?"

"Afraid not." Out from the dim lighting came a midnight green dress, followed by the head of Valeria Mercy on top.

"Princess!" I squawked. "I didn't think anyone else was here. Pardon me, I'll go."

"It's your house," she said tenderly. "Besides, I feel like whenever we're at the same social event, we only exchange a handful of words with each other."

"You mean all two of them?"

"Let's try to break the habit. Sit?"

"Gladly! How is your… I want to say, father?"

"You really know nothing of my family, do you?" the princess contemplated, studying me closely.

"I guess I just don't like politics?" Also it's possible I'm older than your entire family line, princess, but you probably don't need to know that.

"Not the worst trait to have, but you're correct. King Matthias is well. Getting on in years, in desperate need of a royal beard-grooming, but otherwise a fine king and better father."

"Glad to hear it."

"I hope you can meet him someday." She looked back at the house. "He'd like you, I think. This bizarre building is… magnificent. Possibly the work of a madman, but magnificent still."

"Nice to meet you," I joked. "The name's Chadwick, I'm the resident madman."

"Chadwick…"

"Yes, that's my name. I didn't think I actually needed to—"

"No, Chadwick, something's wrong!"

I followed Valeria's eyeline, past the party towards the woods at the edge of my property. Lights were moving frantically, and though it was hard to see in the fading light of dusk, there were columns of smoke rising to paint the night sky a hazy grey.

Then the screaming started.

"Please excuse me, princess," I said to my friend before hopping over the patio railing into the garden. Whatever those lights were had gotten much larger; they must have been big and fast, having made their way to Violet Heights in just seconds. A fire had broken out on a hedge, which explained the mob of guests who were scattering in every direction. I saw a fireball fly from the direction of the woods; it landed on a topiary and set it ablaze.

All around me people were springing into action. Lituin's students, who had been wearing modest formal wear, now revealed blades and armour which had been expertly hidden under their garb. Felsha did a flourish with her hands, producing two curved knives from thin air. I was surprised when I saw Calliope do a similar motion, but she merely assumed a fighting stance. Alan and Hayra shrouded themselves in respective blue and green auras, readying their individual magics. I drew my rapier, feeling outclassed by these champions but grateful to have them on my side. Together we formed a barrier between my guests and our attackers.

It was Lituin who spoke first, shouting something in Elvish. Half his trainees turned around and began escorting guests inside, some needing more forceful persuasion than others. I was momentarily distracted by the scene, and when I turned back around I saw the source of the lights: more than a dozen armed men on horseback carrying torches. Some trailed flags behind them, a skull and crossbones with a defined, jagged slash down the middle.

"Break their ranks!" Lituin shouted, and we all advanced.

"Burn my gardens, will you?!" Hayra roared. Slapping her palm down onto the ground, veins of raised earth burst forth from her position towards the coming horde; a wave of vines erupted mere feet from their advancing line and caused the horses to scatter. One came directly for me, and terror nearly froze me in place. But I recalled Lituin's teachings and found my opening. I dodged the lunge of a spear, sweeping back my blade as the horse ran past me. Blood soaked the rider's tunic at his ribcage.

I looked around for allies, but they had all spread out or retreated, save for Glyph Bonben. His eyeline was aimed towards the woods; I wasn't sure if he even knew I was there. He ripped a grey box off his belt and slammed it with his fist. A thunderous clanging of machinery began, and I saw numerous cannons fold out of my house's roof and walls.

"How long have those been there?!" I squawked.

"Eat iron, you pirate bastards!" bellowed the Gnome, who hit the box a second time. I may lack physical eardrums, dear reader, but the sound of those cannon volleys could have shattered my skull.

"Take defensive positions!" Lituin shouted over the sound of the barrage. "Back to the house, there are more coming from the east!" We did as he ordered. Shattering glass could be heard as we ran, and the space where my heart should have been got very heavy.

"Alan!" I yelled once we were back inside. "You're a mage. Can't you put up some kind of barrier?"

"Yes, but not one big enough for the whole house."

"What about with the Power of Three?" asked Cassandra. Blood was seeping down her arm, but there was an uncharacteristic fierceness in her eyes.

"I think I could manage it. But who else here knows—?"

"I do," she assured him.

"Can someone please tell me what the Power of Three is?!" I realized there was a time and a place for such a question, but panic had made me spontaneous and irrational.

"If three mages can unite in power and purpose," Alan explained. "They can accomplish feats they couldn't do on their own. Hayra, can you help us?"

"But…" she whined, controlling her conjured vines through the window to throw one of the raiders away from the house. "My plants!"

"Bloomkin!" It was Breadalbane, who had been tending to the wounded in the front hall. "If we lose the house, the gardens go with it."

"You're right. Go on, Alan, dear."

The young wizard did a series of hand motions I couldn't replicate if I tried, all while muttering something under his breath. Cassandra played her violin, her tempo seeming to match Alan's voice. Hayra drew roots up between two marble tiles and wrapped them around her wrists. Her eyes glowed emerald green, and she started to chant in a language I had never heard.

Twinkling lights appeared around Alan, knitting themselves into an orb which expanded and harmlessly passed through each of us. It went on through the walls, until a sphere of blue, green, and purple was around the house. Lituin shouted more orders in Elvish once the field had stabilized.

"He's telling his men to kill any raiders who made it inside," explained Breadalbane.

"What do we do now?" I asked desperately.

"We wait," Alan groaned. "Hopefully we can keep this barrier up long enough until they get tired and leave, or the constabulary sees the smoke and comes to help."

"Hopefully?!" I parroted in disbelief. "What happens if you can't hold it that long?"

"It won't come to that," Lituin assured us, wiping fresh blood from his weapon. "I will go outside the barrier and call for parley. As pirates they will have no choice but to let me meet their captain. We will fight one on one, I will kill him, and his men will fall back."

"You can't!" I thought I could feel tears welling up in my eye sockets, but it was, of course, a phantom sensation. "You'll die, Lituin."

"Death is the only Certainty, my friend." With that he smiled and walked out the door.

The other guards tried their best to keep everyone contained in the middle of the hall, but guests and staff alike rushed towards the windows to witness what could be a historic fight. Details were hard to make out through the shimmering magical barrier, but the enemy riders appeared to stop circling the house as the swordmaster approached the barrier's edge. Through a column of smoke stepped a much larger pirate, a Dragonkind with obsidian scales and silver eyes…at least if my squinting vision was to be believed. He and Lituin spoke for a minute before taking their stances, readying themselves to duel.

"Belas above…" Breadalbane uttered, shocked by something none of us had realized.

The Dragonkind captain held a massive two-handed sword, which he used to assault Lituin with several downward strikes. Lituin blocked the first two hits with his own blade, but at the third the captain's weapon began to glow with a dense, golden aura. The blow landed, hitting and instantly cleaving Lituin's sword, and, to my horror, continued down the swordsman's chest.

"No!" I cried. The Elf was downed in seconds, and I was too stunned to move.

"That's the Splitter," Breadalbane hissed. "He's a legend on the ocean."

"Then what the hell is he doing at my house?!"

"The man is ruthless. His blade is enchanted to cut through even the toughest armour. None are safe from its strike."

It wasn't long before the barrier around the house started to ripple and flicker. Swords and arrows hit it from multiple angles, and two more fireballs made thunderous contact from beyond the forest.

"A couple more hits like that and we're done for," said Alan, who looked weak. Cassandra swayed back and forth as she played, and Hayra was sweating profusely. Felsha had a hand on her shoulder, whispering some kind of encouragement in her ear.

"I'm going out there," I announced with no elaboration.

"What?!" shouted half the room in condescending disbelief.

"You'll be slaughtered," Felsha said stoically.

"Uhm, permission to speak freely, sir?" Breadalbane asked nervously.

"Granted."

"You lost a fight with the maid last week." Calliope was across the room tending to more of the wounded; if she heard Breadalbane's comment, she didn't let it distract her from her work.

"I have a plan. Glyph?"

"Yes, boss?"

"We really need to have a talk about those cannons. But I'm assuming you have more surprises inside?"

"A few, but—"

"If my plan fails and they make it in here, I want you to use every one of them, do you understand? All of you, if I can't save your lives, die fighting. Consider that an order." There were words of protest all around, but I paid them no mind. Instead, I took the same path Lituin had walked and approached the barrier.

"Parley?" I announced once I stepped through, waiting for a lull in the attack to do so.

"Who the 'ell are you?" demanded a pirate, one of several that had surrounded me with guns and swords. I noticed their crew was quite diverse; lots of Humans and Goblins, a few Dwarves and Gnomes. A couple were Dragonkind, though smaller than their captain.

"My name is Chadwick Bonesbury and this is my house. As I understand it, you chaps adhere to the rules of parley, yes? So I'd like to speak with your captain and see if we can't find a peaceful solution here."

"There is no peaceful solution here." The Splitter's voice was intense, a throaty growl which sounded like it was coming from the darkest depths of a cave. "But I suppose if you drop this damn bubble and offer a complete and immediate surrender, we'll leave a few of your more prolific guests alive. Ransom rather than rob, eh?" His crew laughed, and the Dragonkind seemed quite pleased with himself.

"Mister Splitter," I began. With subtle casting I used Trick to throw our voices so they could be heard within the mansion; whatever was about to transpire, I wanted witnesses. "I don't suppose you can tell me who sent you here?"

"Can't an honest pirate simply hear about a gathering of entitled, self-important bluebloods and seize the opportunity?" More chortles from the crew.

"I guess I'm skeptical."

"I finished your swordsman in less than six strikes." The Splitter's S-words were very pronounced, more snakelike than I expected of Dragonkind dialects. "I heard you were stupid, Chadwick Bonesbury, but this is almost impressive. Either you think you can best me where your sword man couldn't, or you actually believe you can negotiate with someone who would attack you without warning. Which is it?"

"Neither. My proposal is this: we play a game. You're a pirate, you must be a gaming man. If I win, you take your band of thugs and get out of here. If you win, Violet Heights and everything therein is yours, legally. My people have even been instructed to not put up any resistance if you make it past me." If I couldn't finish off this wretch, perhaps Glyph's battlements could.

"What's the game?"

"Simple: we each get one hit on the other. You're the guest here, so naturally I'd let you go first."

"Naturally," repeated the Splitter, whose head was tilted inquisitively.

"Whoever is left standing after the exchange is the winner. Understand?"

"I don't understand why someone would be so eager to throw away his life, but yes, I'll play your game. Let's make this quick."

We each took our positions, standing about fifteen feet apart. The Splitter's men formed a circle around us and chanted "Split him! Split him!" over and over again, slowly at first, then progressively faster in a most unnerving fashion. I saw that same golden energy shroud the Splitter's blade, and in that moment I wondered if Lituin had had enough time to appreciate how it crackled and whooshed before it cut him down.

"Ready to die, Bonesbury?"

"I'm dead already."

My opponent shrugged and dashed forward, taking huge steps that looked more like leaping than running. Screaming with unbridled battle fury, he raised his weapon and brought it down on me, carving a line from my left shoulder to my right hip.

"Sho!" I spat out, crossing my fingers tightly as I let the syllable go.

Assured of his decisive victory, the Splitter strutted back towards his starting point and sheathed his sword. Seconds passed before he noticed his crew's faces, their eyes wide and their mouths ajar. When he turned back he saw me there, body tense but still very much intact.

"How?!" he roared.

"It was a good hit, captain, I'll give you that. Would have certainly killed an ordinary man. But your first and most fatal mistake was assuming I'm an ordinary man."

"How are you doing this?"

"With a very handy spell I only just learned recently. I've been learning lots of spells, actually. 'Deceptive Defense,' for instance, gives me a protective shield around my body for several hours. I use that one twice a day, truth be told, but it wouldn't have been nearly enough to guard against your impressive swing. No, what I used was the complete mouthful of a spell, 'Ruby's Rapturous Reversal.'"

"Your spell could have a name that fills the mouths of Giants," seethed the Splitter. "And it still wouldn't compare to the power I wield."

"Oh, I think you'll find that it will. You see, the spell is quite powerful, but the tradeoff is it's difficult to use. One must, the second before the blow, cross their fingers and utter a syllable of their choosing. You'll observe," I held up my hand, "my fingers are crossed. This, essentially, holds the damage in a sort of limbo state, neither here nor there."

"Get to the point, rich man!"

"If you insist. To finish the spell, the user need only uncross their fingers while saying the syllable in reverse. Like… Ohs!"

There was a sound akin to thunder when I uncrossed my fingers, but as if the full thunderclap was condensed to the span of a second. A line of red light traced itself on the Splitter's body, running from his left shoulder to his right hip. Before the scaly pirate could appreciate my victory, the line widened to a full slash that surged with the bright golden energy from his sword. Suddenly, his torso ripped apart along that glowing chasm, erupting in a shower of wine-red blood. It all happened so quickly; his eyes were wide and filled with terror as he collapsed to his knees.

"You come into my home?!" I bellowed, dropping the pretense of banter. My voice was amplified by Trick; it was an unnecessary bit of theatrics, but I wanted to make sure these pirates really heard me. Jon had warned me that it was dangerous to cast this many spells in a short span of time and he was right, I could feel my stamina dropping with every word. But I had to press on, and besides, I was nearly done.

"You attack me and my people, unwarranted and unannounced?! How dare you! How dare you treat my staff, my guests, my friends, so shamefully!"

The Splitter's chest heaved up and down, the loss of blood seemed to have addled him beyond rational thought. It didn't matter; no call for mercy from his lips or any other would stop me from raising my umbrella. I didn't need to envision a clock, and I certainly didn't need to picture the Orc; the motion was second nature by this point, and my foe was right in front of me. I cast Magic Blast, aiming directly between the Splitter's eyes.

His body hit the ground first. Despite the vindication I felt in taking this pirate's life, the first life I had ever taken, it was still difficult to look at. The circle of his pirate crew lost its imposing shape as they shuffled around, unsure of what to do next or how to process what they had just witnessed. As more fatigue came over me, I remembered something else Jon had said: if overexertion was expected, you could consciously dismiss a passive spell rather than lose them at random or pass out and lose them all. It was no contest, and the illusory face of Chadwick Bonesbury melted away to reveal the Skeleton underneath.

I screamed, just a pure and primal expulsion of feeling, made even louder thanks to my magic. This sent the pirates scrambling, whooping in terror as they fell over one another trying to get away from me.

With a magician's flourish, I removed the hat from my head and pointed the opening forward, tapping the top with the tip of my umbrella. Emery emerged in his raven form, increasing dramatically in size thanks to the last spell Jon had taught me: 'Embiggen.' The gigantic black bird flew out and picked up one of the fleeing crewmates in his beak, circling around to bring him to me.

"Who sent your crew here?!"

Faced with a demonic Skeleton and corvid of unusual size, the Human man soiled himself. Following that, he wailed, "The D'Graszias! They promised us half your wealth if we cleared you out! Please don't kill me, I'll do anything."

Emery flew him back towards the house for interrogation while I walked in the opposite direction. Lituin's limp body was in a puddle of his own blood, but when I approached he gasped and rolled over, weak but alive. The thought crossed my mind to make some kind of quip about lying down on the job, but I was so weak; I couldn't even register the fact that he had survived. Instead, I merely lifted him to his feet and put his arm over my shoulders.

My Human face was up again before we made it back to the others. I handed the swordsman off to his students, who were ready with magic salves and bandages. Lituin would live, thank the gods. But the gods, I learned, had a poor sense of humour.

"Almost no casualties," Alan reported. "And we're already giving the wounded medical attention. If we—"

"How many did we lose?" was all I could ask.

"Just one…"

That's when I saw him. Lying on a makeshift cot in the middle of my front hall was the body of Fred Avalon, face partially burned and a large wet wound on his side.

"That damned Coglio was right," I croaked. "The bugger didn't live long enough…"

PART 2

CHAPTER 11 – Keep Your House In Order

Hello, reader. We've made it halfway through this little novel of mine. Kudos to you! And a sincere thanks for your… let's call it morbid curiosity regarding my life and times. As I emphasized throughout the beginning of our tale, the purpose of this text is to educate you lot on the ins and outs of Skeleton Business. So let's resume the lesson, shall we?

My duel with the Splitter brought about a plethora of consequences, but thanks to my strategic broadcast of the fight, the majority were to my benefit. For starters, virtually everyone in attendance that night regarded me as a hero. The politicians I had invited each wrote separate, unprompted letters to our head of state, an Elf whose title was the 'Duke of the South,' or so I was told. In recognition of my courageous actions I was gifted an honorarium, along with a plaque which identified me as a 'Guardian of the Realm.' It came with no actual duties or responsibilities, of course; it was essentially just bragging rights given tangible form.

Then there were the businessmen, the ones I had summoned specifically because of their association with Metrion D'Graszia and who suddenly found a healthy, professional interest in me. I had hoped that, upon learning of his highly unprofessional plot against me, they would all break their ties with that fiend of an Elf, but Raeden warned me there was no way to prove D'Graszia involvement in the pirate's attack. Any attempts to cast blame publicly would be met with denial and backlash. However, several partners did cross over to my side. More than half, actually, which Raeden later remarked would prove devastating to the D'Graszia empire as a whole.

Following suit was Sunder Blackstone, who I think I can confidently say was a fan and supporter of mine before the party and, after seeing what I was capable of, began to worship the ground I walked on. He sent countless financial backers our way, even investing a significant amount of his own funds. After this turn of literal fortune, Raeden begrudgingly apologized for ever having doubted me.

Like I said, the majority of outcomes were to my favour, but not all. There was the fate of Fred Avalon, my trusted groundskeeper. As far as Breadalbane could tell, his only family was a sister across the ocean in Mot. I expedited a letter to her, requesting instructions for what should be done with her brother's body. She wrote back:

Dear Mister Bonesbury,

I am grateful that you were so good to Frederick. My brother spoke fondly of you in his letters home. If you could do our family one last kindness, I would ask that you be the one to safeguard my brother's body and soul.

Appreciative regards,
Jenny Avalon

And so I did. We held a small funeral on the grounds, and just about every staff member had at least one nice anecdote about Fred. Hayra had so many stories that she needed to be asked to cede the floor. I spoke last; there were times where I was happy to let my ego rule the day, but this was not one of them. I had taken the time to prepare a speech, but before I could get through the first cue card I recoiled from the stand, turning my back from the podium and hiding my face. Most assumed that I was simply emotional, maybe even ashamed that I was crying in public, but the opposite was true. Damn skull of mine, dry as a bone…

Life, despite our request for an adequate mourning period, went on. Violet Heights had sustained heavy damages in the attack, and to their credit everyone pulled together to start clearing debris and put the estate, our home, back in order. I took the opportunity to start numerous restructuring projects, since much of the house's exterior needed to be rebuilt anyway, and only some were frivolous. Besides, it ensured plenty of work to keep everyone occupied which, I hoped, would help to take their minds off the purveying melancholy.

I didn't have to work that hard to come up with distractions. My four-month anniversary of owning and inhabiting Violet Heights was fast approaching, a date I had been dreading since day one. If you recall, the staff who had served the previous tenant, eccentric Gnome bard Coglio Magella, still had four months remaining in their original contracts when I took possession of the estate; they had agreed to stay on to finish their terms (and help train possible replacements) with the right to walk away from me at the end of that time if they so wished. The fear that the entirety of them would walk out my door had gnawed at me ceaselessly for weeks - what would it say about me and my leadership if the newer staff members saw their elders and mentors bolt out the front gates the minute their contracts were up? But, to my pleasant surprise, only Breadalbane and a handful of support staff chose to go.

"Are you sure I can't convince you to stay?" I asked the butler.

"I'm afraid you can't. You've been… an interesting employer, to say the least. But my retirement is long overdue."

"Then your going away party will be a legendary soiree!"

"That's really not necessary, Mister Bonesbury…"

"Think of it as your living funeral, Breadalbane." It was a rare occurrence when I could control my outward excitement, especially when I thought of an exceptionally good idea; judging by his expression (a mixture of unease and possible nausea) this was not one of those rare times. "It's just as much for us, the people who will miss you, as it is for you."

We went with a much smaller affair, in-house attendance only. Anyone who was leaving had the day off, and everyone else was instructed to do only as much work as they deemed necessary, with a full day's pay, regardless. It would give the party a looser, more spontaneous feel, at least according to Cassandra after we managed to coax an original opinion out of her. I did, however, win the argument to hold the party in the dining room rather than the front hall – I refused to use anything less than the good china and fancy goblets for Breadalbane's send-off.

It felt good to have all my people in one room. I was so used to seeing them in sequences, each one with a place to be and a job to do, all dictated by the passage of time. Their presence here was a reminder that there was life in Violet Heights, not merely by coincidence but by design. I only wished this narration, something I've had years to think about, could have been reflected in the actual speech I gave that night.

"Alright, you buggers!" it began. "Let's not be sad our friends are leaving us after tonight. Let's be happy to have known them, and that their coming absence gives us an excuse to get absolutely sloshed on my good wine, eh? Huzzah to the lot of you!"

"Huzzah!" Alan echoed, prompting the assembly to all drink with smiles on their faces.

I could just barely taste my liquor, which was absorbed by a magic item I kept between my ribs known as a 'Pouch of Vastness.' Jon taught me this trick a while back, allowing me to engage senses I should have no access to, and I had been performing little experiments to see how much I could get away with. I rarely ate with others, but when required I tried to sample some sensation of whatever was mashed between my teeth and funneled into the Pouch. It worked a bit like a memory, but not that simple, either. I had never tasted wine this exquisite in my old life, but I had plenty of experience with bad wine and other drinks. So those memories met the drink halfway, giving me a faint idea of what it was like in the here and now.

"More wine, Mister Bonesbury?" I was asked an hour later.

"No thank you, Breadalbane."

"Sir, it's Alan," said the confused young man.

"Oh, I'm aware," I laughed. "But you said it yourself, you're Breadalbane 2.0 now."

"That was just a joke."

"And a good one!" I cackled again. "But I liked it, and it got me thinking. We really should always have a Breadalbane present at Violet Heights. You don't mind your name being turned into a noun, do you, Pontius?"

"All names are nouns, sir," explained Breadalbane the original. "Proper nouns, specifically."

"We'll make an improper noun out of you yet. If neither of you severely object, that is."

"I have no control over what goes on in this house once I'm gone," Breadalbane sighed, tired but smiling. "But it's a soothing thought, I suppose, to think that a piece of me will always remain here."

"I'll be the best damn you I can be," Alan saluted.

"At ease, you magical twit," instructed the proud mentor.

Later that evening we were privy to one of my most anticipated events. Cassandra had agreed to do a performance, something that should have happened during the garden party (a certain pirate put an end to that notion, but no matter; I put an end to him as recompense). As Cassandra took to the stage in her blue dress, her hair illuminated by the rising moonlight that streamed through the window, the room hushed at her presence.

She took a breath and began to play. Her eyes stayed closed from the moment the melody began, a lively sonata whose notes seemed to physically sway her body back and forth. I saw a faint cyan glow on her fingertips; her bardic magic was enhancing her playing. A light breeze picked up, as if she created the wind just from the strokes of her bow.

I was so caught up in the playing that I failed to notice a shifting tone in the room. People looked around uncomfortably, seeking guidance for reasons I didn't immediately grasp. Then realization struck me like a grand piano: Cassandra had been playing for an unusually long time. Her tempo had changed, too, and she was losing the melody which was not in her nature at all; her notes were coming faster and more discordant with every bar.

"Cassandra?" I called, standing up suddenly from my chair. Every pair of eyes in the room darted back and forth from me to the performing Elf, but she did not stop. The air coming off her grew more intense, whipping her hair into a frenzy as the temperature continued to drop.

"Cassandra!" I shouted again, this time taking long strides towards the stage. I put a hand out, not exactly sure what I meant to do, just as Cassandra took a long, hard drag of her bow across the strings, which sent out a shockwave that knocked me back. Her arms hung loose at her sides, the violin's neck still firmly grasped in one hand and the bow in the other. Somehow, the wild music continued; a trick typical of purple casters, or so I had heard, since they would often use their instruments to cast spells even in the middle of a performance.

The crowd gasped. Cassandra had opened her eyes for the first time since she took the stage. Her irises were now overlapped with a shimmering orange light, and the cyan glow on her fingers had darkened, wrapping in a helix pattern all the way up her arms to the shoulders.

"Gods, no…" Breadalbane cursed. I thought he meant to whisper, but either out of terror or vexation, he was shouting.

"I'm not finished," said Cassandra with a voice that wasn't hers. It was a male voice, heavily distorted as if it were at the bottom of a chasm, and it echoed unnaturally through the room. She began to play again, but her new song was out of sync with the first one still playing and filling the room with its chaotic windstorm. The two sounds gradually merged into one another, equally wild and uneven in meter, and with their union came such a blast of wind that every table and chair was knocked over as if they were made of straw.

And then Cassandra began to float.

A whirlwind formed around the Elf girl, raising and suspending her tiny body at least ten feet off the ground. Her hair became unbound, as if she were floating underwater rather than high above my marble floors and

terrified staff. I could see a distinct sneer on her face, though the way her body bent with the music, she appeared to be gripped by nothing less than total ecstasy. I shouted her name several times; if she heard me, she made no sign of it.

"Do you believe me now, you diminutive halfwit?!" The outburst was so loud and sudden that my focus was drawn away from the horror show which was unfolding before us. Breadalbane was the culprit, his voice tense and his body half-turned towards Hayra, who looked just as terrified of him as the possessed Cassandra. From where I was crouching on the stage I could see his teeth — was he actually snarling at my gardener?

"I don't know!" she returned, needing to shout over the building torrent of wind. Felsha pulled her closer as she began to cry.

"Can someone please tell me what the hell is going on?!" I despised the idea of screaming at my staff, but as the volume around us increased and the resolve among us plummeted, it seemed like a necessary evil to partake in.

"It's him!" Breadalbane pointed towards Cassandra dramatically. The colour had drained from his face along with his aggression, so now whatever anger he had expelled towards Hayra was replaced by sheer and utter terror. "The Gentleman Bard, the Majestic Maestro of the Sapphire Strings!"

"Who?!"

"The former owner of this house, sir…" The old Elf swallowed hard before continuing. "Coglio Magella!"

The music stopped abruptly, creating a silence that made ears ring and eyes wince. We all looked up. Cassandra, or at least her body, was still hovering above the stage, though the tornado winds had died down to that of a strong winter breeze. She turned her head at an unnatural angle and pointed glowing eyes towards my soon-to-be former butler.

"Is that my old friend Breadalbane?" she asked with that same alien voice.

"Hello, sir…"

"Speak up, man!" barked the possessed Cassandra. "And tell me why my house looks so queer."

"That would be my doing," I spoke up, taking a half-step forward. "And I believe you mean my house."

"Breadalbane, who is this skinny boob you're currently trembling be-hind?"

"That would be…" Breadalbane was shaking where he stood, and he had to pause to keep from stammering. "Chadwick Bonesbury, sir. He's, ahem, the new master of the house."

"What?!" The room shook as Coglio Magella, through the body of my favourite violin player, shouted their disapproval. "That's preposterous! A man can't have two masters, Breadalbane. Seems you've gotten sloppy in my absence, my less than faithful butler. Never fret, I'll whip you into shape in no time!"

They raised their arm and drew the bow sharply against the violin, wind-ing down like the ending of a sword slash. A blade of energy, six feet long at least, formed from the instrument and shot towards Breadalbane with foul speed. I did not have my sword at hand, but my training with Lituin was now second nature, and I managed to kick off with my heels to put my body between attacker and target. My torso absorbed the brunt of the attack, Deceptive Defense likely doing most of the work, while the two ends of the blade pulverized my imported marble floor on either side of Breadalbane's feet, causing him to jump.

"Now see here!" Though my absent belly was full of fire, I spoke through gritted teeth; taking the brunt of that spell hurt, as they say, like a son of a bitch. Another one or two of those and I'd be dead all over again.

"You've possessed the body of a dear friend of mine, and you've attacked another. I don't care who you are or what side of death you find yourself on, I won't stand for any of it." To punctuate my stance, I used Trick to shake the room.

"Oh, that's a very intimidating spell," said Coglio, clearly unintimidated. "Let me have a go at that one. And a one, and a two…" Through Cassandra's nimble fingers, they played a steady tune which grew louder and louder. At the exact moment it became unbearable, every piece of glass in the room shattered violently, including the windows and my ridiculously overpriced crystal drinking goblets

"Dispose of them like you did the Splitter!" commanded Jacob. On account of everyone else's terror, I silently forgave my bean counter's audacity.

"I'm sure I could, Ryker. But I won't endanger Cassandra, not until every last option has been exhausted. What are our options, people?"

"A gold caster could probably exorcize her," Raeden put forward. "Their magic draws from the divine."

"Brilliant," I cheered, while Coglio continued to float and cause havoc with Cassandra's violin. "Do we have a gold caster on staff?"

"We don't."

"Then that isn't a bloody option, is it?!"

"We could contain them somehow," said Felsha, half-carrying and half-dragging Hayra towards the huddle forming in the middle of the room. "But my spells[8] only work on beasts."

"Does anyone here know a containment spell?" I asked the group.

"I do," said Alan. "But casting it will take time, and it won't work if they're ready for it. I'll need a distraction."

"I think I can manage that."

"You do excel at being obnoxious," Felsha ribbed.

"Thank you," I replied earnestly. "Oh, Coglio!" As I stepped forward, feet unsteadied by swirling magical winds, I began to wave my umbrella behind my back.

---

8   Fun fact: Felsha is what's known as a brown caster, those whose magic draws from animals and the wild, but in a fundamentally different way from green casters like Hayra.

"Oh, I just can't get this bariolage to work," whined the bard. His words were echoing unevenly, his voice warped and distorted, as if Cassandra's throat couldn't keep up. "Be grateful you're not burdened with any real talent, Bonesbury. You know not the perfectionism that plagues those with expectations put upon them."

"Big talk from someone without his own corporeal body." The playing stopped again, and the ensuing silence felt as if it could push me back. "Is that a sore spot, oh great maestro? Good. And I'll have you know, I do possess a talent!"

"And what would that be?"

"Subtle spellcasting!"

I chose that moment to snare Coglio/Cassandra with the large curtain I had pulled off the wall, accomplished thanks to Lesser Telekinesis. Cocooned in velvet, they thrashed for a moment in the air before falling to the floor. With the pair disoriented, Alan unleashed his spell: with hands outstretched and fingers spread wide, he conjured twenty orbs of light, each no bigger than an apple and glowing like pure gold. Without wasting a moment, they shot forward and zigzagged over, across, and around the thrashing curtain. Glowing lines appeared between them and stitched the orbs together, creating an ethereal, double-walled icosahedron in the middle of my dining room.

"No…" hissed Coglio, managing to free themselves from the lesser of their two prisons. "No! Let me out, dammit!" The curtain fell from their shoulders as Cassandra's fist pounded on the inner wall to no avail.

"Well done, Alan," I applauded, admiring the potency of his spell.

"You can't keep me in here!" Coglio reached for the violin, which had fallen to the floor. I promptly snatched it using Lesser Telekinesis, and smashed the instrument to pieces on the floor.

"And you can't keep possessing my friend," I spoke to them as I would to a particularly aggravating child. "Let her go, Coglio. We'll settle this some other way."

"Never!"

"Then I'm afraid you'll both rot in there."

"There's nothing to settle!" Cassandra's body seethed with the rage of another man. "This house is mine, and I'm free to do whatever I please! Leave, or I swear you'll regret it!" Suddenly they bent backwards, arching Cassandra's spine in such a way that was painful just to watch. Her mouth shot open so quickly I feared that he had dislocated her jaw. Instead, a high-pitched trill escaped, deafening at its onset but gradually diminishing until it was no more, at which point Cassandra collapsed.

"That sound…what was that sound?" I demanded to no one in particular. I saw Breadalbane lying on the floor - apparently he had fainted at some point — and the auxiliary staff were hiding behind the last standing tables at the far end of the room.

"It was likely the spirit leaving the body," Felsha said calmly, though her true fear was betrayed by her trembling body. Hayra was still holding her hand. "The girl will need medical attention."

"Drop the spell, Alan!"

My new butler was shaking with the effort of his spell, but at my command he allowed his
fingers to relax and his hands to drop. I ran to her as soon as the shape disappeared. Cassandra's breath was shallow, her once-luminous skin now pale and clammy. Reaching into my breast pocket, I produced a small bottle filled with a rejuvenating potion; I had been keeping one on my person ever since the Splitter's attack, even though they were of no use to a Skeleton like myself. I uncorked the bottle and put it to her lips, hoping with every hope I had left that the elixir would be enough.

"Ch-Chadwick?" she muttered before her eyes fluttered open. "What happened? Everything hurts…"

"Quite a lot has happened, I'm afraid." I looked to each of my staff, hoping one of them would offer some modicum of comfort. "I'm actually a bit overwhelmed myself. I suppose we should start with something small…

"I think I owe you a new violin."

CHAPTER 12 – Practice Good Negotiating Skills

Breadalbane had come down with a fever, though we could not be sure if it was caused from his close counter with Coglio, his fainting afterwards, or some other ailment. Most of us agreed he wouldn't want to stay at Violet Heights another minute, so I arranged for a caravan to take him to a hospital in the northwest, one of the best in the entire country. He would have a team of no less than five of the best doctors giving him the best treatment money could buy; I knew this because I paid for it. I also arranged for a healer from the next village to accompany him on the journey, as well as several of Lituin's best students for security. We loaded up his few belongings, along with little gifts from the staff, and I bid him farewell, though I doubted he could hear me. He was hard to look at; his already white hair had become almost translucent.

"We're not going anywhere," Alan said, speaking on behalf of the assembled heads of staff. There were nods all around the room. The only one who didn't share their sentiment was Jacob Ryker, who had coincidentally announced after the party that he would be doing some off-site accounting for the foreseeable future.

"I… I don't know what to say." Ever the showman, I mimed the wiping away of a tear.

"Say you've got a plan to get the bastard," Calliope put forward.

"Oh," yelped Hayra. "Calliope, dear, we shouldn't speak ill of the dead… especially when they could be listening at this very moment."

"Okay," I sighed. "I'll tell you what we're not going to do. That."

"What?"

"Live in fear. I don't care if this house is haunted, and I don't care what that ectoplasmic bugger thinks. This is my… our house. It isn't just the money I've put into it, or the work. Violet Heights means something, dammit. It's ours, he can't have it! Raeden, tell everyone what the plan is before I become giddy."

"I've written to the church of Belas about our ghost problem. They're sending a Sol, one of their holy men and a gold caster, to see if they can exorcize the… entity. We should expect them tomorrow."

"In the meantime," I interjected. "We need to treat this like we're going to war. 'Know thy enemy', I read that in a book once. Hayra, you're the only one left who actually knew our enemy, so some insight would be brilliant."

"Oh, he wasn't a bad man!" exclaimed the gardener. Felsha put a hand on her shoulder, which seemed to strengthen both her composure and her voice. "He was a little selfish, and maybe not always as grateful as he could have been, but he was an artist. All he seemed to care about in his last few years was composing."

"How ironic," I said gravely. "In death, all he should be doing now is de-composing!" When no one laughed, I cleared my throat with a "yes, well…"

"My sister's father-in-law became a ghost," added Calliope. "Supposedly he was a bit of a clod in life, but when he died he became a right jackass. I think whatever happens to you when you're a ghost, it sort of strips you down to your truest self, but amplified by ten. Artist types, a lot of them reckon themselves gods. A kook locked away in his own house for a de-cade decides to off himself? Yeah, sounds like he'd be quite the rotter."

"That's actually pretty accurate," said Alan. "We studied ghosts at the

Guild. That's how I was able to make Cassandra's protection bracelet. Coglio likely targeted her because she's a purple caster, like him. Probably felt a shared resonance with her. But the Sol should enhance the bracelet with their own magic, too."

"I have no desire to play host to that… thing, ever again," Cassandra shuddered.

"Nor I," I concurred. My attention turned to the quietest corner of the room. Glyph was tinkering with a supposed ghost trap, although Alan had told me privately it was unlikely to work. Next to the Gnome was Lituin, whose arms were crossed while he stared off into space, still healing from his fight with the Splitter.

"For my security expert, you're awfully quiet," I evoked.

"You speak of war," said the swordsman, whose words were sharper and more calculated than his monk-like demeanour suggested. "Perhaps I'm influenced by the fact that this is not a foe I can cut with my blade. But I feel that most wars, if not all conflicts, are unnecessary precursors to the most simplistic solution: that enemies sit down with one another and talk out their differences, peacefully."

A silence hung over the room after that. I looked at each of my loyal staff in turn; they were supportive but scared, and likely dealing with varying levels of physical and emotional exhaustion. After taking a breath (with what lungs? My form was wonderfully confounding) I turned back to Lituin.

"You're right; of course, you're right. Before we wage war on Coglio Magella… we will speak to him."

The Sol arrived early in the morning. They were a Dragonkind with orange scales, and introduced themself as Veth Skorr.

"I'll admit, I was expecting an Elf," I said humbly after meeting them at my front door.

"Many Dragonkind are in the faith," Sol Skorr replied warmly. "So many are abandoned by our parents at birth[9], but we are found again in the light of the sun."

"Right. So, you think you can help with our ghost problem?"

"I am certain of it."

"Love that confidence."

"Not confidence," said Veth, as they straightened their back to further prove their point. "I have faith."

"That makes one of us. Now, I'm not sure how this works, but…we want to try talking with Coglio before you, I don't know, blow him to kingdom come."

"I can assure you," Veth laughed. "There will be nothing like that. My order helps lost souls into the light, sometimes by force but only if necessary."

"Right."

"I'll have to manifest the spirit in question, though, during which time you can attempt to communicate with it. If you can convince this Coglio Magella to move on of his own accord, it will make my job much easier."

"Then we should get started. Please, come inside. Will you take tea?"

Many on staff had been dismissed for the day, told to occupy their time away from Violet Heights for their own safety. Only those necessary for the exorcism were asked to remain; Lituin insisted on staying behind, along with a small regiment of his students to defend the property at its borders. Our focal point was a bedroom on the second floor: Coglio's old

---

9 Imagine being first-time parents, a young and optimistic Human, Dwarf, or Elf couple, for example, and your child comes out a reptile. Not ideal for anyone in the equation, sadly.

room, where he would lock himself away for months at a time in an attempt to create his masterpieces. It had been the largest one in the house, but that was before I'd had the attic converted into my private sanctuary.

To prepare for what was about to happen, Veth had us cover the bay window with a thick tablecloth so no light could get in, save for a single hole that would allow an intense beam through. They then produced a pristine glass orb, which looked more carved than blown, from a silk pouch on their belt.

"This is the holy symbol of my lady Belas," they explained, holding up the fragile orb with reverence. "It focuses and expands her light. Observe." A small end table had been placed in the path of the window's beam, and when Veth put the holy symbol on it, prismatic light filled the room, beautiful and suffocating in its completeness.

"Are you two ready?" the Sol asked Alan and Cassandra, who nodded.

"You don't have to do this," I said to my bard. "I'd understand if you were reluctant to face Coglio after he…violated you. And it's not like you're our only option for The Power of Three, Hayra is here too."

"No," said Cassandra, a little too quickly for my comfort. "It has to be me, he'll come for me. Besides, we need Hayra to try and reason with him."

"But-"

"And you're wrong, I'm not reluctant. If anything, the opposite is true. I owe him a reckoning."

"There's a fire in you, to be sure," I told Cassandra genuinely. "Just be careful not to burn yourself."

"I would like to go over the plan one more time," said Veth. "I will begin my summoning, supported by Miss Lemos and Mister Miller."

"And I'll be playing one of Coglio's unfinished works," Cassandra continued. "Provided by Hayra."

"I hope this isn't a mistake," bemoaned the gardener.

"Once Coglio manifests," I went on. "Hayra and I will attempt to talk him do[wn] peacefully. If he doesn't cooperate, then we get him."

"Miss Lemos will finish the song," said the Dragonkind. "Symbolically outmo[d]ing Coglio Magella, demonstrating that the world has no further need of him[.] Once that connection is established, I should be able to remove him, or at lea[st] weaken him enough so we may try again later." They looked around at the assembled company, making direct eye contact with each of us; I don't know if it was to assure us of the plan's success or simply to check that we were paying attention. A slight nod of their scaly head in my direction told me they were s[at]isfied.

"Whenever you're ready, Sol," I whispered.

Veth began to chant in Elvish, and the light from their holy ornament seemed to glimmer and grow with every word. Alan echoed their words while makin[g a] series of hand gestures, leading with his index finger and pearl ring, which wa[s] glowing an intense and gilded yellow. Cassandra began the song, and I eyed t[he] protection bracelet on her wrist. It had been further enhanced by the Sol's ma[gic] the moment they had arrived at my door, which reassured me that she was, in[deed, safe.

"We call forth the spirit of Coglio Magella into this chamber!" announced the Dragonkind. "May he find resonance here, the site of his purest creation!"

Something moved across the rainbow light that filled the room, like a dimnes[s] or not-quite invisible object was just slightly obscuring the projection. It pace[d] back and forth, as if it was planning its next move, before stopping near the middle of the space and rising three feet in the air. Sparks began to fly from t[he] dim shape, as the light seemed to knit itself into a humanoid form.

"Chadwick Bonesbury," echoed a familiar voice, one I had only ever heard pr[o]jected through Cassandra's vocal chords before. "As I live and breathe."

"Coglio, you don't do either of those things," I said, trying to keep my tone ev[en.]

"Your Dragonkind friend is holding me here. Have them release me at once!"

"I was hoping we could talk first."

"You and I have nothing to say to one another! After all, aren't I just an 'ectoplasmic bugger'?"

"Oh…" whimpered Hayra.

"So you have been eavesdropping." The plan had specifically called for a neutral conversation; as a being now comprised of pure energy and emotion, making Coglio angry could put us at a disadvantage. "So I guess this just confirms that you're completely without class." Okay, so I'm bad at following plans, I admit it.

"I have more class in one pinky finger than you do in your entire skinny body!" The room shook a little.

"You don't have any pinkies!" I shot back.

"Mister Magella!" Hayra called. "It's me, Miss Bloomkin? Your faithful gardener, sir.

"Yes, hello, Hayra. Am I to assume you've betrayed me, too? Siding with Bonesbury, hmm?"

"H-he really is a good man," Hayra said timidly. "He's taking such good care of your house, and the garden-"

"My house is unrecognizable!" More shaking, and the illuminated vision of Coglio shimmered in an unsavoury manner. "It has been torn apart and defaced! I cannot stand to occupy this garish flophouse!"

"Then leave," I said irreverently.

"Surely, sir," Hayra quickly interjected. "You can't be happy in this state, can you?"

"No more than I was when I was alive," responded Coglio.

"Then can't we help you with whatever unfinished business you may have?

So you can move on, and be at peace."

"What a preposterous notion! How could I, the irrevocable Coglio Magella, have unfinished business? Yes, I hear that insipid girl's sorry attempt to execute the brilliance that is my concerto." Cassandra glared from overtop her violin, playing on with vengeful fervour. "But I had no qualms about the state in which I left. The beauty of the music comes from its incompleteness, the notes I will never write."

"Then…" Hayra squeaked. "Why on Gaiyax did you become a ghost?"

"My suffering in this state was orchestrated!" Yet more shaking, this time strong enough to knock over Veth Skorr.

"By whom?"

"That wretched dog who poisoned me, Metrion D'Graszia!"

"What?!" I pushed Hayra out of the way, perhaps more vehemently than I should have; I would have to remember to install an extra hectare of garden for her as an apology. "You knew Metrion?"

"Knew him? He was my best patron! But for everything that snake gave me, he would take a hundred times over. I was nothing more than a divining rod to him, something to bring him greater fortune and prosperity."

"You said you were poisoned." My mind was trying to put together some kind of important puzzle, but as I am unburdened by great intelligence, it was taking me a while and required further inquiry. "The world knows you to have killed yourself."

"It was a slow-acting poison," said the ghostly light. "Designed to subject its victim to mounting agony. Metrion promised me the antidote once I resumed my role of his subservient miracle worker. But the only thing that dwarfed my pain was my contempt, and so I married the two emotions into a final sweeping crescendo, and took my own life."

"You poor man," Hayra said with tears streaming down her cheeks. "I had no idea you were suffering so badly at the end."

"Yes, he's so hard done by."

"Mister Bonesbury!"

"I'm not denying he suffered. But it wasn't the only thing that brought you into this state, was it, Coglio?"

"Metrion is a master manipulator, with countermeasures within countermeasures!" The bard spoke as if he were doing a monologue in a play. "Decisive sigils etched around my home, so inconspicuous not even my anal-retentive butler could detect them. They barred me from passing into oblivion, and I have lingered here ever since."

"Ha!" I chortled. "That explains a few things. Metrion doesn't give a damn about this house, it's you he wants! But what could you possibly possess that would motivate him to circumvent Death itself?"

"I am a purple caster: arcane knowledge and eldritch secrets are our life-blood, and my career has been a long one. I know the secret location of the Havaras Hoard, I've seen maps that track the floating cities. But the thing Metrion craved most from me is the Immortal Melody."

"Mister Bonesbury," groaned Veth Skorr. "We can't hold him much longer. Even now he's fighting back against my light."

"Just a moment more," I called, before turning back to face the, frankly, terrifying golem of light. "What's the Immortal Melody?"

"It's a song," said Cassandra. "A ritual performed in multiple parts, dozens of them. Most purple casters have heard of it. If it's performed correctly for a single audience member, they become near immortal, with longevity and a constitution that would rival most demigods."

"Yes," hissed Coglio. "But there's a catch. It takes a toll on the caster, and cannot be performed all at once. It makes the target suffer physical and mental hardships while they wait for the song to be completed."

"Metrion's headaches."

"That's why he kept me around," said Cassandra, still playing. "I don't know the Immortal Melody, but my magic can at least help abate the side effects."

"Which will never go away if Coglio never finishes the melody," I mused. "Well, this is an unexpected best-case scenario."

"What are you blathering about?" the ghost demanded.

"Coglio, you and I agree on just one thing: Metrion D'Graszia is a contemptible bastard. But if you're valuable to him, then banishing you has the added benefit of spiting the person I hate most. So tell me, do the sigils trap your spirit here?"

"I have seen into realms beyond," Coglio admitted. "They hold no interest for me. I stay here by my own will because as I have stated, repeatedly, this is my house and my land!"

"Move on, Coglio. I'm asking you nicely."

"Never."

"Then what happens next is your own doing," I said without a shred of pity. "Now, Sol!"

Veth's chanting intensified, growing louder and faster as the passion rose in their voice. Once again the room shook; this time it felt as if the whole building was under a seismic attack. The light figure levitated higher, carried on the colours that permeated the room.

"Chadwick!" it shouted, angrier than before but now with a distinct air of panic. "Call off your Dragonkind, or I swear I'll tear down Violin Heights on my way out, brick by damned brick!"

"Go ahead," I told him flatly. "Assuming you even can do that, there's enough magic users in this room to protect us from your tantrum, and the rest of the house has been evacuated. Besides," I added with a toothy grin, "I can buy a new house."

"Oh, but I've been watching you, Chadwick." Something in the way his inflection changed made my nonexistent stomach drop like a stone, like he had me and he knew it. It didn't matter what he said next; the way he spoke told me that I was in trouble.

"You're sentimental. You don't just like my house, you cherish it. It's a symbol for you, something that represents the life you've built. Destroying it would be tantamount to removing one of your limbs, wouldn't it? And I assure you, I will destroy it if you don't let me go."

"You're bluffing…"

"Coglio Magella doesn't bluff!"

A wind had picked up, emanating primarily from Sol Skorr. Coupled with the now-cataclysmic rumbling all around us, I began to feel new terror overwhelming every bone of my bony body. It felt like a noose tightening around my neck, strangling choice out of me in place of air. Without a second thought, I spun on my heels, drew my umbrella and fired Magic Blast at Veth's glass orb. It shattered completely, shrouding the room in near-darkness.

The rumbling stopped immediately. It was so sudden that everyone was jerked in place, now overcompensating for an earthquake that wasn't there. I was the only one who fell; to be honest, I was relieved to relinquish my autonomy to gravity's pull. Hayra came to my aid right away, joined shortly by Alan. It took me a moment to realize that neither of them were speaking, but their faces were filled with concern, not utter fear. Did they not hear that insidious whispering?

"You'll never be rid of me," it said. "I'll do as I please, and if you try to exorcize me again, this house is history."

CHAPTER 13 – Be Ruthless

To say the rest of the day was a bit awkward would be an odious understatement. Veth Skorr had been struck by several shards of glass, thanks to my little stunt, but their scales offered more than adequate protection. Though they took umbrage with me destroying their god's holy symbol, they weren't overly offended by the outcome of the exorcism.

"We can attempt the cleansing again once my strength has returned," they said kindly.

"I…" My hesitation made me uncomfortable, but I found myself struggling for the right words. "That might not be the best move. Coglio, he… he said he'd destroy the house if we tried to force him out."

"That is a possibility."

"More than a possibility," Alan interposed. "This spirit clearly has a connection to the property, an incredibly powerful one. Even with a more potent exorcist, no offense, Sol, there's always the chance it could start the demolition process before the banishment is complete. Quite the deterrent, I'll admit."

"Then we'll…" I stumbled over my words. "We need to make protection bracelets for everyone on staff. Like Cassandra's, filled to the brim with as many magical safeguards as money can buy."

"Magic doesn't work that way," my new butler scoffed before catching himself. "Uhh, I mean, sir, even magic has limitations. Too much of the same kind in one area, especially magic made to interact with or protect that area, well, it will start to crumble, to undermine itself. That's why some mage hasn't gotten filthy rich selling amulets that make you stronger and smarter and invincible to the entire planet. It's why cities that employ magical defenses usually stick to one magical barrier and not a thousand."

"Well what can we do?!"

"I will do a general blessing on the house," said Veth. "And someone from our order can come by once a month to renew it. It won't remove your un-welcome tenant, but it will keep their negative energy from festering and creating greater problems."

"And I can take the Sol around the house looking for those sigils Coglio mentioned," added my new Breadalbane 2.0. "Make sure this doesn't hap-pen twice, you know?"

"Thank you, Alan." It seemed like an eon since the original Breadalbane's farewell party, when my head was filled with nothing but one last playful tease at his expense. Calling my nephew 'Breadalbane' until it was second nature to everyone was supposed to be a fun game, but I was so exhausted that I didn't feel like playing. "Please do that. I think I'll retire to my room for the afternoon."

When I was sure that I was alone, save for Emery in my hat, I opened up my umbrella. Bizarre, metaphysical darkness came down from it, creating a black curtain around me. As I looked into that void, I saw a strange onyx desert, lit by no sun but still illuminated somehow. I had seen this des-ert before, but my memory of it became fuzzy and distorted after each of these sessions came to their end.

"Jon, are you there?" I called.

"Hello, Chadwick." I heard him before I actually saw him, and even when he appeared, it was difficult perceiving him. Jon was present, but distant, like I was seeing someone through a thick cloud of fog. "We're not scheduled for a lesson today. What can I do for you?"

"We need to accelerate my education, Jon. I need a spell that can kill a ghost."

"That's quite the request." I suddenly hated the way Jon would stare at me before and after speaking, how I could feel his eyes boring into me, even though I couldn't see them.

"I have quite the ghost problem. So go on, then. What's the name of the spell? What words do I need to say, what motions does the spell require? How should I prepare my mind?"

"That's not how this works, Chadwick."

"I keep hearing that today…"

 "Even if I wanted to, spells like that are much too advanced for you at your current level."

"Do you not want to, Jon?"

"Chadwick," Jon sighed. "I'm the teacher and you are the student. That means I set the curriculum. I teach you the spells that I think you need and know you can handle. If you're having troubles with a ghost-"

"I just want to be the only undead thing haunting this house," I grumbled. "Is that too much to ask?"

"You're free to learn spells elsewhere, you know."

"But let me guess. I shouldn't try to overreach, and learning magic is accomplished best when done at a steady pace."

"You do listen," Jon chuckled.

"Jon, are you a ghost?"

"What?"

"Well," I began. "You're ethereal like a ghost, and shadowy like one."

"Not exa—"

"And frankly, you're being a bit of a pain in my behind right now, like a ghost."

"I get your point." I could sense Jon starting to pace back and forth as he spoke, like he was giving a lecture. "That's a complicated question, Chadwick. The short answer is no. I'm closer to a ghost than I am to a man, but I'm as much a ghost as you are a Dragon. Does that make sense?"

"Not remotely!"

"Just as well. Have you tried an exorcism? For your ghost problem?"

"Yes," I groaned. "A fat lot of good that did. It nearly worked, but then the bugger started to destroy Violet Heights."

"So what's the problem?"

"I like this place, Jon! I've put a lot of work into it. It was a house when I got here, now it's a home."

"That's beautiful, Chadwick."

"Are you just going to be sarcastic or are you going to help me?"

"Can't I do both?"

"Jon!"

"Alright, alright," he put up a shadowy hand to stifle me (at least I imagined he did). "Yes, there are spells that can directly harm a ghost. But they're rare, so finding a spellcaster to do it for you, even with your resources, could be challenging."

"We'll call that 'plan B', then."

"The tricky thing about ghosts is that they're halfway between planes. If you could find someone on their level, you could have them fight for you as a proxy."

"What, like another ghost?"

"That's the most direct choice, yes."

"Well that sounds like a chore and a half. What else?"

"You do the damn exorcism, Chadwick." I could tell he was becoming frustrated with me. It's possible I'd used up my daily-allotted goodwill from Jon. "You let the house go, you don't be so fixated on material things. That is your option."

"I wouldn't have all these material things if it weren't for you, you know." In response, my umbrella snapped shut on its own, leaving me all alone once again.

I spent the next couple of days perusing the library, hoping that if Jon couldn't teach me a spell to defeat a spectral maniac, I could find the answer somewhere in the thousands of pages on my shelves. What delicious irony, I thought as I reached for volume VII of The Collected Works of Bartimaeus the Bold, to vanquish Coglio using his own library against him. Sadly, all I found was the encyclopedia bupkis.

I'll be completely honest, ancient tomes of forgotten lore had begun to bore me. Seeking some relief but too lethargic to leave the library, I distracted myself with a book on dragons that was more my speed. As exhaustion caught up with me and I slipped in and out of sleep, or whatever this haunted house of a body did in its place, I thought I caught signs of movement in between the stacks of books.

"Hello?" I called out. "I said I didn't want to be disturbed."

The staff had all returned to the house, but I was disinclined to face them until I could formally announce that they were no longer under threat of ghostly harassment; how could I do any less? Until such time, matters of business were to go through Raeden, and those regarding the house were to be delegated to Breadalbane or Calliope. I even stopped taking tea and meals, although I'd eventually have to give some deception to make sure no one thought I was starving in here.

So the fact that someone was in here right now was rather irksome. I set down my picture book (I did say it was more my speed) and made my way into the stacks. I only made it to the first turn before I was shocked with enough figurative voltage that I mistook it for a lightning bolt. I was suddenly face to face with the snooper; I had assumed they would have either fled or hidden themselves away, so I had prepared myself to find someone, eventually. But the face before me was the last face I had ever thought I'd see again.

"Fred?"

"It couldn't have been Fred," I was told over breakfast the next morning. My experience in the library was reason enough to break my self-imposed furlough and disrupt my staff's morning meal.

"Raeden, I swear on my fortune I saw Fred Avalon standing before me in my library. He was translucent and wouldn't meet my eye, but he was there!"

"It actually would make sense," said Breadalbane as he cleared away Hayra's plate, the gardener having quickly excused herself when this topic of conversation reared its morbid head. "Fred was the only person to die in this house since you took dominion over Violet Heights, and we only just got rid of those imprisonment sigils days ago. He would have been forced to manifest here as a spirit, just like Coglio was."

"What a miserable fate," lamented Glyph, who had been Fred's closest confidante before he died. "I'll whip up a ghost trap to catch Fred, he would have wanted it that way."

"Shouldn't we write to Sol Skorr and have them help Fred to move on?" asked Cassandra.

"I think I've had my fill of exorcisms for a while," I declared. "And we're certainly not going to trap him. I want to try talking to Fred first, see if I can help him do it on his own. Now the question is, how do I get him to talk to me?"

"It's a spell called 'Hither,'" Jon told me later that afternoon, after I had successfully groveled my way back into his good graces. "It compels other beings to stand before you and face you, so long as you haven't done them any recent harm. A simple bit of spellcraft, good for herding and rearing animals, or finding someone in a crowd. And yes, I've heard tell that some use it for manifesting ghosts."

"Perfect, I'll take it!" I exclaimed while rubbing my hands together.

"Focus, Chadwick," he said gravely. "Understand that even simple spells could work against you. If you don't know what you're casting it on, you could invite ruin and chaos."

"How so?"

"Say you want to know who's speaking to you in a dark cave. You cast Hither, and then suddenly you're face to face with a ghastly Dragon or a shadow beast. Or perhaps there's another haunting, the perpetrator of which could be far less pretentious than Coglio Magella."

"Not a difficult feat."

"You could manifest a demon masquerading as a lost soul. Promise me you'll be careful, Chadwick."

"I promise."

My first thought, once I'd learned the spell, was to go back to the library, thus far the location of my only post-mortem encounter with Fred, but

I suspected Fred's choice of haunting venue was just a bit of paranormal happenstance. Instead, I made a beeline for Fred's old shed, which was now a workshop and occupied solely by Glyph.

"How goes it today, Bonben?"

"Oh, just fine, Mister Bonesbury. I've nearly cracked cold fusion."

"Really?"

"I'll show you!" The Gnome hurried over to his workbench and returned with a metallic beaker in one gloved hand and a pair of tongs in the other. Using the tongs, he removed a steaming piece of jagged ice from the beaker. "Two individual pieces of ice, fused together almost perfectly."

"Astounding…" I said bewilderedly. I really was astounded… perhaps not in the way Glyph had intended, but he didn't seem to notice the difference.

"What can I do for you, Mister Bonesbury?"

"I need the workshop for a little while. It's, um, a random inspection."

"You're doing the inspection yourself?" Glyph asked from under a raised eyebrow.

"Alright," I relented. "I'm too tired to think up a better lie, and I don't have the heart or stomach to order you to leave. So we've come to bribery. What will it take to get you to leave this room for a couple hours, Glyph?"

"Oh!" His face positively lit up. "That's easy. I want the green light on my experimental airship project. I've been pitching it to Lockwood and Ryker for weeks now."

"Hmm…" I tapped my chin for dramatic effect. I didn't want to just give in, but an airship sounded fun — a lot of fun, even — so allowing his little project would benefit me far more than it would him. "Could Bonesbury Holdings retain intellectual property and distribution rights?" Hey, I'm nothing if not opportunistic…

"Deal!" Glyph shouted before emphatically shaking my hand. "I just want to build the damn thing. But the only thing I'm going to make right now is a nice cup of coffee. If you'll excuse me."

Once Glyph sidled past me to enjoy his treat, I cleared a space to begin the spell as per Jon's instructions. With my right arm outstretched, I spread my fingers with my palm towards the floor. Then I rotated my wrist so my palm faced upwards, bringing my fingers into a fist along the way one by one, save for my index finger.

"Face me," I whispered, crooking my finger as if I was beckoning someone from across the room.

Because of my damn numbed senses, it took me a minute to realize the room had gotten colder. If I wasn't anticipating a spectral audience, I would have blamed it on Glyph's so-called "cold fusion" but then, I saw him.

Aside from being significantly diaphanous, Fred didn't look too dissimilar from how he looked in life. His hair was messy, balding, and unkempt. His posture? Still atrocious. He wouldn't meet my eye, but I could tell by the way he was standing, slightly lopsided with a hand on his opposing bicep, that he definitely knew I was there.

"Hi, Fred."

"Sir," he replied. His voice was distant, like I was hearing him from across an empty ballroom. Though his mouth moved when he spoke, it didn't match up with the words. Even in death he had trouble looking at me.

"I'm so sorry," was all I could think to say.

"I should be sorry, sir," he said wistfully.

"Why?"

"I failed. Failed you, failed the other staff, and failed Violet Heights. I'm better off forgotten."

"All because you died in that attack? That hardly seems fair, none of us saw those bastards coming."

"I… I don't know. Being this way… it's like I can't breathe. And then I realize I don't need to, and I want to laugh, but instead all I can feel is…"

"Shame?" I asked. The connection was instantaneous; he was describing almost exactly how I had felt when I first woke up in that dungeon.

"Yes, exactly! And then that ch-choking sensation only gets worse, like it swallows you. I don't know what to do."

"I avenged you, you know." It just slipped out. Even as I was speaking I could hear it, the deflection, the need to distract from my friend's pain by making it all about me. But I was powerless against that impulse, an unwilling accomplice to my own ego. "The Splitter, that damned pirate who attacked us, I slew him right where he stood. Sent a message, too, that we weren't to be trifled with again. I hope that's some comfort."

"I suppose."

"It's good to see you." I raised an arm to put a hand on his shoulder, but stopped short when I realized that would be both illogical and a tad insensitive. "Despite the circumstances, that is."

"And now I suppose you want to help me move on, so I can get on with my afterlife?"

"Actually…" Again, I heard it, but I was going to say it anyway. Like I said: powerless. "The avenging isn't done, Fred. You're not the only spirit in Violet Heights, but you're the only one who's welcome here."

"You're referring to Master Coglio?"

"How did you—?"

"I can hear him." Fred stared off into the distance. "Even now. He sings, but it just sounds like a mess. I can't stand it."

"How would you like to silence it for good?"

There was no doubt in my mind that a majority of the staff would disagree with my plan. Though I loved several of them dearly, liked a few others just fine, and happily tolerated the rest, grief compounded some of my less attractive qualities and led me to the conclusion that I was the boss and could do what I liked. It didn't help that I was convinced that this plan was good for the house and everyone therein. Looking back, if I could go back and change my decision, I would. Unfortunately, it is many years and several poor choices later, and all I can do is write about my past deeds as honestly as I'm able, in hopes that you may learn to tread lightly where I've stomped like an Ogre.

My logic was simple: if I ordered another evacuation for reasons related to Coglio Magella, it would be difficult to hide the ace up my sleeve (i.e. Fred Avalon), which would in turn expose the somewhat questionable ethics of my intentions. So I fabricated a cover story instead, in which I brought a rare insect to Violet Heights with the aim of putting it in my menagerie, but it escaped and immediately started to breed with the local vermin. To prevent an all-out infestation, I would need the house to be emptied of all personnel so the exterminators could do their work.

Said exterminators were actually over a dozen Sols in disguise, who were convinced to go along with my charade by way of a hefty donation to their church. Raeden would never catch it; I marked the expense as "research and development." Glyph would just have to pinch his pennies for a while.

"You've gone to great lengths to fortify this subterfuge, Mister Bonesbury," said Veth Skorr. "Why?"

"I wanted the house to feel especially blessed," I admitted. "And truthfully, I feel safer with you here. Shall we get started?"

I dug out two decorative suits of armour which had been gathering dust in storage since I first started remodeling the house. They were positioned facing each other, one with a rake in its hand and the other unarmed. I signaled to Veth for the Sols to be ready, before whispering "Fred?"

"I'm here, sir." No one could see Fred, but he was most certainly there. This time his voice was like a cold whisper on the inside of my skull. "What do you need me to do?"

"Just step into a suit of armour, I think you know which one, and then be ready to throw down. Can you do that?"

"I think so."

A few of the Sols recited prayers. Once they had concluded (a couple insisted on doing it the entire time) I took an opposing stance and cast Hither. To maximize its effectiveness, I held Coglio and the unarmed suit of armour together in my mind's eye.

"Come out, you bastard," I whispered under my breath.

Nothing happened at first, but then the armour suddenly jerked violently, as if someone had grabbed it by its very core and throttled it for a moment. Everything about the way it moved should have knocked it over, but the thing remained upright. Then its head began to turn, as if it was taking in the room.

"What is this, where am I?" came a booming voice; it seemed to emanate from every wall. Many of the Sols' heads twitched in alarm as they suddenly registered a new presence. "Chadwick, is that you?"

"Hello, Coglio." I took a few dramatic steps forward, but made sure to keep Fred between us. "Welcome to your reckoning."

"I'm not sure what your game is," sneered the bard. "But I'll happily wreak havoc in this tin can until such a time as my spirit escapes and resumes its undeath!"

The unarmed suit began to approach me, every individual piece of the armour moving as if they were independent of each other. But the lumbering thing didn't get far before its helmet head was struck by a rake. Before

Coglio could register what happened, Fred delivered two more decisive blows to the bard's shoulders and chest.

"What the hell is this?!"

"I told you," I shouted. "Your reckoning!"

"Oh, I see." My foe caught the rake mid-swing and ripped it from Fred's hands, then threw it across the room. "You're getting creative, Chadwick."

"I'd gladly run you through with a sword if I could," I told him. "But since I can't, I'll give that honor to Fred."

"You've got Fred Avalon in there?!" he bawled incredulously. "I don't believe it." Still moving like the world's drunkest marionette, Coglio seized Fred's helmet with one hand and violently forced open the faceplate with the other.

Fred never spoke. He delivered uninspiring punches to his opponent, the metal clanging weakly as his gauntlet met helmet and breastplate. Coglio accepted the feeble blows, all the while filling Violet Heights with his maniacal echoes.

"I'd say this isn't personal," chortled Coglio Magella, as he punched Fred's vessel so hard across the temple that his helmet spun all the way around. "But it's very personal, Avalon. For siding with Bonesbury," another hit, "for attacking me," and another, "for being a terrible groundskeeper all those years!"

What happened next genuinely frightened me. Coglio picked up Fred's armour and held him horizontally above his head. An uneven sphere formed around the pair that seemed like mist; looking back, I can see that they were being surrounded by an increased density in the air. And for the next few moments they stood like that, like a sculpture depicting an epic wrestling match but with little charges of energy that would occasionally arc off the misty sphere.

"The spirits are fighting outside their vessels," Veth explained.

Fred's armour started to wriggle back and forth, like a fish caught in a net. I could hear little popping sounds coming from inside the metal shell, soft and dull at first but they grew more frequent and intense in a matter of seconds. They reached an ear-splitting crescendo, when suddenly tiny explosions — no, not explosions, more like tiny fireworks — erupted from every chink and joint. Then, just as suddenly, Fred's suit fell apart and clattered to the floor. The abrupt silence was deafening.

"What happened?" I asked.

"I think-" was all Veth Skorr could get out before Coglio moved with illogical speed and drove a gauntlet into their stomach, sending them flying across the floor. This put the armoured figure mere inches from my face. I could see no eyes behind their faceplate, but I could read his expression like a death warrant.

Lituin had trained me for situations like this; the act of drawing my blade to attack or defend as needed had been an unconscious reaction up to that day. But I was paralyzed, completely and utterly. It wasn't just the fear that Coglio could hurt me, would hurt me, but what he did to Fred…

Whether it was because he sensed my terror or he found some sick joy within his own chaotic whims, the armoured ghost chuckled and sped away from me. One of the Sols had rushed over to help Veth, who still lay unmoving on my polished floor; I saw Coglio pick up the holy medic by their throat, lifting them off the ground with ease. The Sol's fingers tried feebly to loosen the metal grip, and I saw true fear in their eyes, which snapped me out of whatever inertia had held me.

"That's enough!" I charged towards him, drawing my sword and driving it with as much force as I could into his midsection, just under the armpit where a lung should have been. How it pierced through the breastplate I'll never know, but I made a mental note to be proud of it later.

"Oh no, I'm dead!" Coglio shrieked. "Oh, wait."

"What happened to Fred?!" I demanded. Despite his over-dramatic feign to my attack, I could feel him struggling to keep this metal body upright. Had I actually managed to hurt him?

"I sent him back to his maker, in pieces!"

"How…? He was already dead!"

"Souls can be destroyed," Coglio laughed. "I applaud you for your ingenuity, Chadwick, I really do. But if you want any sort of shot at besting me, you'll have to do better than just the hired help. And really, Chadwick, how many more people have to die twice before you accept that there is no besting me?"

The faceplate of Colgio's armour lifted by its own power, and I could hear that same high-pitched tone as the one Cassandra made when Coglio left her body. It diminished to nothing and the suit of armour collapsed immediately, save for the breastplate still skewered on my rapier. None of the Sols spoke; I was at a loss for words, and I couldn't blame them for feeling the same.

My thoughts drifted to Jenny Avalon, Fred's sister, and I dropped to my knees. In her letter she had asked me to safeguard her brother's 'body and soul'; that's how she had worded it. What would she say if she knew what had transpired here today? What contempt would I find in her eyes, if I could ever meet her gaze? I had drawn her brother into this fool's endeavour, and now I felt as he had.

Nothing but shame and failure.

CHAPTER 14 – Mind the Importance of Downtime

It's possible you may have noticed that I've been rather lackadaisical when it comes to explaining the significance of these chapter titles. I'll remind you, dear reader, the purpose of this inaugural novel of mine is to teach you how to succeed in Skeleton Business. Though my methods may be unorthodox and long-winded, that objective has not changed.

The purpose of these chapter titles, as I have curated them, is simply to influence any preconceived notions you may have of the material that follows. Sometimes this tactic takes the form of metaphor, a way to sum up the events of a small but particular portion of my existence while still resembling good commerce advice. Other times you're meant to learn from my example, either my great social, financial, and thaumaturgical victories or, most recently, my deplorable failures.

And sometimes they're simply ironic.

My ongoing feud with the ghost of Coglio Magella had been put on hold indefinitely. I found myself a broken man, and gloom was a more steadfast companion than even Emery. When I was most desperate for distraction, something to break this cycle of chagrin, not many could be found. All substantial work on the house had been completed, and Raeden begged me most fervently not to start any more renovations. Even Glyph, who was normally happy to enact whatever madness of mechanical engineering my mind could muster, said he was content with the current projects he had ahead of him.

Initially, Lituin got the brunt of my ennui. I tripled our lessons, justifying it by saying free time was simply an opportunity to better ourselves. At first this significant rescheduling meant that he wouldn't be able to perform his other duties, but by this point he was confident that his handful of apprentices could pick up the slack in his absence. Truth be told, the work we did in those weeks was enough to make me yearn for the ability to sweat.

One day, I believe it was a Wednesday, I entered the dojo for a training session and immediately felt that something was off. Lituin liked things to be a certain way in his workspace, every piece of equipment in its proper place and all that. That day, nothing was where it should have been, like when a child is told to clean their room but they just shove everything under the bed to get it over with. The real giveaway, however, was the fact that my swordmaster was dressed in his casual clothes… and sitting on the floor.

"Something wrong?" I asked apprehensively.

"Not at all, Mister Bonesbury. We're doing something a little different today." He produced a small box and a game board patterned with black and white squares.

"You want to play checkers?"

"I'm actually not familiar with that particular game," he laughed. "Today, I thought I could teach you the game of chess."

"Oh," I groaned, not bothering to hide my disappointment. "I've heard of that one. Isn't it like checkers but with far too many rules?"

"I assure you, they're quite different. Observe these game pieces, I asked Glyph to make them earlier this afternoon."

"He did this in one afternoon?!" I cried in astonishment upon seeing the most exquisitely carved tokens I had ever laid my lack of eyes on. Each ebony piece had an ivory twin. I would learn the names of the pieces later, but the rooks looked like Hayra and Glyph; the bishops were Cassandra and Felsha, and the knights had fittingly been modeled after Calliope and Lituin. Alan was the queen, and seeing as he was the one who kept Violet Heights running, I took no issue with him being the most powerful piece. All of the pawns were Raeden, which I found endlessly hilarious.

And yours truly was the king.

"Not that I'm opposed to the task," I said. "But why the sudden change in curriculum?"

"I'm thrilled that you've taken such an advanced interest in your training," he explained through a warm if not somewhat strained smile. "But your exigency regarding your instruction has been most…incommodious."

"I"m not following."

"Your education is moving at a pace which has become…strenuous for me. As it is my purpose in life to be a great teacher, I took it upon myself to find a solution that would benefit all parties."

"And your solution was a board game?"

"Chess is no mere game," smiled Lituin. "It requires strategy, careful planning across both present and future. You don't simply play chess, you must become a chess player. It is a dance between you and your opponent, one performed with your respective wits, just as swordplay is a dance of blades. If you require extra training, this is acceptable. But as your teacher, I will decide which dance we practice. Is this amenable to you, Mister Bonesbury?"

"Oh, why not?"

While my sword training with Lituin would exhaust both my body and my mind, putting me in a sweet and emotionless coma by day's end, my chess training only frustrated the latter. But try as I might, I couldn't fill all my time with training. Days where I did not have specific plans became seemingly endless missions in my fight against monotony. At some point, pestering Jacob Ryker in his office actually became a desirable activity.

"And what's that form for?" I asked from across my accountant's desk.

"Reallocation of funds," he said sluggishly.

"I see. And this one?"

"A work order being sent overseas."

"I thought we didn't do business overseas?"

"No, I told you that most of our business was done on this continent," said Raeden, swaggering into the office with a stack of fresh paperwork. Jacob eyed the pile hungrily, evidently a masochist. "We've expanded recently. You should be happy about that, Chadwick."

"Hello, Raeden."

"Hello, Mister Lockwood," said Jacob.

"'Mister Lockwood,'" I repeated in surprise. "So formal."

"Ryker knows the pecking order," Raeden chuckled. "Now Chadwick, why are you bothering my accountant?"

"I was actually looking for you!" I declared boisterously.

"You've been here nearly four hours…" Jacob muttered under his breath.

"Raeden, when was the last time you and I spent some quality time together?"

"We were in a meeting two days ago," he said casually.

"No, I meant quality leisure time, not business."

"Uhh…"

"What's an activity two business partners can do for fun?"

"My father was head bookkeeper for an esteemed lord," Jacob interjected. "They went on several hunting trips during their association and always seemed to have a grand time."

"A hunt would be perfect! What do you say, Raeden? You and me, out in the wilderness?"

"Chadwick, you and I have never hunted before."

"You don't know I've never hunted!"

"I'm confident in my assumption."

"Fine, we'll bring a guide. I'm sure Felsha would be elated to do it."

"I won't do it," she said flatly when I asked her later that evening.

"Why not?"

"I have no interest in helping you and that arrogant capitalist traipse through the woods to desecrate nature and murder an innocent animal."

"Felsha!" I gasped. "Do you really hold such a low opinion of me?"

"Nearly."

"Wow." I just stared at her for a moment, hoping she would rescind her hurtful indictment - she didn't. "We're not looking to desecrate or murder anything."

"Hmph."

"You hunt all the time, you hypocrite."

"What I do," she began, puffing up her chest like she was trying to scare me away from her territory, "is stalk exotic and formidable beasts for the purpose of testing our respective mettle and determination, and to occasionally acquire them so they may be kept safe at Violet Heights. I pay the utmost respect to these creatures and the environments in which they reside. I do not 'hunt'. Don't diminish my craft, Chadwick."

"Fine," I moaned. "I'll take this as a lesson in choosing my words more carefully. We don't want to 'hunt,' Felsha. I suppose we…that is I, just want to do what you do, honestly. We'll follow every rule you set out for us. There'll be no killing or maiming or even unnecessary interaction with any creature without your say so. Come on, you must be feeling cooped up. Don't you want to get out, stretch your legs a little?"

After a moment's hesitation, she said "It's possible an arrangement could be made. But we will require a fourth for our expedition. Three is insufficient, especially when civilians make up more than half the party."

"I'm going to pretend like I didn't just hear you call me a 'civilian.' One of the staff can join us. Maybe Hayra could—"

"No," said Felsha with alarming speed.

"I thought you'd jump at the chance to spend time with the gardener."

"Careful, Bonesbury. But no, Hayra shouldn't be there. If I'm to be an adequate guide, it's important I remain…undistracted."

"Ah," I said, finally catching her logic. "Cassandra, then?"

"I have no strong feelings about that girl. If anything, my opal paints her as excessively herself, almost unnaturally so."

"What does that mean?"

"I don't know."

"Right. Well, do you agree to the terms?"

"My regulations will be thorough."

"I'll take that as a yes. Grand."

We set out two days later. Part of Felsha's itinerary was that we leave just after dawn, to allow adequate time for our little adventure but also making it home before nightfall, if necessary. Raeden had hoped to make the journey on horseback, but Felsha quashed the idea, sternly noting that if we encountered an actual threatening beast, our horses would, in fact, be a liability. So instead, Raeden pouted in his 'outside suit' as he called it: a dark olive ensemble topped with an ill-fitting, chocolate brown bowler hat that awkwardly pressed into his ginger hair.

Cassandra had borrowed a cloak from Felsha, a slightly smaller copy of the one my gamekeeper wore on her broad shoulders - I assumed it had once belonged to a younger Felsha, though it was still large enough to drag on the ground behind my bard's tiny frame. Both cloaks were dominated by a hue that lay somewhere between green and beige and dark brown - not by magic, just well made - to camouflage the wearer as they trekked over multiple terrains and seasons.

I, of course, was dressed in the same dashing black suit and top hat I always wore.

We stopped to make camp shortly before lunch. We would have gone an hour or two longer, I reckon, had it not been for Raeden's repeated complaints: the aches in his feet, or the humidity, or the ravenous swarms of mosquitoes feasting on his tiny Halfling body.

"This is nice," I sighed as we all sat around a small campfire Felsha made. "It's a gorgeous day. There's good company, better tea. I think this might be a perfect moment."

"And naturally, you're ruining it by opening your mouth," said Felsha.

"I still can't believe you brought tea to this…" Raeden mumbled.

"Why don't we all go around and say something interesting about our-selves?" I suggested.

"Oh gods," Raeden and Felsha said in unison.

"I'll go first. I've learned not one, but two new spells recently." I waited for a response; truly anything at all would have sufficed. But everyone just sat on their logs and exchanged awkward glances.

"Really, Chadwick? Two whole spells?" Felsha finally said sarcastically, failing to stifle a smile.

"That's so many!" continued Raeden, catching onto the bit. There was a pause; I could have shot back any number of snappy responses, but I was afraid of being too mean, or giving the comedic duo even more ammuni-tion.

"You're becoming quite the little spellcaster." Everyone turned in shock to Cassandra, who was trying in vain to hide a smirk behind her plate of rations. Her remark was like a pinprick in an already crumbling dam; not much on its own, but enough to unleash a torrent of laughter from all four of us.

"Brava, Cassandra, that was too good. I think you've earned the chance to go next."

"Oh."

"Better you than me," laughed Felsha. "I might maim the man who asked me to say 'something interesting' about myself."

"Alright, so we'll skip Felsha," I chuckled.

"Can I make a similar threat?" asked Cassandra innocently.

"No."

"My mother is dead?" The statement sounded like a question, almost like she was asking if it was an adequate contribution to the conversation. Suddenly, the forest seemed a lot quieter. "It happened when I was young."

"I'm sorry," was all I could think to say. "What about your father?"

"He's a cruel man who never wanted me. Metrion took me in when I had nowhere else to go."

"How… altruistic. What was your mother like?"

"She taught me to love music." There was something about the way Cassandra smiled when she said that, like she was in the memory and not just recalling it.

"That's wonderful. Raeden, I think it's your turn."

"I hear a weird noise…"

"Raeden," I chided. "That's hardly an interesting fact about—"

"Shush!" hissed Felsha. She was on her feet at once, curved knives poised and ready in her hands. Her back was to us, her eyes focused on the trees and, possibly, the source of Raeden's mystery sound. I held my breath (or I would have if — oh, you get the picture by this point) when all of a sudden, a massive black bear leapt out from the brush.

Drawing my sword at the sight of danger was second nature to me at this point, and this ursine monster was undoubtedly dangerous. Its fur was matted and patchy, covered in mud and bits of grass or some other kind of plant matter. Its eyes were glazed over, and its jaw hung open in a sickly kind of way.

"Nobody engage it," Felsha warned, never taking her eyes off the befouled apex predator.

"But—" I protested.

"Cassandra," commanded the Pursuer. "Do you know a song of beast-calming?"

"I…" the bard hesitated. "Yes, but—?"

"You pacify the creature, then I'll perform a spell to contain it. Once it's down, we run."

I tried to protest again, but the look in Felsha's eyes silenced my arrogance. Cassandra began to play a slow, soothing refrain that sounded a lot like a lullaby. The bear didn't seem any more calm than it had a moment ago, but it also wasn't coming at us. Meanwhile, Felsha sheathed her blades and crouched down slowly, not daring to make a sudden move. From the ground she grabbed a clump of dirt in one hand, and a couple of small sticks in the other. She spat into the dirt, and rubbed the hasty concoction on the sticks.

She threw them into the air, making a few complex hand gestures as they descended. The muddy sticks glowed with a light green aura and hung in midair just in front of her face. They began to spin in a circle, stretching and knitting themselves into a large wreath. The twined hoop shot forward, securing itself around the bear's neck like a collar. As the beast writhed in discomfort, Felsha signaled for us to get ready to run.

But then the bear charged.

Naturally, it went for Felsha. She quickly opened her palm wide to summon one of her blades, but the bear was surprisingly fast, almost too fast. She caught her weapon just as a giant paw swiped at her, huge claws outstretched and shining like polished sabres; she managed to block the attack, but the sheer force knocked her down. I ran towards the bear, managing to plant myself between it and Felsha before it could ready another blow. A few shallow slashes from my blade drove it back, only a few feet, but enough to get Felsha out of immediate danger.

"We need to finish this quickly!" I shouted to everyone and no one in particular, fearing our foe could charge again at any second. My instincts brought me into a fighting stance: feet planted, sword raised. My mind, meanwhile, was screaming for help.

"Chadwick!" Cassandra called. I forced myself to tear my sight away. I saw Raeden hiding under a pile of our travel bags, but Cassandra stood poised and ready with her violin. "Get ready to hit it with one of your spells, nothing fancy!"

"Nothing fancy, eh?" I whispered to myself as I turned back, grip tightening on my umbrella. I was tempted to simply cast Embiggen on myself and decapitate the thing, but it seemed like Cassandra had a plan. Magic Blast was about the least fancy spell I could think of, which hopefully meant it was the correct choice.

As this thought process played itself out in my mind, Cassandra began to play. But it was not so much a melody or even a tune, more like a chaotic collection of sounds as each note she produced ran awkwardly into the next. And for whatever reason, the composition invigorated me. A wave of such confidence and optimism washed over my being, I felt as if I could challenge a god and come out the victor. The bear roared, a bestial thunder that would have, a few moments earlier, made me figuratively wet myself; now, I almost pitied the creature.

"Enjoy your hibernation… in Hell!" I taunted as I aimed my umbrella square between its beady eyes.

What happened next was the most potent Magic Blast I had ever generated. The spell's core was solid, the most turgid beam of green energy I'd ever seen, with crackling lightning bolts, also green but brighter, running up and down the full length. And it had a tail! Like a shadow made of light, it trailed behind the main attack, giving my spell the appearance of a violent comet.

It hit my snarling opponent on the forehead, just off-center but still as much of a bullseye as any caster could hope for. The bear's skull shattered, and its headless corpse staggered for a moment before collapsing in a massive heap on the forest floor. It was over, I did it, and the woods were quiet again.

"Nice shot," groaned Felsha, refusing my hand as she picked herself up off the ground. No matter, I knew she was grateful. I turned my attention to my bard, her instrument still in hand.

"Cassandra, what exactly did you do to me? And, a follow-up question, are you able to do it to me for the rest of my life?"

She giggled. "Art has an effect on others. The magic of purple casters hinges on that influence. I just gave you a little boost, helped you be the best spellcaster you can be."

"Speaking of…" I said, and we all turned to Felsha. "How come your spell didn't work? Or Cassandra's, for that matter?"

She walked over and began examining the body, being careful not to touch it. I heard her sigh, a deep sigh filled with, what? Disbelief? Disappointment? "Because they were designed to target beasts, natural animals."

"Then what the hell makes this bear so unnatural?"

"Simple," she said, unaware of how much her next three words would unnerve me. "It was undead."

When we got back to Violet Heights later that night, Felsha presented Hayra with a clipping of the bear's fur. From the plant matter she found within it, Hayra was able to grow small yellow flowers called Gold Evolvus, pretty little things but a bit underwhelming for my tastes. She told us they only grew in one place in this region, a domain south of here called Highrake Mountain.

I refused to take supper. It wasn't like I would starve, but I was too perturbed to put up the pretense of being human tonight. The day's revelations made for a puzzle that only I had the displeasure of solving. An undead bear had wandered away from Highrake Mountain. Mountains had tunnels; tunnels made for good lairs and dungeons… like the kind I woke up in.

Dungeons and undead. There was a potential threat in the south, one which was far more existential, alarming, and personal for me than it would be for anyone else…

Highrake Mountain could be where my necromancer was hiding.

CHAPTER 15 – Just Have Fun With It

nd then, somehow, a full year had gone by.

To be clear, I don't mean a year from the previous chapter, nor do I mean a year from when I first took possession of Violet Heights. I realize either of those would be the common meaning behind such words, but I pride myself on being unconventional. No, it had been a year since all of my core staff had officially joined us, a pivotal moment when Violet Heights became, in my humble opinion, a home.

And with the changing of the calendar came an event which, at first, I had been dreading. But as the first annual Violet Heights Showcase poked its head over the horizon, I found myself giddy with excitement. You know, in spite of the fact that it was the anniversary of that time I got my butt kicked by my maid.

It was to be a veritable festival, one held entirely on the grounds of Violet Heights. Every nearby settlement was invited, from Humble Corners to… well, a bunch of others whose names I hadn't yet committed to memory. Mostly politicians and businessmen, yes, but families as well. Enough to make the corporate sponsors happy, while ensuring we were one of the most-liked and well-funded institutions around.

Glyph built half a dozen different rides, with my stipulation that each must hold no less than a dozen people at a time. The most popular of his creations was a gigantic spinning wheel that stood upright, with small carriages along its circumference for people to ride in. Glyph had dubbed it, quite creatively, as a 'Glyph Wheel', and happily discussed its design with local engineers and inventors, many of whom were members of the very guilds that dismissed his ideas as dangerous and/or insane just a few years earlier.

Felsha's staff oversaw a petting zoo she had set up for the day, meticulously curated so that only the most suitable animals were put within arm's length of the public. Yes, you read that right: Felsha's staff, as in actual people doing actual jobs. And the only person more surprised than me by this fact was Felsha herself. Apparently, they had just been quietly following her lead and cleaning up after all her creatures, too intimidated by their "boss" to ever actually introduce themselves or ask for guidance. This arrangement suited Felsha just fine, especially since she was determined to watch today's main event.

The Violet Heights Showcase was founded with the intent of being just that: a showcase. Six of my staff had volunteered to participate in a tournament of sorts, with only light beseechment from me. Cassandra, Calliope, Breadalbane, Glyph, Lituin, and Hayra would draw random lots to determine their opponents. The entire exhibition was focused on their unique talents, so the goal of each fight was to render it figuratively pointless for your opponent to continue, though not necessarily through physical dominance. The three winners would get some sort of covetable prize, but that little detail was a carefully-guarded secret.

We invited the gathered crowd to witness the lottery, which took place just one hour before the scheduled fights. Contestants would draw coloured marbles out of a small, sealed box; matching colours would determine fighting pairs. What I neglected to tell a single soul was that the lottery was entirely rigged. I'm of the firm belief that a small degree of mischief is inherently healthy, so I hid Emery in the box and telepathically instructed him to distribute certain marbles to specific people.

Glyph would be fighting Hayra. Technology and nature, two opposing forces I was ecstatic to see in a head-to-head battle. Calliope was set to fight Lituin. I'd be lying if I said revenge played no part in my logic, with

Calliope fighting the experienced teacher when she had so effortlessly demolished the student. But I genuinely gave them both a lot of credit; they were undoubtedly the best fighters amongst my core staff, and with such different styles it was sure to be one hell of a fight.

That left Breadalbane and Cassandra. Admittedly, I'd put the least amount of thought into these two, a bit of oversight on my part as they both possessed incredible magical abilities. Wouldn't that make for a more interesting fight, though? I'd never witnessed Alan give it his all before, at least not in direct combat, but his background coming from the Wizard's Guild surely meant he was powerful and capable. And Cassandra was full of surprises.

"Contenders have one hour to prepare!" Raeden announced, looking like he was actually having fun for once. "Make sure you come back early to get the good seats, people!"

I had planned to make smalltalk with random guests until the main event, a skill I had woefully neglected up until that day. But I had barely made a quarter-turn before a gaggle of local children nearly bowled me over, caught up in some game that required running around like maniacs but not looking where they were going. They all froze, regarding me with fear. One little boy's eyes were wider than all the others, and he began whispering to his friends, never taking his gaze off me. It took me a second to realize he must have recognized me as master of the house, and was now alerting his co-conspirators to the fact, and how much trouble they were in.

"Having fun, are we?" I bellowed, doing my best impression of a half-intact memory of my father scolding me several lifetimes ago. "Let's see if you find this fun!"

I brandished my umbrella, holding the thing so that it was hard to tell whether I intended to cast a spell or use it as a bludgeon. The children cowered, and several of my guests had stopped to watch, no doubt astonished by the thought of Chadwick Bonesbury taking time out of his day to assault the youth.

At the height of their terror I cast Trick, projecting over a dozen colourfully wrapped pieces of candy from the tip of my umbrella. The children were so dumbstruck that my sweets hit most of them square in the face. But their panic quickly subsided, and they began to laugh as they collected the dropped pieces, so I released a second wave of sugary treats. The gathered crowd began to laugh as well, a few even clapped. Suddenly feeling eyeballed and very insecure, I tipped my top hat to the nice people before taking my leave.

For anyone curious, the candy had been in my pocket; Trick merely summoned it out into the open. And you might be asking yourself, 'why did Chadwick, both a grown man and also a Skeleton with no taste buds or stomach, have candy in his pocket?' First off let me say, don't you judge me! Plenty of people love candy! But my exact reasoning? I suppose it was a combination of nostalgia, another half-intact memory of pilfering sweets from my mother's pantry, and a sense of practicality: offering someone a candy was as good an icebreaker as any.

…social situations are daunting, okay?

Before I knew it, the hour had passed and it was time for the main event. The spectators gathered around the fighting ring, a thirty foot circle placed between the house and the edge of the forest. A raised platform had been constructed on one side of the arena for the judges: Felsha, Raeden, and Jacob. Glyph and Hayra were the first to fight; Gnome and Halfling stood equidistant from the circle's center, bodies facing each other but faces turned towards me, waiting for my signal. As I pointed my umbrella skyward, the crowd leaned in with anticipation. I fired off Magic Blast, a green bolt went screaming into the clouds above and the crowd cheered with gusto; the fight had begun.

It was Glyph who made the first move. He threw a metal cube, about the size of his fist, towards the middle of the circle. It hit the ground and dug itself in, spreading itself wide with quick and sudden jerks all over my manicured lawn. It took less than a minute for the entire battlefield to be covered in metal sheeting, and both parties found themselves struggling for balance on the new floor.

"Ha, I've got you!" laughed Glyph. "How are you going to grow your precious plants now?" From his hip he drew a pistol that looked like it was made from scrap metal. It had a long tube that extended from the base of the barrel, over Glyph's shoulder, and into a huge canister which he wore on his back. He aimed at Hayra and pulled the trigger; from my position at the base of the judges' platform, I could hear several loud fans churning inside the canister, and I felt the air change — did the barometer just drop? No, Glyph's weapon was sucking in air, apparently great gusts of it, which it then fired from its barrel with a deafening "BOOM!"

Two shots was all it took to knock Hayra on her behind. Felsha stood up abruptly, and I feared she might jump into the ring if her beloved was harmed. Hayra began to get up, but another blast of air sent her back down. I stole a glance at Felsha, who was glaring daggers at the Gnome; to her credit, she remained on the platform. Suddenly, Hayra began to cry, great heaving sobs that everyone present was sure to hear. Glyph took visible pity on her, I could even see the regret in his eyes as he lowered his weapon. And that's when the tears stopped.

Hayra was on her feet immediately. I was used to her movements as a gardener, which tended to be slow and methodical; imagine my surprise when she began to run at top speeds towards Glyph! As she ran, she reached into her coat pocket and produced a small brown bag with a sprout growing out of it. She held the bag to her right forearm, and the sprout had a sudden growth spurt, sending out great twinning vines that latched around her bicep. In the other direction it grew a single long branch, one which darkened to a deep olive green with thick, burgundy thorns, as it extended past her worn palms and peat-filled fingernails. It grew quickly, until it was twice the length of her body, but it did nothing to impede her pace, nor did it dampen the fiery resolve in her eyes.

Glyph, eyes wide, somehow managed to fire off two more blasts of air, but they were easily sidestepped by the bolting Halfling. She took a running leap, easily closing the gap between them, and swung the branch like a sword towards the weapon. The hit landed with such force that it launched the gun a good four feet into the air, severing the tube with impressive damage. The Gnome spun around, partly from the impact and partly due to fear that his body may be next. Hayra saw her opening and took it, thrusting her plant sword directly into the canister on Glyph's back.

A hideous sound rang out, a popping noise overtop of an explosion, as the compressed air was suddenly and violently freed from its container. The crowd gasped, as Glyph and Hayra were thrown in opposite directions and knocked out. After a minute of waiting, during which time Felsha made some less-than gentle demands that she be allowed into the ring, Hayra let out a groan and struggled to her feet, followed soon after by Glyph. The judges named Hayra the winner due to her impressive adaptation and by virtue of being the first one to get back up. The crowd cheered, shaking the ground with the passion of their volume.

The uproar only continued as Lituin and Calliope stepped into the ring. Lituin's students cheered for their master, but the housekeeper's staff were equally supportive. The two opponents stared each other down. Calliope opened her mouth to speak, but before a quip or a taunt could leave her lips, Lituin made two decisive and brutal slashes in the air with his sword. At first it seemed like a nonverbal taunt of his own, a demonstration of my swordmaster's skills with the blade; they were still several feet apart, after all. But the wind changed again, this time as if it was struggling to dodge out of the way of that blade. The crowd suddenly shut up and held its breath. Calliope put a hand to both her cheeks, and when it came back bright red, she understood what Lituin had done.

"You cut my cheeks!" she shouted indignantly.

"The wind cut your cheeks, Miss Baines," said Lituin, faux innocence anointing every word. "I merely influenced it into action."

"I'll influence you into submission!" The Dwarf touched her cheeks again, making both hands sufficiently bloody. Neither party, nor the crowd, seemed to have noticed that I had yet to signal the start of the fight. That was just as well, as I was having nightmarish recollections of my own pummeling by my housekeeper. And just as before, both her hands turned to malleable iron, and she screamed that gut-wrenching scream as she charged towards Lituin.

Their collision reminded me of a bird accosting a birdfeeder: Lituin bobbing back and forth like the feeder in the tree while Calliope came at him from as many angles as she could manage. But Calliope had no beak, just two metallic fists which clanged furiously against the Elf's sword. Lituin hardly ever moved his feet, defending his position effortlessly while Calliope continued to throw her fists like two sledgehammers, even leaping into the air a few times as she tried to strike her opponent in her face. As I watched the two powerhouses uppercut and parry each other, it suddenly struck me how equally matched they were. Their fight felt more like an intricate dance than actual combat.

For every ten strikes from Calliope, Lituin made just one. His moves were clearly methodical, never daring to expend more energy than necessary. When he suddenly began a quick series of attacks, the crowd gasped. Calliope's iron skin, which extended several inches past her wrists and up her forearm, was more than sufficient for blocking, but the shift to defensive strategies had clearly rattled her. Using the flat of his sword, Lituin swept Calliope's legs out from under her and knocked her onto her back. His face tight and his eyes bulging slightly, the Elf stood above her and brought his sword down vertically, looking as if he meant to skewer the Dwarf.

Calliope caught the tip of his blade in her left palm, and using her right hand she chopped at the sword; at least six inches of high quality steel broke free in her iron grip. Lituin's balance was thrown off, but Calliope was still on her back. In one smooth motion she brought her knees to her chest and raised her hands up beside her head. Then, with lightning speed, she pulled her legs in tight, rolled onto her shoulders, pushed off with her hands and kicked Lituin square in the chest with both feet. She rolled far to the left and hopped back upright. Still holding the tip of Lituin's sword, she roared again and aimed for her opponent's neck. But Lituin recovered faster than she had anticipated, and he held his broken sword at the perfect angle so that, if Calliope continued with her attack, she would drive her throat into the jagged edge of his weapon. She saw his move and stopped her attack just in time, the tip of the blade just an inch from Lituin's throat.

"Bravo!" I shouted from the perimeter of the arena. "Good show, a good show indeed! I'll leave the final decision to our illustrious judges, but I'd like to propose that both these fighters are winners today. How do we feel about that, ladies and gentlemen?" The crowd cheered, and one by one Felsha, Raeden, and Jacob each gave a thumbs up.

I didn't envy Breadalbane and Cassandra having to follow such a display, but I was nevertheless curious to see what they would do. I sounded off another Magic Blast to start their duel, and Cassandra began playing almost immediately. Little points of light appeared all around her, both in the air and on her person. Some were like clouds of light, while others were more distinct and angular sigils. I had never given much thought to what it would look like if Cassandra went 'all-out,' but I imagined it was something like this, and my excitement grew exponentially.

And then my nephew dashed my dreams and hers.

He spun his hand in a circle in a familiar fashion, causing his pearl ring to grow a familiar shade of baby blue. Cassandra was suddenly enshrouded in a bubble of the same colour, and all notes from her violin were immediately stifled.

"Zone of Silence," I muttered to myself. "Alan, you magnificent bastard."

Cassandra caught on to what was happening right away. She cried out some kind of protest, but no one could hear her. Naturally, she tried to move out of the bubble, but Breadalbane extended his arm towards her while snapping his fingers, and a wave of force knocked her back. She made three more attempts, and each one was met with the same result.

There was a moment where neither combatant did anything. Then my butler started rubbing his hands together. Visible static could be seen building up between them, which quickly grew and spread around his body. Storm clouds covered his eyes, and he raised a hand above his head. Lightning arced up his arm and crackled loudly.

Out of viable options, Cassandra put down her violin and held up her hands in surrender. A smile crept across Breadalbane's face before he dismissed both his electricity and the bubble with a final flick of his wrist, and the crowd cheered for their fourth and final winner.

"Wasn't that a fantastic show, folks?" I called to the crowd once Breadalbane, Calliope, Hayra, and Lituin were assembled before me. The gathered masses whooped and hollered for them, which did my heart good. "But they still have to claim their prize, something to ensure both your enjoyment and theirs!" All four of them looked around uncomfortably, not sure if they should be expecting a trophy or a kick in the pants.

"Haven't you figured it out yet, ladies and gentleman?" I really amped up my showmanship for this moment, a trait which I was sure people found endearing, though Raeden called it 'obnoxious.' "The winners will get an opportunity to take on yours truly!"

What would make this fight different from the others, besides the sheer absurdity of it, was that my staff would have only minutes to heal up and prepare their gear, virtually no time at all. I wanted them on their toes, ready for anything. Surely most people here knew I was a capable fighter; my elimination of the Splitter last year was proof enough of that. But I played the role of the fool so earnestly, and I'd imagine many still doubted my proficiency in combat. Not to mention the fact that I was usually seen using my trademark umbrella like a cane, giving me a moderately incapacitated sort of air. That's what made this so fun.

My four opponents stood before me. The crowd murmured in speculation and intrigue. Since I was no longer officiating, Raeden rang a bell to signal the start of the fight, but no one made a move.

"Come on, you lot!" I taunted. "We are losing daylight!"

Lituin looked to the others. "Would anyone mind if I made the first move against our employer?"

"Fine by me," said Alan.

"Go right ahead, dear," chirped Hayra. Calliope just nodded with a smirk.

The swordsman came at me as I anticipated he would, an unconventional jog meant to confuse the opponent. His first attack was made with less than a third of the strength or ferocity I knew he was capable of; a thinly-veiled insult, to be sure. The cheer from the stands when I parried it didn't make it sound that way, though. To them, I may as well have deflected the swing of a Dragon's tail. Our swords locked twice after a series of blows, and though Lituin's face was calm, his eyes were alive with a firestorm.

I broke the second lock and struck my teacher in the face with the hilt of my blade, prompting the crowd to wince in unison. The move bought me a few precious seconds, so I created some distance between us and waited for Lituin to come at me again. As soon as he moved to attack me, I raised my umbrella and cast Magic Blast. The beam struck him in the shoulder, and he spun a full rotation on his heel before he fell to the ground. The crowd gasped, then went silent.

I knew he felt that attack. It was imperative in our training that I kept my spellcraft out of it, lest it become a crutch. But it was only logical that as my skill in both grew, I would learn to weave them together effectively. Lituin was ready for anything I could throw at him as a swordsman, but I am so much more than a swordsman. When going up against four adept opponents, giving it anything less than your best is tantamount to suicide.

"Try that on me, I dare you!" screamed Calliope as she ran towards me, her still-iron fists out and ready. I swung my sword at her, just enough to keep her from getting too close. But she was fast, ducking and dodging my blade all the while inching closer to me. She delivered several intense blows to my midsection, and I was overcome with astounding gratitude for my lack of a stomach. I could sense she was building up to something, so I intentionally left an opening between her and my head. When she flew upwards like a compressed spring, I made my move.

"Sho!" I barked. A powerful blow connected with the side of my skull, but I felt nothing. My fingers crossed, I uttered "ohs" before uncrossing them. Red sparkles appeared on the side of Calliope's face, the calling card of Ruby's Rapturous Reversal, before a sudden invisible force knocked her down, head first.

With two down, I turned to the others, but the act of moving my body had become arduous and strained. It felt as if I were moving through jelly, and I soon saw why. Breadalbane was flailing his hands and wiggling his digits in some overtly arcane fashion. Whatever magical snare he was conjuring was meant to slow me down, and it had succeeded. He had evidently been conspiring with Hayra, because I could see her summoning a wave of vines just as I'd seen her do on at least one previous occasion. There was no hope in dodging; within seconds I was caught in them.

It took most of my already limited strength (in my defense, I literally don't have any muscles) to wrestle an arm free, and I began hacking wildly at my restraints. The slowing effect still plagued me, but if he used it as a forerunner to Hayra's vines, I figured that I wouldn't stay slowed for very long. As if on cue, my bones started to move more freely, but not before I saw Lituin and Calliope pull themselves together, poised to attack once more.

"I guess it's now or never," I whispered to myself.

Mostly free of vines, I crouched down and shot up into the air with as much force as I could from my static position. When I reached as high as I would get, I opened my umbrella and shouted "Fala!" My spell took effect, and I was carried by a magical updraft about twenty feet into the air.

More gasps from the crowd. Even my opponents were stunned, which made sense; no one but Jon had seen me perform my new spell, which he said was called 'Minor Levitation'. I couldn't stay up here for long, but I had more than enough time to win. My hat tipped open and Emery emerged in his blackbird form. Along with a dozen shadow copies, he descended in frantic flight patterns to beset my challengers.

"Sorry, boss!" Breadalbane called up to me before hurling a fireball at my head. It would have landed and set my bones ablaze were it not for the second spell I'd recently learned. Jon had presented me with a small list of spells with brief descriptions, saying he would only teach me two and the rest would be lost to me forever.

"Can't I learn the rest eventually?" I had asked.

"Sometimes tough choices are necessary," he had said in his difficult way. "You'll appreciate your chosen spells more if they were obtained through some semblance of sacrifice."

Before my nephew's spell hit, I cast Telekinesis on my own body and flew out of the way. I don't think I need to convey to you, dear reader, that I would have picked Telekinesis in a heartbeat (if I had one), being that it was something I'd wanted ever since learning Lesser Telekinesis over a year ago. But when I learned the specifics of Minor Levitation, I realized I could use the two in conjunction with one another to create a unique ability: flight. It wasn't true magical flight - only mages far more powerful than myself could accomplish such a feat, or so I was told - so the way I moved through the air was awkward and bumbling, never quite straight or steady. But I did a sweep over the crowd for dramatic effect, and while everyone was busy looking at me, I set my final gambit into motion.

The real Emery, hidden amongst his shadow copies, clutched a knockout potion in his talons. After sneaking up behind Alan, he returned to the form of an Imp, uncorked the bottle, and threw its contents right in the butler's face. With the only real threat to me (at least while I was airborne) now taken care of, it was time to finish it.

Using both these spells to fly expended much of my energy, but I risked firing off two final Magic Blasts; one hit between Hayra's feet and knocked her down, and the other disarmed a surprised Lituin of his sword. One more spell could have very well sent me plummeting to the ground, but my opponents didn't know that, so I tried to look as intimidating as one could while brandishing an umbrella.

"Do you yield?" I called from above. Lituin smirked and looked to Calliope, who rolled her eyes before they both put their hands up. At that, the stands roared to life in applause. When I finally made my descent, I took a bow before helping Hayra to her feet.

The first annual Violet Heights Showcase proved to be a huge success. After taking a short sabbatical to recover my stamina and magical faculties, I spent the remainder of the afternoon being chased around by the local children as I flew through the air and magically distributed more candy, their suppers be damned.

Later in the evening, as people began to take their leave, I overheard conversations in which the children referred to me as 'Rich Uncle Chadwick' despite their parents' protests. After hearing that…it's hard to say what it did to me, exactly. All I know is that all of my losses and failings of the past year seemed to wash away, just a little bit, and life didn't seem so bad.

Never underestimate the power of a good time.

CHAPTER 16 – Seek New Enterprises

I first became aware that something was amiss on the morning Cassandra joined me for tea.

"How is your training coming along?" I asked her.

"Brutally," she groaned while massaging her shoulder. "They both have such different teaching styles. Lituin is endlessly patient. He never loses his temper, and he's always encouraging me to do better, but the lessons are so intense. Calliope, on the other hand, is like a drill instructor. I've never been called a 'clod' so often in my life. Sometimes I feel like Metrion treated me better."

"Let's not entertain that notion."

"I feel like I'm ready to drop at any moment."

"You know you don't need to do all this training." I tried not to worry about her so much, but her hand was literally shaking as she lifted her teacup.

"I do, though. It's been weeks now since that tournament, but I just can't get it out of my head. There was so much I could have done, but Alan rendered it all meaningless. My intention is still to be the best purple caster I can be, but that can't be all I am."

"I admire your passion," I told her truthfully. "Just don't destroy yourself in the pursuit of greatness."

"Can you honestly say you'd take your own advice?"

"Really going for the jugular, aren't you? They're teaching you well."

I was grateful to hear her laugh at that. Before I could join her in earnest, my attention was drawn to the gaggle of staff running by the parlour door. Even more concerning was the fact that most of them were security personnel.

"What's going on?" I demanded as I rose from my chair and bolted out of the room.

"There's been an incident, sir," said a young Elf. "Upstairs. We've been called to assist."

Cassandra and I were already on the move. There was a fracas going on all around the second floor landing. I pushed past the assembly and saw that a Gnome, whom I knew to be called Bert, was being wrestled by three other staff. He was thrashing wildly, and I could tell from the way his body moved that he was not well.

"What's wrong, man?" I called.

"Chadwick." Bert's head jerked in my direction like an invisible hand had grabbed him by his chin. What unnerved me most were his eyes; they were whiter than snow. "Just the man I wanted to see."

"Coglio?" The distortion in his voice was unmistakable. There hadn't been any paranormal activity in months, long enough to make people nearly forget the terrifying hold he had on Violet Heights. "What the hell are you doing?"

"Hell is exactly what I'm doing, Bonesbury. Unleashing it, in your life. I've been possessing Bert for two days, and I've set plans into motion which will completely shift the balance of power in your world!"

"You're…you're lying! Someone would have noticed."

"I don't think he's lying, boss." It was Alan, who had been watching from the periphery. "He was acting strange, sure, and missing a lot of his duties, but I assumed he was sick and didn't want to tell anybody, or maybe off canoodling with someone. Whatever…this is, it wouldn't have been my first guess."

"What did you do, Coglio?"

"Oh, just threw a highly flammable log on the fire of war!"

"Gods, these riddles!" I wailed. "I would strangle you if you weren't so impotent as to not have your own neck."

"I've got him," said Cassandra, stepping forward and taking off her protection bracelet. Silently I admired her valour; when she first got it, I don't think Cassandra would have taken it off for anyone, but here she was risking her own safety to help someone she barely knew. Everything I knew about magic, which wasn't a lot but more than people typically assumed, told me that putting the bracelet on Bert's arm would expunge any unwanted passengers from his body.

"Wait!" Coglio screamed. The word was stretched out and reverberated horribly around the house. "I can tell you everything, Chadwick. Believe it or not, my machinations would be better served if you were not ignorant to them. Hear me out, and I promise to leave Bert willingly and without damage or struggle."

"…someone grab a rope." Damn my curious nature.

We restrained Coglio in one of the unused bedrooms. He requested a piece of parchment and a quill, as well as a free hand to write with; he argued that if he were to try anything, there were enough mages and warriors around to stop him. We gave him what he asked for, begrudgingly, and he began his tale of deceit and mischief.

He sketched some sort of map while he spoke. Coglio explained that he had sent a letter to the D'Graszia family the previous morning, one which contained an identical copy of the map and instructions on how to use it. It would be too far out by this point to be easily retrieved, but not so far out as to give Metrion and his brood an unfair head start.

"What's so special about this map?"

"Treasure, Bonesbury. Treasure to rival whatever wealth you've accumulated, and by a great deal. I discovered it in my exploration of this land, but I lacked the resources to take it, resources you and the D'Graszias both possess."

"Why should anyone believe you?"

"Don't want to get richer, Chadwick? That hardly sounds like you."

"I already have plenty of money. I'm not so greedy that I'd fall into an obvious trap just to get more." That was a half-truth; I did like the idea of getting richer, and a genuine treasure map sounded nice.

"Doubt me if you like, but Metrion has the same map you have. Even if you don't believe the treasure is there, or even if you do but somehow delude yourself into thinking your soul isn't wild with avarice, can you really risk letting the D'Graszias have it? They would overtake you completely. The gap in power between you would make for a fall you could never survive."

"Why are you doing this?"

"Because you know I'm right. This conflict between you will submit to the drums of war. The enemy of my enemy is not my friend but my enemy, Chadwick Bonesbury, and it would entertain me greatly to see my two foes continue to tear each other down with newfound brutality."

After that, Coglio did as he promised and made his egress from Bert, who reacted as one might after being jolted from a listless sleep. In my private study, I waited for Alan and Felsha to go over the map individually and make their assessments. Raeden and Cassandra were there as well, round-

ing out the four to make a sort of inner council. They were wise, knowl-
edgeable, and strong of spirit, and I trusted them to treat me and my ideas
fairly.

"The end of the map is definitely Highrake Mountain," Alan determined.

"The wizard is correct," added Felsha.

And that's what cinched it for me. Coglio was a devious mastermind, but
not even he realized what fantastic bait this was. After our encounter with
the undead bear some time ago, I'd authorized Alan to employ investiga-
tors and inquisitors to gather as much information as they could about
Highrake Mountain.

There wasn't much in the way of written history on the area, but many
of the locals did report issues with undead over the years. Now knowing
there was supposedly a large treasure within as well, the similarities between this place and the dungeon I woke up in were impossible to ignore.
Was there a chance my necromancer had taken Highrake Mountain for
their base of operations? Could the answers behind my existence really be
this close?

I, of course, shared none of this with the group. Alan and Cassandra still
didn't know I was a Skeleton, and I was afraid how the others would react
if they knew this endeavour was as existential as it was desperate. Raeden
was no help; I think the issue actually broke him. He was terrified of going to war with the D'Graszias, but generally agreed with Coglio that they
would crush us if their financial power were to increase by such a ridiculous amount. It was clear that whatever I did going forward in this, it
would be without his input.

We made plans to set out with the remainder of the group; Lituin would
take Raeden's place. When the sun rose the next morning, though, there
was another holdout I probably should have anticipated, but didn't.

"What do you mean you're not going?"

"I'm sorry," said Cassandra woefully. "I just can't."

"But why? Is it… oh, it's Metrion, isn't it?"

"Yes. I can't enter into a conflict like this, not with him."

"But you're so much stronger now, and you'll have us there with you. He can't hurt you anymore, so there's no need to be afraid of—"

"I'm not afraid!" She looked as if she regretted the outburst immediately and quickly composed herself. "I mean, of course I am, a little, how could I not be? But there's more to it than that."

"Explain it to me?"

"Is it so peculiar to have complicated feelings about where you come from, even if it was no good for you?"

"A mighty tree doesn't have complicated feelings about the dirt, Cassandra."

"I don't think that's true. But it isn't like they're all as bad as Metrion. A couple had a kind word or two to spare when I was a victim of his acrimony."

"'A kind word or two?!'" I spat. "Is that all it takes to cool your resolve?"

"My resolve isn't cooled, Chadwick. I'm simply choosing to divert it elsewhere."

"I—" It had been a long couple of days, and my temper was short. I wanted to shout at Cassandra. After all I had done for her, could she not support me in this, especially when my aim was to deliver retribution unto her very tormentor? But the look on her face, lip quivering but eyes steely and resolute, halted my anger. She had presented me with a line she would not cross; yes, I could drag her over to my side, but in doing so I would lose her forever, and that was a risk I could not take.

"You can hold down the fort here," I said at last. "I'll talk to Calliope about taking your place."

"I've been ready to go for ten minutes now," the maid suddenly shouted from down the hall.

"Calliope! I'm surprised you're so eager."

"Can I speak freely, boss?"

"Don't you always?"

"I'm eager to kick some ass."

So that was that. I set out with Felsha, Alan, Lituin, and Calliope, each of us getting a horse this time. We must have looked like an odd bunch, all different races and fashion choices, riding five thoroughbreds and bounding across the landscape with the sunrise behind us. Is this what it felt like to be an adventurer? If it weren't for the high chance of war with my arch nemesis, I could get used to this…

After a few hours of riding, Highrake Mountain was within view. The map's directions were pretty straightforward, pointing us to the base of the mountain. We went another twenty minutes before Felsha's head shot up, suddenly alert to something the rest of us could not sense.

"Hold!" she cried, and one by one we each stopped our horses in our own awkward ways. It was silent, and I looked around for whatever Felsha had seen. Suddenly, an arrow shot out of the trees that flanked our right. It sailed closest to Calliope, who easily snatched it out of the air and broke it before tossing the pieces to the ground.

Our attackers revealed themselves, nearly a dozen of them. Men on horseback who wore dull-coloured suits with wide-brimmed hats, thick leather gloves, and capes. I recognized their family attire immediately. They moved quickly, surrounding us in a well-practiced circle formation. It was only after we were completely enclosed that I saw him, wearing a wicked smile and the biggest, dumbest hat of the whole lot. Entering the circle on a golden mare was Metrion D'Graszia.

"Hello, Chadwick."

CHAPTER 17 – Remain Confident Under Pressure

"Metrion," I seethed. "Out for a stroll? Or just airing out your clown costumes?" I looked to the quartet around me, but they were too preoccupied to give me props for my scathing remark.

"Cut the bullshit, Bonesbury," said the head of the D'Graszia clan. "You were clearly sent on a fool's errand by the ghost of that wretched Gnome whose house you stole from me."

"You're on the errand too, fool." I took pride in seeing his eyes narrow at that; more than enough props. "There must be something to it after all."

"Oh, you're not a fool for believing the treasure exists, Chadwick. No, you're a fool for thinking you'll get to it before me."

"Use your head, Metrion." I got down off my horse and took a few steps towards the tasteless Elf. "Why would Coglio send us both to some horrid mountain in the middle of nowhere? It's probably some trap meant to destroy the two of us."

"Let me be clear," announced my most-hated foe. "We give you but one opportunity to turn back, one warning. That was it."

"And if we refuse?" I asked. In response, the D'Graszia family began brandishing swords and bows and wisps of magical energy.

"If you refuse?" repeated Metrion. He reached behind his back and produced a staff the colour of maple, and with an arrogant twirl of his stupid cape he drove it into the ground. Yellow light flowed out of the big stick and formed a fence around us that reached nearly seven feet high, trapping us inside with the D'Graszia clan. "If you refuse, we can't be held responsible for what happens to you."

"What do we think, friends?" I asked in a hushed tone.

"Though we are outnumbered," said Lituin. "I estimate our two groups are fairly evenly matched. Many of their warriors look inexperienced and nervous. And with you, Mister Bonesbury, as well as Alan Miller, we might just have a varied-enough skill set to compensate. I would suggest we—"

"Attack!" shouted Calliope at the top of her lungs. She jumped off her horse and shot forward, her fist clenched and leading the charge.

"...yes, that was the stratagem I was going to suggest."

Lituin and Felsha rode forward and began slashing, while Alan hung back and conjured shields around each of us while lobbing the occasional fireball. Calliope was leaping from D'Graszia to D'Graszia, content to simply punch some in the face, but with others she held her place on their shoulders and assaulted them repeatedly until they shook her off or, more often than not, fell down. I wanted to chastise her for such random fury, but I quickly realized it was anything but random. Her targets were exclusively the spellcasters, and thus less likely to have melee weapons to fend off her close-contact fighting style, not to mention the fact that they likely couldn't take a punch as well as the soldiers.

"Quit gawking, you skinny idiot! Metrion's getting away!" Felsha's cruel words snapped me to attention. I scanned the chaos and found she was right; Metrion's golden horse had touched its nose to the fence; the light began to ripple and weaken, just enough so that rider and mount could pass through, along with two other comrades.

"I can't go after him," I cried while Felsha fended off two attackers at once.

"For the love of — you're the only one of us who can fly!"

"Oh," I muttered. Truthfully, dear readers, the idea hadn't occurred to me, and I don't much care to dwell on it any further. After parrying an attack from one of Metrion's sons, I shouted "Fala!" and rose into the air, flying forward with all the grace of a rag caught in a cyclone.

It was a straight shot to the base of the mountain, and if I were a better pilot I could have beaten Metrion there easily, but my lack of skill meant I had to dive to avoid being walloped by the tree canopy. I was about a hundred feet behind my foes; the treeline became denser as we grew closer to our target, leaving a path just wide enough for two horses to run side by side. I was able to stay ten feet in the air, but most of my magical stamina was spent keeping me airborne, so my spellcasting options were limited. I cast Magic Blast towards the base of a grizzled old oak, knocking it right into the path of the horses. The two subordinates were cut off — one horse was spooked into retreating while the other collided with the tree and fell on its side. Metrion, meanwhile, sidestepped it completely and kept on his course.

There was no hesitation with my next move, though looking back perhaps there should have been. I fired off two more shots, both directly at Metrion. One missed him completely and disappeared into the woods, sending a flock of birds into the sky. The second shot failed to find its intended mark, but instead struck the horse in its flank. It pained me to know I had caused harm to such a majestic creature, but when I saw its rider fly over the reins, the grief became tolerable. Metrion's body hit the road hard and rolled several feet; he was just rising to his elbows as I flew by and our eyes locked. A spark of mutual hatred flashed between us before I left him behind in a cloud of dust.

I continued to flail erratically through the air until, finally, I reached the end of the path at the foot of the mountain. My feet landed clumsily on solid ground - if you've ever seen a dog try to stop itself mid-sprint then you get the idea. A calm wind was the only sound that accompanied the sight of staggering peaks, but what surprised me the most was how green Highrake Mountain was. My perception of mountains that I had acquired from books was that they were cold, unfeeling juts of rock which pierced through serene and remote landscapes. But here was this place, teeming with life, and it was beautiful.

I pulled the copy of Coglio's map from my inner jacket pocket, silently grateful that I had elected myself its bearer before we set off from the estate. I allowed myself a brief pause to wonder about the fate of my staff, my companions, before I turned my focus back to the task at hand. The map alluded to a cave on the mountain's western slope, 'slightly bigger than the other caves, and shaped like the maw of a great beast,' according to the bard's note. Luckily, I was already on the correct slope and so took my chances with a cave that seemed to fit the description. All the map said to do next was 'find the path with no wind.' I could only assume that this meant Highrake was home to a labyrinth of caves, most of which would eventually just lead me back outside if I failed in making my ingress. Hesitation held me back, but the knowledge that I had very limited time pushed me forward.

Upon entering, I was immediately reminded of the dungeon I had woken up in. At first it was only because of the all-encompassing darkness, which was no issue for me as my vision took on a familiar monochrome filter; I imagine the adjustment would have been harder if I actually had eyeballs. You would think that being able to see within shadows would remove the frustration of stumbling around in the dark, but really it just led to more stumbling and more muttered profanities. To try and reduce the injury to my remaining toe bones, I sent Emery off ahead to explore potential routes.

There was a greater familiarity, though, a sense that I was not alone. I made my way down pathways and corridors, trying my best to feel the wind, or rather the lack thereof, but all the while I felt that someone, or something, was down there with me. After turning down a promising new path, my suspicions were confirmed: another Skeleton. Its back was to me, but it too must have sensed my presence because it quickly turned my way, facing the intruder in its domain. Its face was veiled in thick cobwebs, and whatever clothes it had worn in life were now mere rags hanging off its ribcage.

"Well, aren't you a sight for sore eye sockets?" I greeted. When it gave no visible reaction, I added, "what, aren't puns and jokes the native tongue of our kind? Or does lacking a tongue impede us from having a native one?"

The other Skeleton responded by attacking me. Oh well, some people just don't get comedy. It didn't seem particularly strong, as I was able to draw my sword and slice through its sternum with little difficulty. The bones collapsed but were still twitching after they hit the ground, so I sliced at its skull until it stopped.

As I left my latest critic behind and continued on my journey, I quickly discovered that, just like my old dungeon, there were other obstacles. Paths that led me to either dead ends or circled back to where I started from. Pitfalls that dropped the floor from under me; those made me grateful for my quick reflexes. I was becoming more convinced that this lair was exactly like the one I came from, but at least this time I could predict and prepare for whatever magical defenses had been put in place. And of course, more undead. I was attacked, repeatedly; it felt like every five minutes but was probably closer to every twenty. At one point I was completely beset by a horde of Skeletons and Zombies, practically drowning in a sea of reanimated flesh and bone. It was only then, as I slashed at rotten flesh and bones, that it dawned on me: I was afraid… truly afraid for my life.

"Enough of this!" I exclaimed from under a mountain of undead foes. It took some wriggling, but I managed to gain a modicum of room around me, just enough for me to cast Embiggen on myself. I grew several feet, slicing and hacking my enemies to pieces before the spell could finish, taking advantage of my increasing size before I ran out of room. The walking corpses crumbled at my blade, but my frustration didn't fall away with them.

"You could have prevented this!" I screamed at them. "All you had to do was answer me when I talked to you. Are really none of you like me? Not a single one?! Just mindless monsters, the lot of you? Am I so horribly unique in this world? Answer me!"

"Boss?"

My heart would have skipped a beat if I had one. Was that a genuine response, recognition among Skeletons? Then I saw that it was merely my Imp, returned from the survey I had sent him on almost forty minutes ago.

"Emery! What have I told you about interrupting me when I'm in the middle of a crisis?"

"Not to do it. But given how much of a mess you are as a person, we'd never talk at all if I followed that rule."

"Would that really be so horrible?"

"Do you want to see what I found or not?"

 My body halted, sword still in mid-swing; apparently, I had been mindlessly hacking at air for several minutes at least, with not a single undead enemy left standing. But there was no time for me to stroke my own ego, as I quickly followed my arcane companion down a dizzying series of lefts and rights. With every turn I tried to feel for wind, but everything feels a bit like wind when you have no skin. Finally, our path ended in a wide hallway with a massive boulder on the far wall.

"This is another dead end, you stupid Imp."

"People in dumb houses shouldn't throw stones, Chadwick."

"What the hell are you talking about?"

"I'm saying this ain't no dead end, bonehead!"

"Watch it."

"Would you just look at the stupid rock?"

I did as he asked and inspected the stupid rock. Something about it was off, I could feel it, but trying to place it was maddening. It took longer than I would like to admit, but I finally realized what was so strange: faint light was coming from behind the stone.

"Have you been back there yet?" I asked.

"No," said Emery. "Not enough space for me to squeeze through."

"Why didn't you just shapeshift into one of your smaller forms?"

"None of your business!"

"You forgot you could do that, didn't you?"

"Just blast the rock already."

"Gladly."

I took a step back and composed myself, rolling my shoulders back and locking my jaw into a stern grimace. With my stance set, I stabbed my umbrella forward and cast Telekinesis. Despite the spell's utility, I had only ever used it in conjunction with Minor Levitation in order to fly, so I had not yet developed a sense for its limitations. The boulder was very large, I'd wager about the size of a teenage elephant. I would have never been able to move it without magic, even if I had unlimited stamina and a week to attempt it. So as an assurance, I cast the spell with the maximum amount of force in mind. I was going for 'sufficient' but what I got was 'cataclysmic' — the boulder was immediately launched from its sitting position at a speed that would make bullets blush.

Emery and I were immediately blinded by searing light. It seemed like an eternity of blinking and cowering behind raised hands before our eyes could focus, but when they did we saw a massive cavern, imperfect and spherical, nearly a hundred feet high. But what was truly impressive was not its size, but its contents. Piles of gold and jewels carpeted the floor and rose nearly halfway up the walls, littered with what could only be described as countless magic items and weapons.

"I don't believe it," I whispered.

"And what don't you believe, little intruder?" The voice was pulverizing, filling up the entire room and bouncing off every wall a thousand times. Instinctively my hands shot up to cover my ears, but it was a twice futile gesture; even if I'd had ears, the sound would have vibrated through my bones just the same.

"Hello?" I called once my skull stopped shaking. "Is someone there?"

"Such a tiny voice the intruder speaks with!" This time I was nearly driven to my knees by the reverberation. "Speak up, tiny thing. My ears are older than the wind and too good for your words, but I will humour you for now!"

"I was given a map to this place!" I shouted. "The one who produced said map sought to lure me here with the promise of treasure, but I—"

"There is none of my treasure which is promised!"

"Yes, I understand, sir! But you see, I am under the impression that you and I have more pressing business."

"Business?" Finally, a word uttered by the voice that didn't try to shatter me. "What business could an insignificant speck like you have with me?"

"I'd like to reveal that to you, sir. Perhaps if I could see you, we could discuss the matter at length?"

"I don't care to reveal myself to you. Begone from my mountain."

"But…" I stammered. "I've come all this way."

"Then you surely know the way back."

"I…" My emotions boiled inside me like a potent soup; I dipped the ladle of introspection into the broth and brought it to my lips, concluding that the flavour was indignant and salty. "You will reveal yourself to me!"

"There is no power in your words, tiny thing. Be grateful I'm bereft of my appetite for havoc today, and pray I do not find it soon."

"Oh yeah?" I scoffed petulantly. "I'll show you words with power."

I pointed a finger outward, palm facing the ceiling while my other three fingers aimed back at me. The spell was ready to cast, a bullet loaded in an arcane chamber. Jon's words played back to me, about needing to be careful with this one, but I saw no other options; I needed answers. I could be careful later.

"Face me," I spat, curling my outstretched finger back towards me to cast Hither.

"Oh," said the voice, almost quiet now. "A summons? Now this does change things." The room began to shake, the treasure shifting and falling over itself. "Tell me your name, little thing, and state your business. I would like to know the name of the creature with such unparalleled audacity."

"My name is…" I began, but the room was shaking so intensely that it was hard to compose my words. "My name is Chadwick Bonesbury, and I believe you are the person responsible for creating me!"

The shaking stopped, replaced with deafening laughter. I demanded an explanation, but my words were drowned out by derisive echoes and the sound of shifting treasure. Swaths of gold coins and magic goblets were suddenly caught in both a whirlpool and a tornado, as the piles spun down and rose up all at once. The culprit, I realized too late, was moving underneath the hoard, a massive thing rising to its surface. Suddenly the pile erupted, and the great monster rose until it barely brushed the ceiling. Wealth fell down around me like a deluge. I raised my arms to shield myself from the debris, but when I lowered them, I feared for my life a second time that day.

"So, Chadwick Bonesbury," said the Dragon. "Tell me, how would you like to die?"

CHAPTER 18 – Learn to Find Success in Failure

There were many books on Dragons in my library. On account of my casual interest in the subject, repeated attempts were made to read them. I say attempts because, well, they weren't particularly good books. Purely technical and dreadfully dull, for the most part. Genealogical records, biological breakdowns and studies, etc. One book simply titled 'The Numerology of Dragons' did nothing more than break down the math that goes into everything a Dragon does, such as flying or breathing fire. There was no meat to those texts, and certainly nothing even remotely relevant as to how one should go about interacting with Dragons or relating to them on a personal level.

In other words, nothing even a little bit helpful to me in my current and very dire circumstances.

"I asked you a question, Chadwick Bonesbury."

"I'm thinking!" I yelped. "C-could you repeat the question?"

"Certainly," the Dragon hissed. It bent its neck slightly so that the tip of its snout was not ten feet away from me. There may not have been any wind in this part of the mountain, but its breath more than made up for its absence. "I said, how would you like to die?"

"W-what an interesting inquiry." My knees were shaking, and I lacked the necessary emotional fortitude to stop them. "If I may, allow me to answer your question with one of my own. Am I to assume your intent is to kill me, sir Dragon?"

"Intent?" the Dragon chuckled. "It is not my intent, no."

"That's a relief."

"It shouldn't be." The Dragon got even closer now, turning its head so my entire view was dominated by its one giant, reptilian eye. "You dying by my effort is still entirely possible, just not my specific aim. The likelihood will change depending on whether you displease me or not. My question, short-life, answer it!"

"Right, how I'd like to die." I scratched my head, trying to spur some brilliant improv which would endear me to this creature. "I suppose I am uniquely qualified to answer a question like that, seeing as how I've done it once already."

"What?"

"Oh, I suppose that must be confusing. You see, I'm—"

Before I could finish my thought, the Dragon turned its head so quickly that it created a draft and knocked the hat off my head. Emery brought it back to me and proceeded to hide inside it. I found myself staring into one gigantic nostril, a cave unto itself, which flared before hitting me with a blast of hot, putrid air. I felt strange when it hit me, almost relieved, and that's when I understood. Though I couldn't see myself, some preternatural awareness told me that my long-used Tailored Illusion had been dismissed.

"I thought you smelled peculiar," observed the Dragon. "An ensorcelled Skeleton, but not one of mine. You're not one of mine, are you?"

"No, sir. But those other undead I encountered in this mountain… you're responsible for them?"

"I am."

"Do you call yourself a necromancer, Dragon?"

"I engage in the occasional necromancy, an easier effort than summoning living minions. But I am not a necromancer."

"I suppose that makes sense. Not every person who can toast a slice of bread can be called a chef, right?" The Dragon only narrowed its eyes in response. "Right, I don't suppose you have any other caches of treasure, say, a few days' ride from here? Maybe an underground dungeon filled to the brim with Skeletons?"

"This is the only hoard to which I lay claim."

"I see. Well, that's rather disappointing."

"There have been many words used to describe the great Havaras," laughed the Dragon. "But 'disappointing' has never been one of them. Explain yourself, before you are but dust and atoms by my will."

Fear can do strange things to the body, especially in conjunction with other emotions. I had no bowels to loosen, so instead what spilled out of me was the unapologetic truth of my existence. In an abridged fashion, I relayed my entire history to Havaras, culminating in how I was herded here by the dual needs of defeating an enemy and meeting my maker. All the while I spoke, Havaras listened intently, shifting his position occasionally to stretch amongst his riches.

"Your tale is a satiable one, Chadwick Bonesbury. You have spirit, but I am not he who raised you from oblivion, and for that, your coming here was but a fool's errand."

"People keep telling me that today."

"Perhaps it is because you are a fool."

"May I ask you something, oh great Havaras of the mountain?"

"I will allow it."

"Why did you ask me how I'd like to die if it wasn't meant as a threat?"

Havaras did not answer me right away. He paced back and forth as much as his giant girth would allow, half swimming in his pile of treasure, sometimes stopping to admire a gilded cup or radiant sword. With his attention no longer fixated on me, my fear relaxed its hold on me just enough to appreciate his being, and to pick up on details I hadn't noticed before. I had no frame of reference for what a Dragon was supposed to look like, at least not up close, but there were things about Havaras which were… not right. His scales were not vibrant or shiny, but instead bore a resemblance to worn and rusted metal. The leather canopy of his wings was full of clusters of holes, with ragged edges and bits of skin dangling from some of them. And his eye, which had stared me down just moments before, was murky and clouded, something that surely could not have been a sign of good health. Havaras was old; ancient, even.

"You're dying, aren't you?"

"Were I of greater vitality, I'd smite you where you stand for suggesting such a thing," said Havaras. "But I am old, Chadwick Bonesbury, and I am tired. As the first articulate being to converse with me in many seasons, I grant you this insight into Havaras the Dread Wing, Havaras the Bright Calamity. Yes, I am dying, and it is a fate which brings me great discontent."

"I don't know what to say," I admitted. "I suppose… you have my condolences for your suffering?"

"You would dare offer me pity, pitiable thing?" Havaras did not have eyebrows as such, but the look he gave me could only be described as irked irritation.

"No, never pity, sir!" Grovelling was second nature to me, not one of my proudest traits. "Call it… call it compassion."

"Strange," the Dragon sighed. "Compassion is known to Dragons, and we are capable of it, but it is not an emotion which comes to us naturally."

"I think it's important to practice compassion," I told him honestly. "Especially when it doesn't come to you naturally."

"There may be some wisdom in you after all, man of bones."

"Why is dying such a disconcerting thing for you?" In some remote part of my skull was a tiny Goblin, a metaphorical agent of pure logic begging me — no, screaming at me — to end the conversation immediately. It made the most sense to warn Havaras about the D'Graszias, to ask if I could be of assistance in stopping them, and then be on my merry way. But curiosity pushed me further, and I didn't much care to listen to that logic Goblin.

"Oh, many reasons," sighed Havaras. "Too many to navigate with the time I have left."

"If you were alone, perhaps," I reassured him. "You yourself said that I was the first articulate person to talk to you in some time. Maybe I can help you?"

"You would help me, Chadwick Bonesbury? To what end?"

"Being perfectly honest?" I chuckled. "I think it's simply that I'm too dumb to quit."

"Ha! Very well. Let us see what you can make of my ennui, tiny Skeleton. I think the core of my problem lies in the guilt I would feel."

"Feel guilty? For dying? That's preposterous! Everyone dies."

"Yes, but my kind are dying all across this planet. What right do I have to pass on and reduce our numbers even further?"

"You have the right to — wait a minute." Suddenly, I became uneasy. "What do you mean Dragons are dying?"

"In the Dragon Wars." He said those words as if I should know what they mean. I didn't have the heart (or other organs) to admit that I had no clue as to what the Dragon Wars were, so I remained awkwardly silent.

"Surely you must know of the Dragon Wars," Havaras continued. "I haven't left this cave in decades, but even I am kept informed by the birds of the air."

"I have no proficiency in politics or current events," I admitted honestly. "Please, educate me."

"There were once many powerful Dragons in this world. Even today, they still exist in formidable numbers, though not what we once were. Dragons of all alignments engage in schemes and plans, endeavours which can take centuries to complete. This is true of evil Dragons as well, their plots typically threatening the balance of life and power on this plane."

"That's awful." I lamented as I sat down on a small pile of gold coins; I expected this story to go on for a while. "Someone should stop them."

"Someone does, usually," said Havaras. "While hundreds of you mortals get slaughtered in your attempts to stop my kind, one sporadically gets lucky and becomes a dragonslayer. Well, these lucky ones train others, and then suddenly they're going after all Dragons, including those who have no business being slain. And before long, our numbers start to drop.

"This happens in cycles. Dragonslaying guilds get established, some of my kind wipe them out, and then it repeats. But more and more wicked Dragons have begun setting their plans into motion, wanting to take their chance before they're cast down by some up-and-coming heroes. It is the absence of competition from their contemporaries which makes them bolder, which makes them more dangerous. The cycle gets exacerbated, Dragons form alliances, nations ally together to combine their armies to fight them, and those same armies turn on each other when infighting inevitably begins. The process is horrific, but the end results are the same: the gradual decline of the Dragon population."

"It sounds like a nightmare," I gasped.

"I'm surprised you were unaware," Havaras analyzed. "It is my understanding that this conflict touches many corners of the world."

"Like, you, Havaras," I began, "I've been underground for a while. Although if I'm being honest, I'm privileged to live a pretty sheltered life. You haven't been outside in a while, but this is a nice little country we both live in, and I myself occupy just a small piece of it."

"The borders of your maps mean less than nothing to me."

"Right, well… Dragons are dying, which is a tragedy. No one wants to be part of an endangered species. But it looks like you're on your way out already, friend. Erm, I mean great and terrible Havaras, the… I want to say Dread Calamity?"

"Close enough."

"Okay, so if you're dying one way or the other, wouldn't it be better to do it peacefully? To not struggle, and go out on your own terms?"

"You raise a good point. In my younger years I would have raged against this fate, gone out in a righteous blaze of passion, or sought to master magics which could have prolonged my life. But I am… too tired for those things now."

"There you go!" I declared.

"But I would surely manifest as a spirit afterwards. Even as I tire of life, the Draconic insistence on prolonging ourselves permeates my very essence. And I loathe the idea of haunting this miserable cave, entombed with treasures I can never again touch."

"That's… a lot to unpack." A potential opportunity existed just outside my field of vision, but it disappeared whenever I eyed it directly; I hoped to coax it out if I just kept speaking. "Have you considered haunting somewhere else?"

"It would be a statistical improbability."

"I've had some dealing with spirits lately. I understand the need for an anchor, so what if my home became your anchor?"

"You speak in riddles, Skeleton."

"What if you die, and I bring you back with me? Violet Heights is a paradise, Havaras. Extraordinary people work for me, brilliant creatures with unique perspectives and talents. And there is always some new adventure happening, so you'd never be bored. It would be as entertaining an afterlife as a respectable Dragon could ever desire. I even have my own treasure hoard, another thing we have in common."

"Your boldness is… surprising," Havaras mused, bringing his face uncomfortably close to mine yet again. "You forget that I could still kill you without a second thought."

"I forget nothing," I asserted, gambling my plan, and quite possibly my entire life, on a single step forward in the hopes that such a move would impress my potential partner rather than enrage him. "That's a possibility regardless, so I may as well say my piece and see where it gets me."

"You're quite the gamesman, Chadwick," Havaras laughed. "I would call you 'he who games with Death.'"

"Does the fact that you're not using my last name anymore mean you would call me… a friend?"

"Be careful with your presumptions, Skeleton. Even if I were to consider taking up residence in your dwelling, I would not leave my own hoard unprotected."

"I considered that," I started, already fearing what presumption and boldness were about to spew from my non-existent lips. "You know… we could transport your hoard… to my dwelling? Keep all the treasure in one place…"

"Your greed is transparent and pathetic," spat Havaras. "My hoard does not leave this mountain, under any circumstances."

"Alright, yes, that's a valid caveat," I grovelled. "You mentioned protecting it somehow. Could you do that with some sort of enchantment, or a charm, or perhaps—?"

"I would settle for nothing less than a curse."

"A curse is good! Why not curse the treasure?"

"I…" for the first time since I met him, Havaras hesitated. "My will is not what it once was. Even as I decay before you, my body swells with un-imaginable power, but there is more to spellcraft than just power. You clearly have some knowledge of magic, so you must understand this."

"Emphasis on 'some,'" I laughed uneasily. "But I hear what you're saying. What are our options, then?"

"You could cast the curse for me."

"Me?" I shouted. "Why me?"

"There is no one else." Havaras locked eyes with me, his giant bulbous spheres to my empty sockets. His were terrifying, and mine were terrified, but there was something else, something beyond sadness beneath those scales. If a Dragon could ever look grave…

"I will guide you," he continued. "Once my body expires, my essence shall flow into your bones, and through your will we will manifest a curse, one potent enough to safeguard the possessions I have acquired over ten of your lifetimes. Do this for me, Chadwick Bonesbury, and swear to forever be a worthy guardian of my soul, and it will leave this mountain with you."

The mention of guarding a soul dredged up old shame in me. Not wanting to be at the mercy of my own emotions, I turned that shame into deter-mination and found yet another opportunity amidst the wreckage of my choices.

"I do swear, Havaras. I, Chadwick Bonesbury, will be a friend to you for as long as both our souls persist. And in exchange, you will help me avenge a wrong born from the hubris of my good intentions."

"Let us persist then, friend."

Havaras took a step back and closed his eyes, his great jaws slightly ajar.

A light emanated from his mouth, growing in intensity; I could see the fire building in his throat. It expanded outward, not a quick-moving fiery blast as one would expect, but rather a slow cloud which enveloped first his face, then his neck. As the fire travelled down his massive body, refusing to slow or stop, I realized with moderate horror that I was witnessing a self-immolation.

It was not an angry flame, no more intense or passionate than your garden variety campfire. When Havaras was completely covered, there was a burst of air and a rush of smoke which filled the entire cave and rushed out the doorway behind me. I coughed from the force, not out of need but from instinct. A great deal of gristly material fell to the cave floor, like a wet sail collapsing from its mast. Apparently, there was a considerable amount of non-combustible material inside a Dragon's body. Maybe one of the books in my library could identify it; I made a mental note to check after I got home.

"Are you ready, Chadwick?" I looked up and saw a dark, Dragon-shaped cloud where Havaras had sat just moments before. Two glowing points of light were in place of his eyes.

"I think so?" I called. "What exactly do I need to do?"

"Just don't resist," Havaras whispered ominously.

The cloud expanded outward before coalescing into a snake-like coil, which wormed through the air. I was entranced by its smooth movements, and before I knew it I was surrounded by its mass. The smoke froze in the air for a second, taking on the appearance of a solid rather than a gas, before each individual molecule of it shot at me, coating my bones until they resembled sparkling charcoal.

"Oh, good gods!" I screamed. My insides felt like they were on fire — lack of insides notwithstanding. A light blared in front of my face, and it was several uncomfortable seconds before I realized the source was my own eye sockets. I looked down at my hands, which were crackling with lightning that ate away at my gloves.

(You're doing fine,) said the voice of Havaras from inside my mind. (Brandish your instrument.)

"My instrument?" I realized he meant my umbrella, and it suddenly flew into my hand without me casting any sort of spell. Was it responding to my subconscious desire? How powerful was I now?

(You must aim it at the treasure and speak the conditions of your curse. But be specific. A curse is more alive than any spell, an arcane thing which will persist long after we are gone from this place.)

"Protect the treasure in this mountain," I began. "The hoard of Havaras, the Bright Calamity, shall never leave the confines of Highrake Mountain under any circumstances! Those that seek to take the treasure…"

No! My mind went blank, struggling to find the words. Had my talent for improv been expended already? More power than I ever thought possible was coursing through me, but my senses were past their breaking points and robbing me of my focus. Colours were beautiful melodies, sounds were wonderfully abstract compositions of form and shape. I could taste the magic in this, and the past and present gave off a pungent odour.

Desperately I tried to ground myself. Why was I here? To meet my maker, but my maker wasn't here. In that case, I was here to stop the D'Graszias from acquiring this treasure. Metrion… Metrion was on his way here!

"Let those who seek to liberate the Havaras Hoard from this mountain bring great suffering upon themselves!" I started. My thoughts drifted to Cassandra. Would she want me to tailor such a specific curse to destroy the man who had raised her, wicked and hateful though he may be? I told myself she would understand… she'd have to. Despite what I told Havaras about the importance of practicing compassion, I found myself unable (or unwilling) to take my own advice.

"Should even a single piece of treasure be removed without express license, the perpetrator will see their livelihood expended! Their prospects will wither, and they shall live just long enough to see every happiness ripped from their existence. Those who deem to steal from Havaras will know a miserable life, a relentless nightmare from which they can never wake!"

I took a breath, briefly ignorant of my lack of lungs, as I felt a crescendo building; the curse was happening, and it was too late to stop it.

"Let those who seek to take this treasure see the ruination of their house and everything they hold dear!"

The result was nothing like a spell, there was no visual signifier or physical change to the room once the curse had been cast. A taste filled my mouth akin to rotting meat, seasoned with petrichor and topped with a rancid egg. My legs buckled as if I'd been drained of all energy, but I could still feel the power in my bones.

"Is it done?" I gasped.

(Yes,) said Havaras. (Your casting was crude, but it will suffice.)

I don't remember leaving the cave, but when I stepped out into the daylight, the sun shone like a rainbow. If an actual rainbow were to appear in the sky right now, would it look to me like ordinary sunshine? The air vibrated as time passed through it.

"You okay, boss?" asked Emery, only now brazen enough to speak after the death of our new Draconic ally. "You're acting… kinda funny."

"Emery, I need you to do something for me."

"W-what?"

"I need you to pass along a message. Two, actually, so you'll need a shadow copy. Tell our friends in the forest to retreat, and that I order them to go home. And fly to Violet Heights and tell everyone to evacuate immediately. I'll be back soon."

"But —"

"Now, Emery. Amic Arcanus!"

The Imp's body convulsed, flying backwards and changing into a huge black bird, far larger than his typical raven form. It took off with great speed, cutting an obsidian shadow across the sky before splitting in two and disappearing over the treeline. My vision followed him for as long as it could, before I lowered my gaze and saw five men on horseback approaching the mountain.

My Tailored Illusion was back up before I could give it a moment's thought; I was Chadwick Bonesbury again, not just the skeleton of Charles Miller. But the facade rippled, the illusory flesh barely containing the heightened power within me.

"Chadwick!" shouted the lead rider, his horse rearing as its reins were pulled taut. It was Metrion D'Graszia, now sporting a black eye and lacking his signature hat. His arm sat at an odd angle, perhaps it was broken?

"Hello, Metrion," I greeted steadily as I made my way down the path. "How goes it?"

"The treasure!" he grunted, trying in vain to hide a grimace as he dismounted; yes, definitely broken. "Did you see it? Were you inside the mountain?"

"I was, Metrion, and I won't be leaving with that treasure today. I think I have enough of my own."

"Feh! An obvious trick."

"No trick, Metrion," I sighed. "In fact, as a conscience-clearing courtesy, I'll offer you a warning. Under no circumstances should you attempt to take the treasure out of that mountain."

"Try and stop me," he scoffed before pushing past me.

I walked until I was sure I was out of sight of the D'Graszias, not hurrying but not lollygagging either. When I felt confident there was no one around save for the squirrels and the elks, I put a foot in the air. And then another, and another, and… well, you get the picture. I don't precisely know how I knew that would work, but if regular Chadwick could fly, sort of, then Dragon-enhanced Chadwick could surely tear through the air like an arrow fired by an archer vindicated by the gods.

It was hard to tell how long I flew before I was back at Violet Heights. It was still bright out, so this whole ordeal hadn't yet carried us into the evening. As I touched down, no sign of my staff anywhere, I was briefly held in awe of wondering what the stars might look like with my current perception.

"Boss?" Emery had landed on my shoulder, an Imp once more. "I did like you asked and got everyone out. It took some doing, but Cassandra helped."

"Where are they now?"

"A mile or two down the road. They don't know what to do or where to go."

"Go meet them. Tell them to wait an hour and then make their way back, cautiously!"

"What are you going to do?"

"Simple, be the boss."

The front doors flew open as I approached. The house was impeccably clean and put together, save for some errant baskets of laundry that had been abandoned after my evacuation order. The foyer surrounded me, devoid of anyone that could get caught in the crossfire of what was about to transpire.

"Coglio!" I screamed. "Coglio, get out here, now!" Hither was such a simple spell; casting it with my current powers felt like overkill, but what better method was there for dealing with a ghost?

"Hello, Chadwick." His sudden appearance caught me off guard, if only for a moment. There was no big show of his spirit being conjured, no lights or wind or garbled musical notes. One minute I was alone, and the next I was face to face with a translucent, glasslike Gnome with a furrowed brow. "I didn't expect you back so soon."

"Coglio Magella," I enunciated. "Ever since our first meeting, you have done nothing but harass me and my staff, damage my property, devastate my confidantes, and threaten everything that matters to me in this world. No more."

"What the hell are you talking about?" Coglio folded two ghostly arms and raised an ethereal eyebrow at me. "You're stuck with me, remember? We've been over this."

"No more! Ever since I left that mountain, I've thought long and hard about all the words I would say to you when this moment finally came. But I concluded that only one would suffice: caesura."

"Caesura?"

"Yes, caesura. I came across it in your library. A break or stop in a piece of music. Only fitting, because your song is about to end. This is where we part ways, you foul, odious little malcontent."

"What are you—?" If a colourless, see-through entity could blanche, then Coglio became whiter than white. "Oh gods, Chadwick…what's wrong with your aura?"

"Coglio, I've made a new friend with whom I suspect you're acquainted. His name is Havaras. Come and say hello, Havaras!"

My head bent back violently, and my jaw bone shot open so fast that it was nearly ripped from the rest of my skull. Smoke poured out of my mouth, thick and inky tendrils which swelled and expanded, filling the room in seconds.

"Chadwick!" Coglio cried. His spectral form was no longer visible in the haze.

"Havaras, send him back to his maker… in pieces."

"Call him off, Chadwick! You don't have to do this! I'm sorry, okay? Chadwick! Chadwick, I'm sorry! I'm—!"

The thunderous and deafening screams of Coglio Magella rang out loudly. It was distinctly his voice, but the sound contorted and twisted for over a minute, then shifting to something which more closely resembled a dying animal. From there it decayed into a high-pitched, alien cacophony. It wasn't the sound of anything living, merely pain itself made audible. It reached its crescendo, shattering four windows in the main hall and then…silence, sweet and pure.

The smoke slowly dissipated into the house, visibly seeping into its walls and going between the tiles of its floor. When all was clear, I fell backwards onto those cold and expensive pieces of marble, my limbs sprawled out around me. Now that Havaras and I were no longer sharing a body, I was left physically and emotionally exhausted. It felt as if my very bones throbbed, and the stark change in my senses gave me terrible vertigo.

Have you ever spent so long working towards a goal that you aren't sure how to actually cope with your life once you've achieved it? My mind grappled with this as I lay there. I had purged my home of an irritating and hazardous influence, and filled it with a…questionable but likely more benign influence. My staff could once again work and sleep soundly, and I had the personal satisfaction of having crushed an enemy.

But it all counted for nothing, didn't it?

I still failed Fred.

CHAPTER 19 – Give Back to the Community

etrion D'Graszia was dead.

Oh, I don't mean to imply by the suddenness of that opening that his death was in any way quick, or even relatively soon after my return from Highrake Mountain. The whole process took a little under two years, as it turns out.

It started with a brief but unprecedented boom in the D'Graszias' business interests. Stolen Dragon gold tends to do that for a company. Raeden and Jacob were panicking, convinced that we were finished. When they asked me how I could remain so calm in the face of utter corporate and financial disaster, I simply kept stone-faced and maintained that we weren't to engage with our rivals under any circumstances.

The winds of fortune changed overnight. Whispers in the corporate world said that the D'Graszia family had been betrayed by no less than three different business partners in quick succession, each one working independently to undermine the family for their own selfish practices. Shortly after, a pirate began targeting any and all ships that bore the D'Graszia seal; apparently, he had been allied with the Splitter, and was seeking retribution for his comrade's demise. I wanted to be offended — after all, it was I who killed the Splitter — but in the end, I was getting what I wanted, so I didn't feel entitled to complain.

From there, public appearances by the D'Graszias became fewer and farther between. Rumour had it that Metrion's sons had died, although how many children he had to begin with wasn't exactly clear. As he struggled to fight an economic war on multiple fronts, grappled with insolvency, and mourned the loss of a large percentage of his immediate family, Metrion finally collapsed in the dead of winter. A simple fever, or so I've been told.

The ruination of the house of D'Graszia created a power vacuum in this region of the world, a considerable one that Raeden was quick to use to our advantage. And it turned out we didn't even need the Havaras Hoard; once we snapped up the contracts and business partners lost in the fall, we became too big to fail. In anticipation of the Bonesbury Holdings expansion, along with the sheer amount of planning and work such a project required, Raeden made sure I had even less to do.

"You'd just get confused," he laughed. My old friend had gotten more distant as of late, but it was impossible to deny his spirits had been lifted into the heavens after all our recent good fortune. "No more than a signature or two a month, that's all I'll need from you. Enjoy your free time, Chadwick."

I did my best to do as he said. When you didn't need to sleep or eat, and virtually every other need you could possibly have was provided for by your vast wealth or dense infrastructure of servants, finding purpose was easier said than done. Havaras and I got to know each other a little better in the interim, and he revealed to me a truth about our brief union which intrigued and unnerved me in equal measure.

"You… gave me a spell?" I gawked.

"That is correct," said Havaras, whose voice came to me as a distant echo from within my azurite dragon statue; a bit obvious, but still fitting for a king of the mountain such as himself. The odd servant or two gave me strange looks as they passed by our conversation, but I'm confident that I convinced them I was merely admiring the art I had procured for my front hall. There were other places we could have spoken: a specific corner in the library, under the table in the dining room. But Havaras was always so insistent about where he wished to manifest. He was particularly fond of the deepest level of my vault, but I had long ago paid for substantial security measures, so it was a hassle to be going in and out of there whenever I wished to have a chat.

"I did it as thanks for your help in transitioning me to this next stage of my existence," continued the Dragon. "When our essence was one, I allowed the magic to imprint from mine to yours."

"I see…" It was imperative that I didn't seem ungrateful, even if the thought of someone altering my mind, or my 'essence,' without my consent was alarming at best. I knew how much trouble a petulant ghost in my house could be, and there was no way I could pull off the same trick twice to get rid of Havaras. "What do you call this spell?"

"Its true name would be unpronounceable with your mortal language. But I've met your people's mages before, and I suppose they might call it something like 'Draconic Insight.' You establish a fleeting connection with your target, granting you preternatural intuition as to how best to do them harm."

"How morbid."

"If you succeed in slaying this opponent while the spell is in effect, you will add a fraction of their power to your own."

"I suppose that could be useful," I surmised. "What are the components of this spell?"

"I don't understand."

"Funny words? Kooky gestures? Aggravatingly specific materials that only a madman would be able to find in a timely fashion?"

Havaras laughed. "These things are irrelevant. You merely need to will the spell into being, and it will do as you command."

"Oh," I smiled. "That, I like. I like that very much."

While my magical abilities could only increase, my martial proficiency was involuntarily stagnated. Lituin's school was growing, as was only natural; Bonesbury Holdings, and by virtue Violet Heights, were both becoming illustrious operations, so of course there was a need for additional security, and thus more warriors had to be trained to our high standards. Lituin was happier than I had ever seen him, as his dream of becoming the world's greatest teacher was closer than ever. But it also meant that his free time had thinned to practically nothing.

"Fear not, Chadwick," he said warmly after what would be our last sparring session as teacher and student. "Ending your training is not a decision I make in haste. You've become a great swordsman, and I'm overwhelmed by pride. Our education never truly ends, but I have taught you all I'm capable of. One day you may surpass me, but it will not be from my teachings."

"You mean the day that Hell freezes over?" I laughed.

"That would be something," he beamed back. "Certainly the day you can beat me in chess."

"Ha! That's what I love about your jokes, Lituin. I never see them coming."

I hoped I could live vicariously through Cassandra's training, but she had become steel-faced and private in recent months. How heavily did Metrion's demise weigh on her? Did she blame me for what happened? She'd be right to, of course, since it was my fault. What happened inside Highrake Mountain was not something I shared readily with anyone, apart from Raeden, and even that conversation was weeks after the fact. But I made it clear that the Havaras Hoard was not worth taking, and that I had found within it a powerful 'something' which disposed of Coglio Magella for good. Most of my staff took my explanation at face value; whatever I did had obviously worked, and all our lives were easier, so why question it? Cassandra was more perceptive than that, though.

"I'm fine," she said coldly when I finally worked up the nerve to talk to her.

"Of course, of course. But you're feeling okay? What's been on your mind lately?"

"What is this, Chadwick? What are you trying to accomplish?"

"I'm…" I mumbled. "I was just worried about you."

"Well," Cassandra sighed. "To reiterate, I'm fine."

"Then why do I get the feeling you're not?"

"Because you're an idiot?"

"Wow," I chortled in disbelief. "Someone's been spending time with Fel-sha, I see."

"You're right, that was harsh." We both chuckled, but only as one does to fill an awkward silence. "I'm sorry. It's just been a lot, everything with the D'Graszias, and I can't shake the feeling that you had something to do with what happened to them."

"I see."

"You did, didn't you?" she challenged. When I wouldn't make eye contact, she added, "Chadwick…"

Confession is supposed to be good for the soul. At least, that's what Veth Skorr told me once. The standards and practices of their church didn't quite align with me, but I figured there must have been something to it, or why else would the idea have persisted for as long as it has? So, I gathered whatever fragments of courage existed in my marrow and told Cassandra everything. Meeting Havaras, our conversation, and how his need to protect his treasure in death paralleled my desire to destroy a foe, sweetened by the poetic justice of it all. Throughout my entire telling, Cassandra wouldn't look at me.

"I tried to warn him," I pleaded with her. "I looked Metrion dead in the eye and warned him not to take that treasure."

"Knowing full well he would do the opposite of what you told him!" she spat back, suddenly boring into me with her eyes.

"Is that my fault, though?"

"Yes, Chadwick!" I would have never believed that Cassandra's face was capable of projecting such vitriol. She only broke her gaze to begin aggressively packing up her things.

"What are you doing?" I asked.

"Leaving."

"Leaving? To go where? And is it forever?"

"I don't know."

"Please don't leave," I begged.

"I feel like I don't know you," she shuddered. "There's nowhere else in this world that would have me, but if this is your true face, then I don't think I can stay." She picked up her bag and violin case and started for the door.

"Wait!" I called. As I watched her walk away, something broke inside me, and out poured a feeling that I was not prepared to grapple with. "You want to see my true face? Okay, look!"

Cassandra turned to face me, but the man she knew as her friend and employer was no longer there, replaced instead by a Skeleton wearing his clothes.

"Chadwick?" she asked timidly.

"In the flesh," I shrugged. "Or, well… poor choice of words, I suppose."

"Why do you look like a Skeleton?" Her eyes were opened wide but neutral, as if all her rage and resentment towards me had drained away and was replaced by… nothing.

"Everyone looks like a Skeleton if you think about it," I chuckled clumsily. "Some just have more meat and hair and clothes in the way."

"Chadwick…"

Even I had enough self-awareness to know I was being cruel; she was confused, and my attempt at humour wasn't helping. Cassandra got my full story this time, from my awakening as Charles Miller, animated and articulate Skeleton, to my dark baptism in an underground treasure tomb, all the way to the Chadwick Bonesbury who stood before her, a fraud with an eye for fashion. I watched her closely; I could see the cogs turning in her mind as she pieced together the clues, moments and occurrences previously missed and dismissed as just weird ol' Chadwick. A wave of comprehension slowly washed over her face. 'It's so obvious!' I imagined her thinking. I emphasized that I went into that mountain expecting to meet my maker, the person or creature who had animated my bones, an existential conundrum that still weighed heavily on me. When I was robbed of that sense of finality, Havaras offered it back to me, and my weaker nature compelled me to oblige.

"I'm sorry," I said after a long pause. "I'm sorry for any pain my actions may have caused you. I don't understand it, but that doesn't mean it's not real."

"Why would you tell me all this?" Cassandra asked after another pause.

"I wanted you to understand me…" I sighed.

"But this makes me dangerous to you now." I looked at her face; she was staring off into the distance, pondering the severity of that statement, or so I hoped. "I could report you to the constabulary, or the local magistrate. You'd be ruined. I could ruin you with this information."

"I trust you," I told her honestly. "And I suppose, even if it's a bit naive, I hoped that by letting you in on my secret, it might make you trust me, too."

"You have a lot of faith in me," she smiled, weakly but still a smile.

"Of course I do."

She turned to me. "Would you kill me to protect your secret, Chadwick?

You killed Metrion when he crossed you, is this some ploy to keep me from leaving? I can't leave if I'm dead, and you can't allow me to reveal your secret. Is that it?"

"No!" I shouted, somewhat offended. "Why is *that* where your mind goes?"

"I've been hurt a lot in my life. Assuming the worst is just second nature, since I'll either be correct or pleasantly surprised."

"You're right, I would kill to protect this life I've built for myself," I admitted, perhaps realizing it for the first time. "But not you, never you."

"Why? What's so special about me?"

"You're somebody I've come to care for in this world, and a world where I don't look forward to seeing you every day is… well, it's simply unacceptable to me."

We just sat after that. At some point my illusion went back up; we were alone, yes, but that didn't mean someone wouldn't come looking for us, or stumble upon our council of uncomfortableness purely by accident. Cassandra had my trust, but the random chance of the Universe did not.

"I'll stay." Cassandra's words broke the silence, and for that I was grateful. "I don't know if it will be forever, but I don't need to go right now. I could use some space, though."

"More than fair."

Our friendship did endure after that, but not without a lengthy breather. About two months later, I went to Cassandra to ask for help kickstarting a new charitable endeavour. Maybe my conscience had been eating away at me, or maybe I was just bored, but I felt like I had enough wealth that it would be morally and socially reprehensible to hoard it like a Dragon in its lair (no offense, Havaras). I wanted to do something for the common people, and being blessed as I was with a flair for the dramatic and cursed with obnoxious sensibilities (or maybe it was the other way around) I could see no better way than with a party.

If it hadn't been for Cassandra, the soiree would have been a disaster. She kept my ideas grounded and efficient, namely by sticking to what we already knew would be a hit: rides and games, which put Glyph in an overly enthusiastic mood. Petting zoos, live entertainment, and of course, gifts for all in attendance. These were all planned with exceptional detail and craft, but we decided that the focal point of the event would be a feast, the kind typically reserved for kings.

I wanted anyone and everyone in the region to feel welcome at Violet Heights, so we arranged for a caravan to run a loop every half hour to bring our guests to the estate. However, there was some concern about being able to procure enough food.

"You'll starve the realm by feeding the realm," was all Raeden said with a dismissive huff when I ran the quandary by him. I spoke to four more members of my core staff before a solution finally presented itself.

"There's horrible waste in marketplaces," Breadalbane explained. "Vendors usually can't sell their entire stock before some of it spoils, which means it all just gets thrown out. The real problem is time. Even if they were willing to give it away at that point, there's no way to get it into the hands of those who need it most."

"Unless… some eccentric rich man were to pay a fleet of couriers to go buy the food and get it to the plates of the needy?"

"I suppose," Alan sighed, the impish smile already creeping onto his face. "But where would we find such an eccentric rich man?"

"Where, indeed."

It would have been reasonable for me to conclude that the event was a smash hit by the number of attendees, the overall satisfaction level of the crowd, or the adulation I received from local community heads, despite my intent to make this a day devoid of business or self-aggrandizing. But no, I only deemed the endeavour a triumph when a child identified me in a crowd by my favorite title, Rich Uncle Chadwick, and his friends' faces lit up when they recognized me.

Once the feast was underway, I stood up and made a speech highlighting the importance of community and togetherness, the usual sentimental drivel that no one completely believed but still liked to hear. Once I had the crowd eating out of my metacarpal, I made the announcement that Bonesbury Holdings would be funding a new enterprise: food distribution. The same couriers I had enlisted to gather today's provisions had been contracted to make regular acquisitions in hubs of commerce, buying up unsold goods that could then be resold to those in more remote and impoverished areas for a fraction of the price. The name of this enterprise? The Violet Caravan. Credit to Breadalbane for that one, so much so that I put him in charge of the whole thing.

To the surprise of no one, least of all myself, the declaration was met with thunderous applause. However, its popularity diminished significantly in the following weeks. The head of a local merchants guild came to Violet Heights, proclaiming that his institution could not allow the Violet Caravan to exist, as it would drastically lower the value of food and other trade goods.

"So?" I balked. "We're helping those less fortunate than ourselves."

"With all due respect, Mister Bonesbury," said the merchant, unable to completely veil a patronizing tone. "This is basic economics, something you're clearly not well-versed in. You're rocking the boat, as they say, and the waves made by said boat could drown you if you're not careful."

"And with all due respect to you, you arrogant, pretentious stooge, what exactly can your little band of shopkeepers do to stop me?"

"Excuse me?"

"You're not excused!" I shouted, as I pushed him towards the door with an intimidating and methodical stride forward. "Violet Heights and Bonesbury Holdings are, quite frankly, bigger than you. So what exactly can you do that could hold a candle to my resources, reputation, and capital, hmm?"

"You're not seriously suggesting opposing the merchant's guild?" he stammered. "Are you?"

"Just watch me." Dear reader, I've slammed many doors in my life, but this one was one of the most satisfying.

I will admit, ever since I acquired my wealth and my magic I'd been a bit of a bastard at times. I refused to see myself as a villain, but only a fool denies the scarcity of space between sinner and saint. After all, was I not at least trying to do good in the world? Did that not redeem me for any wrongdoing I may have been responsible for? No matter how many times I asked these questions, the answers would not come. What I got instead was a dark disquiet, one which gnawed at my bones for days or even weeks at a time. At my lowest, I felt like I was alone in a dark sea, isolated from my emotions and all the things that enriched my life, that gave it meaning.

And then, there came a night filled with bad dreams.

CHAPTER 20 – The True Meaning of "Skeleton Business"

I've made it clear that I do not sleep. There are times when my body shuts down, almost involuntarily, and I have to assume that this state is equivalent to rest. As long as I don't overexert myself during the day, I can maintain a certain degree of control over its timing; I have found waiting until nightfall, when everyone else is asleep, creates the fewest problems, at least socially. Contrary to how I run my house, I need very little amenities in my personal quarters to be content. However, to keep up appearances, I made sure my bedroom in the attic was fully furnished; I even put in the effort to crumple the bed sheets every morning, as if a normal, non-undead person had been lost in their dreams through the night. On this particular morning, though, I genuinely tossed and turned, beset by the most foul nightmares of my life. But that should not be possible.

I do not sleep, and therefore I do not dream.

"Havaras?" I whispered after bolting upright in the dark.

"Yes, Chadwick?" With my unique perception in shadow, I saw the grains in my mahogany bed posts stretch and open to reveal a great Draconic eye staring back at me.

"Is… is there anything wrong with Violet Heights?"

"Wrong? In what way?" came the voice of Havaras from somewhere around me I couldn't quite place.

"Is anyone hurt, or in danger? Any spirits afoot? Or worse?"

"Hmm." The eye closed, and I could feel the tiniest, nigh-imperceptible vibration run through the room, presumably the whole house. When it stopped, the face of Havaras appeared to me on the underside of the especially decadent velour canopy that stretched across the four posters of my bed. "There's nothing like that going on right now, Chadwick. What's this about?"

"Likely nothing," I mumbled, more to myself than the ghost of a Dragon. "Just a nightmare…"

Unable to return to my non-slumber, I wandered downstairs far earlier than usual. A few servants gave me uncomfortable stares, their daily schedules interrupted by the sudden and unannounced presence of their boss. I dismissed them, more for my own comfort than theirs, when suddenly there was a knock at the front door.

"Yes?" I answered.

"Mister Bonesbury!" shrieked the mail courier.

"…yes?"

"Sorry, Mister Bonesbury. I'm just not used to giving you your mail directly."

"It's a morning of firsts. What have you got for me, Stewart?"

"Looks like just the standard post today," smiled the courier, hauling a large satchel bag from over his shoulder. "Except for this one package, expedited shipping and addressed to you directly."

I took my mail into the dining room and pried open the package. Inside was a note, which read:

Calliope received her flowers and chocolates, and I threw in the cigars as well. They would be wasted on my lack of lungs, and I figured they might endear her to Sunder just a tad better. She seemed happy to receive them, but made no mention as to whether she would write Sunder back or even plan to see him again. That made me laugh; maybe there'd be more gifts in my future.

For now, though, I studied the ones Sunder had given me thus far. The monocle was indeed nicer than mine, a platinum frame with glass in a shade somewhere between lilac and periwinkle. I put it on, but no magical effects were apparent to me. Oh well, a riddle to be solved another day. The second magic item, though, was far more peculiar.

It was a tiara made from dull silver, with a single square-cut pink gem in front. It weighed almost nothing in my hands, and had no markings which might indicate what it was capable of. It didn't seem like Sunder's style or mine, but then I remembered one relevant character trait we both shared: our superior taste in headgear. After a moment's hesitation, I slipped the tiara over the brim of my top hat.

There was an immediate splitting sensation from within my skull. I keeled over, nearly collapsing, but managed to steady myself. I pressed my fists into my temples, trying to alleviate the pressure — how could my brain throb if I didn't have one?! Then, just as suddenly, the pressure eased and my head was no longer in a vice grip. I slowly brought myself upright once again, and my jaw dropped. Every tiny, minute detail around me in the room was sharpened. I looked at my dining room table, and I instinctively knew its weight, the kind of wood it was made from, even the method its maker used to give it a mirror-like sheen. A quick glance at the fireplace told me how long since the fire had been extinguished, based entirely on the pattern of soot left behind. And that's when it hit me.

"The tiara vastly increases my intelligence."

My nonexistent nerves were so alight with comprehension that I didn't notice or care that I had said such a ridiculous statement. But the sight of the room was quickly becoming chaotic, and my head began to swim. Out of cautious humility, I ripped the thing off and threw it to the floor. Where putting it on had produced a splitting migraine, taking it off made me feel as if I were sinking into the floor, weighed down by a lack of something vital in my being. This was no doubt the hangover Sunder warned of in his note.

Suspicion began to set in that the tiara was too staggering to use exorbitantly. True, one might assume that repeated trials would lessen the negative effects, but there was no guarantee of that theory, nor that somebody could ever be proficient with a magic item such as this. Therefore, I saw it necessary to find a single worthy use of the tiara and go from there.

I chose pranks… in my defense, this was more power than I really should have ever been entrusted with.

The perfect practical joke was literally within reach. The remainder of the mail was all business documents, things like quarterly reports and income statements, and other important-sounding things I couldn't comprehend. But that was a limitation I could now forgo, if I so chose. My plan was simple: look over these forms and, with my new advanced intellect, develop a thorough understanding of them which would be sure to baffle Raeden. It's hard being this clever and funny, but somehow I make it work.

I cast Trick on the envelopes, removing their contents without breaking seals or tearing paper. My giddy joy was palpable; it felt like I was a small child again, sneaking a peek into an adult world I was not permitted to see. As I read I became dizzy, my cognizance needing to catch up with my progress. The more I took in, though, the more a pattern began to emerge. It was an ugly pattern. Panic began to set in, and I went over the pages two or three more times to make sure the tiara wasn't manipulating my understanding. But my conclusions were the same, so I put everything back, sent the mail off where it needed to go in Violet Heights, and retired to my room.

I'm not a perfect man, I freely admit that. When it comes to the day-to-day, I prefer to keep things breezy and easygoing. It's a wretched thing to be blindsided by an uncomfortable conversation, to be sure, but knowing one was on the horizon was somehow worse, and I preferred to put them off entirely if I could help it. But this, this was more than just an uncomfortable conversation; this was serious. Thanks to that damned tiara I had uncovered a problem, a veritable worm in the apple of my life. A sickly vein of chartreuse in my violet rainbow. A…complicated bit of imagery in my confusing metaphor. They can't all be winners, okay?

Raeden had the answers I wanted, but there was no way of telling how he would react to such a line of questioning. Privacy was the key, and I knew how to get it, with a bit more help from the tiara. After scanning the staff schedule, there was a clear window when the house was less occupied than all other times. From there, it was simply a matter of assigning aimless tasks and pointless busy work to as many servants as possible, and giving strict instructions to the others that I was not to be disturbed. Raeden himself was easy enough to procure; I just had to tell him the truth.

"There's some things about the business I don't understand, and I have a few questions."

"Oh, yeah?" He didn't look up from his paperwork. When you tell Raeden Lockwood you want to have a business meeting, the man is going to do business.

"I glanced at the mail from the other day. There were some… inconsistencies with how I understand our company runs. "

"Mhmm." His responses didn't even match what I was saying anymore. If I was going to do this, I may as well take the plunge and get it over with.

"Raeden, are we war profiteers?"

That got his attention. He looked up at me and, without breaking eye contact, folded the papers in front of him before leaning back in his chair, hands resting in his lap. "Why on Gaiyax would you think that?" he asked in a calm, incredulous tone.

"I told you, I looked at the mail. I saw what kind of undertaking bypasses me to land directly on your desk."

"You're an idiot, Chadwick." There was no venom or aggression in Raeden's voice; he spoke as if he were stating the sky was blue. "Even if you did look at my documents, you must have misinterpreted them, because there's no way you could have understood what you were looking at."

"See," I groaned, rubbing the back of my neck out of stress with one hand, and reaching into my jacket pocket with the other. "On most days, you'd be right, but I had a little help this time." I threw the tiara in front of him, knocking over an unlit candlestick in the process.

"I'm guessing that isn't just some costume piece," he said, eyes widening slightly.

"I'm afraid not."

"Some kind of cerebral enhancement magic?"

"No," I scoffed. "It makes me smarter."

"That's what 'cerebral enhancement' means, Chadwick."

"Oh."

"Maybe you should wear that thing more often."

"Shut up!" I roared. In the moment I regretted doing it, but looking back, I probably should have gone on the offensive sooner. "We're selling weapons to soldiers, Raeden. Private militias, rebel groups, fighters in the Dragon Wars. But we're also funding their enemies, prospering off of both sides. That doesn't seem right."

"Okay, Chadwick…"

"Oh, but wait, there's more! Labour shops, set up in wartorn cities where citizens have no choice but to work for a fraction of their worth. And we got a lovely little confirmation that one military unit successfully made a group of detractors just… disappear! With our support! It was encoded, of course, wouldn't want anyone stumbling upon our war crimes."

"Chadwick!"

"And I have to wonder how deep this goes, Raeden. Because while I didn't look into the entire operating history of Bonesbury Holdings, it really didn't seem like this was a new endeavour. What evils have you committed in my name, Raeden? What wickedness and rancour have you made me complicit in?!"

"That's enough, Chadwick!" screamed Raeden. His whole tiny body moved up and down with the weight of his breaths, and a vein throbbed in his temple.

"Tell me it isn't true," I begged. "Make me believe this is all some complex misunderstanding, that we're an entirely ethical, above-board company who never hurt anyone who didn't deserve it."

"I don't owe you an explanation," he said defensively.

"Actually, you do," I spat back. "You're my business partner, and it's my name on the company."

"I didn't realize we were called Miller Holdings…"

"You know what I mean."

"Fine," he said after a short pause. "It's all true. I signed off on all these things and more."

"Why? How could you do this?"

"'Why?'" he repeated back. "You really have the gall to ask me that?"

"What d-do you mean?"

"You made it nearly impossible for us to be successful, Chadwick!" He was seething at this point; evidently I had really touched a nerve.

"I… I didn't—"

"Yes, you did. At every conceivable turn you made decisions which held us back, spurning the D'Graszias being chief among them. You told me to make it work, so I made it work. This is what that looks like."

"But Raeden… war profiteering. It's… so ugly. I don't want that for us."

"Oh, grow up, Chadwick. You think Metrion didn't do this stuff?"

"I wanted us to be better than Metrion. We're more successful than he ever was, and we're the only one left standing now."

"Yes," Raeden chuckled derisively. "Because I did what was necessary. You should be thanking me, not interrogating me. Put on that tiara again and maybe you'll be smart enough to see that."

"I just…" Anxiety hung off me like a thick tar clinging to my bones. This wasn't at all how I wanted this conversation to go, and I felt out of my depth. "I just don't understand how you can be so nonchalant and callous about it."

"About what?" he jeered.

"All the death!" I shouted, throwing my hands above my head. I was so devastated that I had somehow looped back around to plain, stark annoyance. "We're richer than kings, with more influence and esteem than I know what to do with. But…at what cost? How many dead bodies are we responsible for? What amount of suffering? How many innocent lives would still be intact were it not for our influence?"

"That's how things are done, buddy. Necessary sacrifices. You know what they say," Raeden began, but he was cut off by his own laughter. It's my personal opinion that significant moments have their own gravity, pulling in perception and emotion the way stars pull planets into their orbit. The next words out of Raeden's mouth would break me, and I'd never forget them.

"It's just skeleton business."

I don't remember sitting; perhaps that gravity pulled me down and the chair just happened to be between me and the floor. But I do remember that we sat in silence for what felt like a long time, though it couldn't have been more than a couple minutes. "We're stopping immediately, of course," I said once I had regained enough composure to speak.

"No, Chadwick."

"A complete overhaul," I went on, ignoring his objection. "Bonesbury Holdings needs to be reworked from the ground up. Cut out the rot, as they say."

"It doesn't work that way," said Raeden, more condescending than I had ever heard him, which was a feat. "Even if I'd allow it, this isn't hacking a diseased limb off a tree, it would be tearing it up from the roots. Too much of our operation is interwoven with these practices."

"Then we'll dissolve the company." If my mother were here, she'd accuse me of having an answer for everything.

"We have obligations, Chadwick. To powerful people. If we keep doing things for them, they're our best friends. If we suddenly stop, there will be retribution."

"I'm a man of means," I bragged. "Let them come."

"No, Chadwick! Things will continue as they always have."

"I outrank you, Raeden." I stood up, using my height to try and intimidate him for the first time since we met, back in his little shop. "Socially, financially, and physically. This isn't up for debate, and it certainly isn't something you want to test me on."

"Ha."

"I mean it!" I whined.

"Oh, I'm sure you do." The Halfling crossed his arms and leaned back in his chair, steadfast and unbothered. "I laughed because you're mistaken about the power disparity between us. If you try to upset the natural order of things, I'm prepared to tell people what you are. They'll come for you, Chadwick, and they'll take away everything you have."

"They can try."

"I wasn't done. You think it would end at you? The people you care about wouldn't fare much better."

"You wouldn't…"

"I can frame Alan for illegal magic, it would be child's play. Glyph, too. You know, a lot of his inventions aren't quite above board. I'm fairly certain Calliope has confessed to me that she killed a man once, more than enough to have her thrown in prison."

"Stop…"

"Felsha has a warrant for her arrest, did you know that? Yeah, two kingdoms over, just one letter and she'd be done. Poor Hayra, she may not be able to handle that. Even if she could, though, she doesn't have a life outside this house, so it would be far too easy to put her in her garden permanently, if you know what I mean. And then there's Cassandra, your little pet project."

"I said stop!"

"She was a part of the D'Graszia operation for years. Things haven't gone so well for them as of late. I bet it wouldn't take much effort to send some of that heat her way, make a little trouble for the white-haired harpy."

Do you know what the problem is with spells that don't require magic words or special gestures? It's that there's very little one can do to prevent less-than-voluntary castings when one's emotions are incited. Like, say, when somebody threatens everyone and everything you love. I cast the spell Havaras gave me, Draconic Insight, and a writhing mass of darkness emerged from my shadow, crawling across the floor with the speed of a highly motivated rat, before embedding itself in Raeden's shadow.

"Chadwick, what did you just do?" he asked, looking alarmed.

"Just a bit of shadow play," I teased, my annoyance now looping even further back into contentious taunting. "But I'll give you one chance to take back everything you just said. The Raeden Lockwood I know would never threaten good people so wantonly."

"You never really knew me," he sneered. "You just knew what I could do for you, and that was enough."

"That's not true…"

"It is. Now stand down, Chadwick. I'm good enough at what I do that I can give you everything you've ever wanted and still accomplish my goals in full. If you jeopardize that, though, I swear I will ruin you and everyone you've ever cared about."

And that was enough. I grabbed my umbrella and cast Telekinesis; my prized Ripple Gun flew off the wall above the mantle and landed right into my arms. It was a horribly awkward thing to hold, too many external and asymmetric parts that failed to conform to my arms or grip. It was long enough that it stretched a third of the way across the table. But all that couldn't stop me from aiming it directly at Raeden.

"What are you going to do with that?" I'd had dinner guests who looked more intimidated than he did at that moment.

"There's an old bard saying about introducing a gun in a story, and how it needs to be fired before the story is over. I have absolutely no idea what this ridiculous weapon does, but I'd love to find out."

"And you won't."

"Are you sure?" I jabbed the gun forward a few times to try and accentuate the potency of my threat. "I'm a wild and dangerous Skeleton man who's been pushed to the brink!"

"You said it yourself, you think you know me. I'm important to you, and I'm also the one who runs your business. You'll kill some random pirate, you'll curse an enemy straight to oblivion, you'll tear a hostile soul asunder if it crosses you, but you won't hurt me. We're friends, Chadwick, whether you like it or not."

I stood there regarding him, letting his words hit me with an array of emotions I didn't care to identify. Eventually, I put down the gun and bowed my head. Things were silent for a moment, but then out of the corner of my vision I could see Raeden start to get up. My arm whipped upright, extending my umbrella in front of me.

"My story doesn't end with you!" I announced powerfully.

Draconic Insight made everything heightened; my aim, my power output, and even my stance were all bespoke to causing the most harm. Raeden had been right, we were friends, but casting Magic Blast felt just like it did when I fought the Splitter. There was no clock, and no Orc, just my foe standing right in front of me.

Heartbreaking.

The blast hit Raeden square in the chest, his chair sent tumbling as his body was launched over the back of it. He spun in the air before hitting the ground on his side, his limbs falling at unnatural angles. I heard my umbrella clatter softly as it hit the floor, though I don't remember dropping it. All I saw, all I sensed, was that my friend was dead and I couldn't bear it. Despite being his assassin, I ran to him and took his hand in mine to check his vitals, a gesture made futile by my dulled senses. If I were physically capable of it, I would have wept.

At some point I must have started cradling him; I remember cupping his face when I felt the tiniest twinge of movement from his head. Had I failed? Was he wearing magic-dampening clothes, or naturally immune somehow? Looking back on it now, I'm astounded by just how quickly the violent avenger melted away, replaced instead by a blubbering mess of bones in an expensive suit, who was ready to take it all back and find a way to let bygones be bygones.

Fate has an irritating sense of humour.

What I mistook for signs of life was actually Raeden's jaw being pried open…from the inside. My own jaw hung open in disbelief, and my non-existent eyes went wide. If I had the power to blink, I doubt I could have done so in that moment; the shock was overpowering. I could not move and I could not look away.

Eventually, what crept its way out of my departed friend's mouth was a tiny, pale pink Fairy. Its body was no bigger or brawnier than the stem of a rose, and its skin was so smooth. Its wings were like those of a dragonfly but carved from opal. A mop of turquoise hair hung over pointed ears and golden eyes, and were those orange irises? It wiped a good deal of Halfling saliva off itself before it noticed me staring at it. It shot me a hateful glance, stuck out its tongue, and flew up into the air and out an open window.

It didn't occur to me until hours later that I could have cast Telekinesis to keep it from escaping. Maybe then I'd have gotten some answers, some closure. Maybe I'd have had one less problem to deal with in the future.

Instead all I got was heartache.

CHAPTER 21 – Never Stop Reaching For New Heights

I destroyed the tiara. A pragmatist may have held onto it for a rainy day, but given that using it caused physical pain, and the one thing I used it for led to the death of one of my closest friends, I concluded that ignorance was bliss.

No one suspected I was Raeden's killer. Why would they? I was his beloved business partner, and his closest known associate. My role in his life made it believable when I said I knew he wouldn't want a funeral, and I cited grief as my reasoning for wanting a quick and simple cremation. I should write a book, apart from this one, that is. 'A Skeleton's Guide to Getting Away with Murder'. It would be a bestseller, and wouldn't that be something?

Not that I didn't try to keep up appearances, or keep trying to better myself. Lituin humoured me by agreeing to spar, perhaps he could sense the growing depression within me. He encouraged Cassandra and me to match blades as well, to test our respective skills. When my former teacher pointed out I was even lighter on my feet than in my previous matches, I realized that I had Raeden to thank for it. You see, by killing Raeden while he was under the effects of Draconic Insight, some of his natural Halfling dexterity was given to me. This got me excited, at least when I managed to suppress the morbid feeling afforded to me by the context of the whole situation. I started to research whether Halflings had any other unique abilities; some believed that they had an inherent, elevated luck, but this had been widely dismissed as superstitious hokum.

Maybe he'd had some luck, but took it with him to whatever afterlife he ended up in, because the matter of my business became uncomfortably complicated without him there, just like he said it would. So I did the only logical thing there was for me to do: make everything far more complicated than it needed to be. Raeden and Jacob's jobs were combined into a single job, and that new job was then split into five. The positions were filled by Jacob, two of Raeden's least ambitious but most efficient assistants, Alan (who I practically had to beg to do it) and myself. My own contributions were only a fraction greater than what they were before; my ego had been hit hard, and I could reasonably conclude I wasn't smart enough in this field to make any real input.

Dismantling the darker deeds of Bonesbury Holdings proved to be easier said than done. We danced around the topic, because no one wanted to flat out say what this company really did. Raeden wound up being right again, this time about it being far too tricky to simply pull out of so many crucial ventures without warning. At best, it would take a decade to completely change the course of our enterprise, maybe more. I lobbied for other, quicker alternatives, but this is where my inexperience hurt me the most. Everyone at the table took turns explaining why my ideas didn't account for literally dozens of factors of business, commerce, and economics. No one was cruel or stupid enough to say so out loud, but it was clear they saw me as Metrion did, as a child playing at business rather than an actual businessman.

"Well, shit," I exclaimed before rising to my feet suddenly and making my way out of the room. My emotions had been stretched so thin as of late, I feared if I had to deal with the immutable consequences of my actions for one minute longer while in the presence of others, I would snap. A knot had been forming in the pit of where my stomach would be, an insipid emotional clot that had only grown over the past few weeks. At first I thought it was the Pouch of Vastness which sat in my ribs and caught my food and drink, but upon inspection I found that it was operating fine.

"You know," chirped a voice I wasn't expecting in the slightest. When I came to the garden to clear my head, Jacob Ryker was the last person I

thought would come after me. "I…oh, perhaps it isn't my place to say anything."

"You came all this way," I sighed. "You may as well speak your mind. It can't be any more disobliging than what's on my own."

"I know you don't like me very much."

"This is off to a fantastic start, Ryker."

"Most people don't. I'm better with numbers than I am with people, and I'm highly motivated by money. Those aren't inherently endearing traits, but that's just how I am. Most people who are good with numbers are usually talented at seeing patterns, as well. I have a lot of experience in business, and if there's one pattern I've picked up on, it's that small, meaningful changes are more effective than big, drastic ones."

"What are you getting at?" I asked, caught off guard by more words than Jacob had ever said to me in a single sitting.

"I see what you're trying to do," he smiled. "The way things are now won't necessarily be how they are forever. Have faith in the process, and try to accept that if something is worth doing, it's worth doing poorly. At least for now."

"Well," I sighed. "Colour me surprised, to say the least. Thank you, Jacob."

The emotional boost I got from that astonishing moment of sincerity proved to be just a fleeting high, not a lasting solution to my problems. I attempted to fortify relationships with my staff, but the fruits of my labour were lacking and bland. Lituin had indulged me enough and had fallen behind with his own students' lessons, and Cassandra was present but distant. Calliope told me to my face that she had no interest in "hanging out" socially, and I had made the mistake of giving Alan far too many responsibilities, expunging much of his leisure time. Hayra and Felsha were occupied with each other, which did my soul some good, but it wasn't enough. I wanted friends. Were I not in a fog of despair, I may have been able to see that the truth lay somewhere in the middle, but at the time, it was evident to me that my staff only saw me as their employer, nothing more.

But then, as if in bald-faced opposition to this conclusion, there was Glyph Bonben, my mechanic and head architect, who seemed overly enthusiastic to spend time with me. The weeks following Raeden's death had been filled with his multiple requests for an audience with me, each one being declined because I was either in meetings or too depressed to be around people. There reached a point where I had run out of meetings, but my boredom had yet to overtake the lingering gloom. Fully aware that I may not be able to keep my promise, I told Glyph he could have his audience the following week.

There were times in said week where I was almost tempted to accelerate our plans; I had nothing else to do, after all. A wickedly dreary rainstorm had taken up residence in the skies above Violet Heights, leaving me housebound and even more miserable than usual. Flashes of lightning cast frightening shadows, and only then did I think to turn to Jon for support. He had been my first friend since becoming a Skeleton, after all, and it was because of him that I had met Raeden. If anyone could understand, it would be him.

"Fine, nothing to report," was all I managed to say when he asked me how I was and what was new in my world. New anxieties had crept up inside me. Would I just be burdening Jon with my troubles? Could I drive him away if I was a nuisance? Or would he simply be indifferent, revealing that there truly was no one in the world who cared for me? That wasn't something I was eager to confirm. Equally likely was that Jon would be mad that I killed Raeden. He had never elaborated on what their relationship was, so who's to say he wasn't more dear to Jon than he was to me? Regardless, I may not have gotten my desperately-needed catharsis, but I learned a couple new spells, which I had to believe was almost as good. I had to…

My 'sleep' schedule had become much more erratic as of late. What was the point in acting like an ordinary Human being when I felt as awful as I did? I retired to my room when I grew weary of the waking world, and stayed there as long as this haunted mess of a body would let me. In an effort to hold onto some sense of routine, I made it a habit to greet Stewart the mail courier whenever I was active in the mornings, and the staff learned to leave this to me if I was roaming around.

"How are you today, Mister Bonesbury?" he greeted me warmly.

"On the edge of the abyss!" I said with manic, insincere enthusiasm. "Yourself?"

"Oh, I can't complain," replied Stewart, completely oblivious. "Looks like just the standard post today, save for this black envelope."

"...black envelope?"

My misfortune, despite a request for some bloody respite, went on. The letter read as follows:

Dear Mr. Bonesbury,

We regret to inform you that your former employee, Pontius Breadalbane, passed away early this morning. He had been fighting an illness for several months now, and had trouble staying conscious in recent weeks. We are sorry for your loss; his passing was relatively peaceful and occurred in his sleep.

Our deepest condolences,

— The Sisters of Hipchala

I crumpled the letter in my hand until it was utterly pulverized in my fist. I set the thing ablaze using Trick and watched as it fell to the floor. I ordered Emery to spread the ashes far from here.

"Alright, Glyph," I shouted to announce my arrival in the workshop a short time later. "You're in luck. I'm desperate enough for a distraction from my troubles that I'm willing to indulge your tomfoolery. What have you got for me?"

"Oh, you won't be disappointed, Mister Bonesbury!" he said giddily. "Someone find me the remote! No!" One of Calliope's sons, who was doing an internship with Glyph, had brought him a brass remote, but the Gnome slapped him on the shoulder. "Not that one, you dunce. Do you want to kill us all?! Bring me the copper one, on the double!"

He led me out into the field which lay between the main house and the woods. We were on the edge of the property, far away from Hayra's garden and Felsha's animals. After gesturing to me that I should pay attention, he pressed the only button on the small copper box, and the ground began to shake. Fertile earth with thick blades of grass began to rise and tear itself out of the ground. Wide metal rivets soon became visible, followed by an entire domed platform. When it was completely revealed, with huge chunks of dirt and plant matter on every side of it, the dome split down the middle like a giant eye and retracted.

"Oh, Glyph…" I sighed in awe. Before me was something I had only ever seen pictures of in books, and those had not done justice to the majesty that was an honest-to-goodness airship sitting right in front of you. It was the size and shape of a small whale with its fins and tail shaved down. Over half a dozen different metals could be seen in its exterior, from bronze to iron to steel, and several others I had trouble naming at that moment. A large glass sphere was embedded in the front, and upon closer inspection I would see that it housed the cockpit.

"She's finally finished," smiled Glyph, looking like a proud father about to see his child off to university. "Took a couple years and a few hundred barrels of elbow grease, but she's finished. I'm so grateful to you for believing in me, so I wanted to offer you the only other seat on her maiden voyage."

A smile involuntarily appeared on my face, although the simple expression masked complex emotions. There were so many things I wanted to say; a sincere thank you for the opportunity, a joke about how we'd have to discuss the illicit working space beneath my house, or how I had completely forgotten I'd given him permission to make the airship in the first place. But my mind was still a victim of considerable stress and grief, and so my resulting idea reflected those conditions.

"We'll leave immediately!" I declared, doing my best to let my enthusiasm take the lead over my other feelings. "Just let me do one thing first."

I waded through a gathering sea of staff who had come outside to see what sort of shiny commotion had literally erupted on my lawn. There were even more when I made my way back from the house, and some of them attempted to flag me down, no doubt wondering what was going on. None of them could have stopped what was about to happen, though.

Glyph showed me the controls once we were in the air. Altitude was controlled by a series of three levers, but the actual direction was operated via a large wheel that wouldn't have looked out of place on a pirate ship. It was truly a thing of beauty, and I told Glyph as much.

"It's hard to resist a classic," he laughed.

"How high can this thing get, Glyph?" I asked as we did laps around the property, about fifty feet above the gawking crowd. "To the stars?"

"Heavens, no, and pun intended. In its current state, I think the ship could maybe hit the lower stratosphere before it would begin to break up, but I wouldn't recommend getting anywhere close to there if you want smooth, safe sailing."

"Right." We touched down not far from our departure point. The assembled crowd had thinned slightly, I suppose due to their exemplary work ethic. The second we were on the ground, I pointed at a random spot of people and said, "I think I see Cassandra out there. Could you fetch her for me? I want her to see this, too."

Glyph did as he was told, but I didn't wait for him to bring her. I wasn't even sure if Cassandra was out there; silently, I hoped she wasn't. When I was confident there was nobody immediately in range, I seized the controls and aimed the airship skyward.

This next part may get a little morbid, dear reader, but I implore you to keep reading. We're nearing the end of this inaugural novel of mine, and it's my sincerest hope that you crave finality and closure just as much as I do.

A person can make poor decisions when they're sleep-deprived. I wasn't sleep-deprived; I don't sleep, you'll remember. But my rest cycle had been uneven and choppy, so perhaps that was a contributing factor into my decision to find oblivion in the sky. It's so difficult to say 'no' to an idea once it grips me, and I suppose I have my ego to thank for that. As soon as I saw Glyph's little project rise from my manicured grounds, I knew the only suitable end to my misery, a flashy one, was attainable.

My little jaunt into the house had been to collect a few things. It's said ancient kings and queens of the past would be buried with all their finest belongings, anything and everything they might need in whatever awaited them in the next life. It was my intent to bury myself in the sky, and I was too lazy and skeptical to bring more than I could carry, but the principle was the same. I had a fresh suit and top hat, my umbrella and my sword, the monocle gifted to me by Sunder Blackstone, an inkwell and some paper in case I wanted to attempt some writing (it was never too late to start), a travel-sized chess set, and a large pouch of gold, in case there was some cosmic ferryman or gate guardian I needed to pay off.

You might think I'm being flippant with the idea of my death, but you see, that's the thing; I died a long time ago. Everything that's come after? The dungeon, and Jon, and Chadwick Bonesbury? That was a bonus, what I thought was a second chance. But at some point I came to the conclusion that it was more an experiment to see if I wanted a second chance. And right now, at my lowest point, drowned in nightmares and reminders of all my greatest failures, it felt like that experiment was a failure too, so I was putting a stop to it.

My mind wandered to the nightmares, which had been a recurring annoyance for weeks now. They had begun the day that Raeden and I had our confrontation, which made me assume they were herald to something awful, warning me of Raeden's betrayal and the toll it would take on me. But they haven't ceased, so what more could be ahead of me? What other horrors did the Universe have left to deal out, and did I want to wait around for them to happen?

No, not really. I was a failure in every sense. The empire I had built for myself, the life I was so desperate to make perfect, was all founded on lies, greed, and bloody warfare. I had lost a groundskeeper twice over, a butler, and a best friend and business partner, all because I was either too weak to protect them or too stupid to see them for what they were. I destroyed a family, even if it was one I hated that had brought nothing but turmoil to my life. And I was no closer to understanding the nature of my undeath or the necromancer that imbued me with it. By these demerits, it was clear that my destruction would be no great loss to the world.

Glyph's airship continued to ascend at a sharp angle. Rain belted the front window with such force and volume that one might have assumed I was being pulled up a waterfall. Cracks of lightning could be seen in the distance, and it was only then that a twinge of fear went through me. The storm clouds were getting closer, a great black wall of darkness and hate accelerating towards me at an unpalatable speed. As it got nearer I began to scream, and Emery joined me; I think he had only just realized what was happening. We only stopped when the ship finally made contact, and we were suddenly alone in the dark.

The cloud cover choked out all light and hope. Even its own storm was a stranger here. I had assumed since childhood that storm clouds were simply full of electricity, and when there was a flash of lightning, it was just the electricity leaking out. This dark void of atmosphere was nothing like I had ever imagined, and it was suffocating me. Without much strength left in my body, I kept my hands on the controls to keep us moving forward (which is to say up, for you ground-bound readers). Scarred both mentally and emotionally, I pushed on, expecting the ship to fall out of the sky or explode… and I was immediately blinded by sunlight.

The other side of the sky was nothing like it was below. The sun was so big and full, the way you only ever saw it in sunsets, but directly overhead. Beneath me was a sea of clouds, as white and fluffy as newly fallen snow on a bowl of whipped cream, but glazed with golden orange light and just enough room for slight highlights of blue reflected from the expanse above. The fog that had been clinging to my mind and soul was literally burning away, as this little slice of heaven assaulted me with comfort and understanding.

"I… I want to live," I stammered in amazement.

Now, let me be clear about something. My detractors have often said that I'm especially susceptible to influence, that my morals and convictions are flimsy things. While that may be true the odd time on a case by case basis, I would overall deem this sentiment to be a gross oversimplification of my character. It is important to be malleable in the face of new information, dear reader. Very few of us are gods, and the ones who are gods, I have to believe, are divine works in progress. It's possible to be wrong, which should be a joyful thing, because it givesus the opportunity to learn and do better. The ability to change one's mind is a wonderful power, the ability to change your heart even more so. Although, every now and then, it can come at inopportune times…

"Gods above, I want to live!" This time I was shouting, because several of the dials and gauges in front of me had become erratic, some with their own alarms to accompany their activity. A few had definitely broken entirely, because I heard a long metallic screech and a small bursting sound, but I was not well-versed enough in this equipment to identify what was precisely wrong with it.

"That makes two of us, you unbelievable jackass!" Emery screamed, peering out from under the brim of my hat. "Do something or start praying, quick!"

I fought with the controls, but nothing I did stopped the ship from going into a sharp nosedive. Being the highly suggestible type (do me a favour and read that with a dash of sarcasm, would you?) I took Emery's idea to heart and began praying to every god I could think of.

The gorgeous sunlight reminded me of Belas, goddess of the sun worshipped by Veth Skorr's order. I'd heard sailors invoke the name of Abelos, a divine and mighty Giant who had domain over sea and sky, to clear the air of storms, which would be terribly useful right now. Even in the midst of this new disaster, the woes of my recent past played in a non-consecutive loop, and I recalled my last words to Raeden: 'My story doesn't end with you'. Taking inspiration, I prayed to Nattwen, a diminutive god of games and stories, asking him not to end my story here. I even prayed to Hipchala, a lesser healing goddess, simply because I recollected reading her name on the letter from Breadalbane's hospital. I'd take what I could get, and promised any god that delivered me back to the ground safely my undying devotion. Surely they'd be falling over themselves in the heavens to save me.

The cloud wall was fast approaching, now a floor like living coal and ink, and still no divine intervention to be seen. I was expecting floating chariots, or a cadre of angels to lift me from my descent, but all I got was a headache as we reached terminal velocity. If I didn't save myself then no one would, and the thought of returning to that void sickened me. Taking my umbrella firmly in hand, I cast Telekinesis on the front of the ship.

We were moving faster than any target I'd ever tried to use this spell on before, and I was only able to focus on the general area, not a specific spot or object, which was the exact opposite of what Jon said to do with this kind of magic. Still I fought, straining my very will in an attempt to lift up the ship's nose. With no instruction from me, Emery flew to the back of the ship and pushed down on the floor, trying to achieve the same effect from a different angle.

"That's it, my friend! That's it!" I shouted, keeping my fears that our efforts were equally futile to myself.

I began to let out a prolonged, primal scream, the kind that would have lacerated my throat if I still had one. It felt silly, but to my credit, the craft did begin to point up. Soon we were gliding above the clouds instead of penetrating them. The instruments in front of me were still very much broken, but I could feel a response, albeit only slightly, when I tried to steer us.

"I think I can get us home!" I announced triumphantly. "It'll be a bumpy ride, but if I can just—"

All the glass around me suddenly shattered.

It was followed by a jarring, earth-shattering boom unlike any thunder I had ever heard in my very long existence. Wind roared all around the cockpit. Emery had crawled back inside my hat just seconds before it all happened, and if it weren't for him I likely would have lost my favorite piece of headgear. Instinctively I shielded my eyes, even though there was no flesh to be pierced by the flying shards. If I'd had eyes, though, I wouldn't have been able to believe them, because before me was something which absolutely should not have been in the sky.

A city, absolutely massive and wide, blocked out the entirety of the panorama before me. Had it been hidden in the clouds? That was the most logical explanation, but there was no way I wouldn't have seen it before now. That boom…had it teleported here? The city itself derailed my train of thought. Numerous glowing auras of different colours hovered over different districts, too big to be creatures but too irregular in shape and motion to be ordinary spells. Tall spires of metal and crystal and stone gave the whole place a distinct silhouette. It made me think of someone creating a diorama out of many upside down panpipes, all arranged at odd angles and different intervals, with the rest of the city built around and within that assortment. It was breathtaking, which distracted me from a most-pressing issue right up until the last minute…

We were about to crash.

TO BE CONTINUED

well, obviously...

SPECIAL THANKS

Wow, so we're really here. If you're reading these words, that means I'm officially a published author, a dream I've had since I was too young to even put that into words. And since we're at the back of the book, I'm hoping that means you actually read the darn thing. Regardless, thank you so much for being here. (Does that make you my first acknowledgement?)

I have to start by thanking my wonderful friend and publisher, Jen Frankel. Doing something as big and complicated as publishing a novel can be soul-crushingly terrifying at the best of times, let alone when it's your first time and you don't know what you're doing. What started as a simple lunch to get a few pearls of wisdom about self-publishing turned into one of the best decisions I ever made. I don't know what I would have done without someone by my side throughout the whole process, my Yoda, my Mr. Miyagi.

One person who definitely made a difference for the better was my editor, Debra (Siemens) Lawson. It's hard for me to dissect my work with a critical eye, and I've never liked deviating THAT far from the first draft anyway. Debra got it all done with professionalism, efficiency, creativity, and kindness. You're one in a million, Deb. Expect to hear from me soon about book 2.

Believe me when I say Jenna Skold put honest to goodness magic in the interior artwork you witnessed in these pages. There's something so inherently satisfying about not getting exactly what you wanted, but instead in what you get being better than you could have hoped for. Jenna exceeded all expectations, and I'm unbelievably grateful. It was important to me that "How to Succeed in Skeleton Business" had personality, and what better way to do that than by evoking the feeling of picking a fantasy book off the shelf in grade school and seeing fantastic illustrations inside? Because I'm pretty confident that you don't stop liking stuff like that once you become an adult.

And on the subject of art, a big thank you to Tommy Devoid for completely nailing the cover. I had a good friend in mind to do it when I first set out writing, my only choice at the time, really, so when they were unavailable I felt a little defeated. When I saw Tommy's portfolio I knew he'd understand the tone and style I was going for. Chadwick Bonesbury may not have a face, but thanks to Tommy, my novel does. A rather handsome one at that, which doesn't hurt.

And finally, last but not remotely the least, thank you mom and dad. I wouldn't have been able to get nearly this far if not for you. For all the meals, the pep talks, the love and support, I'm eternally thankful.

^{THE} BONESBURY CHRONICLES

BOOK TWO

Ever since waking up as a dead man, Chadwick Bonesbury has spent practically every moment trying to foster relationships and hone impressive skills, all in the pursuit of being better than he was when he was alive. But now those relationships are out of reach, and his skills will be put to the test like never before.

Trapped in a logic-defying city that floats in the clouds with no clear way home, Chadwick might have to rely on fate, the kindness of strangers, and his own obnoxious inability to quit if he's going to make it back in one piece.

ABOUT THE AUTHOR

Steve Bernardi has been telling stories for as long as he could speak. Frankly, he can't stop. Now, in an attempt to get out of his own head (and make his dreams come true in the process) he's bringing some of those stories out with him. Writer, cinephile, York University graduate, jack of all trades, perpetual dreamer. His current projects include a Halloween anthology, the second book in the Bonesbury Chronicles, and trying to find happiness and fulfillment in this crazy world. Steve currently lives in Ontario where he can be close to his loved ones.